A
WOMAN
in the
WILD

A
WOMAN
in the
WILD

a novel

TAD CRAWFORD

ARCADE PUBLISHING • NEW YORK

Arcade Publishing books may be purchased in bulk at special discounts for sales promotion, corporate gifts, fund-raising, or educational purposes. Special editions can also be created to specifications. For details, contact the Special Sales Department, Arcade Publishing, 307 West 36th Street, 11th Floor, New York, NY 10018 or arcade@skyhorsepublishing.com.

Arcade Publishing® is a registered trademark of Skyhorse Publishing, Inc.®, a Delaware corporation.

Visit our website at www.arcadepub.com.

10 9 8 7 6 5 4 3 2 1

Library of Congress Cataloging-in-Publication Data is available on file.

Cover design by David Ter-Avanesyan
Cover image by Shutterstock

Print ISBN: 978-1-64821-112-6
Ebook ISBN: 978-1-64821-113-3

Printed in the United States of America

「言亦不可盡,

情亦不可極。」

What is the use of talking, and there is no end of
    talking,
There is no end of things of the heart.

From "Exile's Letter" by Li Bai (701–762), as "translated"
in *Cathay* by Ezra Pound (1885–1972)

1

The wild man didn't speak. Whether he refused to speak or had lost the ability to shape words into sound, no one knew.

After the media uproar—the hyperbolic newspaper stories and earnest journalists on the evening news describing him as dangerous as a beast—it was a miracle that he was saved from the wilderness alive. When pursued, he ran with unnatural speed, often on all fours. The constables shot dozens of tranquilizer darts that missed their mark. In the end, the two that brought him down might have just been lucky shots. In any case, the hunt for this man who kept company with a bear excited the journalists like a pack of hounds. The image of the wild man unconscious and restrained on a stretcher carried by two strong men was broadcast across the country.

Thea Firth watched the interview with the hunter again and again. A strapping man with close-cropped peppered hair, he sat in his study with a scoped rifle across his lap. Behind him, the stuffed head of a buck with six-point antlers looked out from above a fireplace mantel.

"I saw the opening to the cave," he said, choosing his words with care. "I wanted to go in but something, a sixth sense maybe, warned me not to. I stayed at the entrance and slowly moved my rifle barrel across the interior. It took time for my eyes to adjust to the light, so I didn't see him until I brought the rifle back across the cave. Filthy, naked, crouching in the darkness, he didn't look like a man. He was emaciated, starving maybe, but alert like a wild animal. I was afraid he might rush at me. I kept my eyes from meeting his. Acting as if I hadn't seen anything, I backed away. I could barely keep myself from running. I'll never forget those eyes."

2

Thea didn't consider herself a romantic or a superstitious person, but the wild man arrived at the institute near the end of April, on an afternoon flooded by sunlight, only three days after she began her residency. The Institute for Healing and Transformation was high up in the mountains the man had roamed with such freedom. Five large, vine-covered buildings of stone faced a pentagon of grass. Each building was named for one of the great continental rivers— Danube, Nile, Amazon, Yangtze, and Mississippi. The walkways, made of bluestone from nearby quarries, met in a circular patio at the center of the lawn, where a golden sundial marked the passage of the minutes and hours. Built more than one hundred years ago, the institute was a center for retreats, healing, and meditation.

The wild man occupied a small room with yellow walls and no windows. It reminded Thea of the rectangular aquarium pool in which she once watched a ghostly beluga whale swim endless laps. The room had no features except for fluorescent lights recessed in the ceiling, a stainless-steel toilet without a seat, a sink, and a twin mattress on the gray tiles of the floor. A small one-way mirror in the entry door allowed Thea, or anyone, to remain unseen while peering at the new patient. The switch for the lights was not in the room but in the hallway, beside the door.

The man was near her own age, fifty give or take a few years, painfully thin, barely aware of his surroundings. His eyes, when Thea could see them, looked glazed. The matted mass of hair had been shaved, so his bald skull gleamed in the bluish-white light from the fluorescents overhead. His facial expressions, even his postures as far as she could tell, were distorted from the months he'd lived in the wild with a large bear for his companion. Thea could hardly believe this was true, but eyewitnesses had seen him running on all fours beside the bear. More definitive proof came from an infrared motion-detecting camera a ten-year-old boy had set up in the woods for a science project. In the images it captured, the man and bear looked wary but at ease with one another. They entered and left the area together.

Ordinarily, Thea paid little attention when people would say that this or that event happened for a reason. "If I hadn't gone to the wrong platform and missed my train, I would never have met her." "If I hadn't failed the accrediting exam, I wouldn't have found my true calling." Thea heard reason after reason in her sessions with clients. The reasons could be almost a relief. Without reasons, unpleasant and tragic events simply happen. They lack explanation, context. Her work as a therapist convinced her that the essential ingredient of any life is meaning. This was true even when the meaning was that life can be lived with suffering and unbearable losses.

Yet she believed from her first glimpse of this man through the one-way glass that their arrivals so close together connected them. The strong feeling defied her ability to explain, even to herself, why this should be the case. Often, he would rest on his side facing the wall. Staring at his back, uncertain whether he slept, she wondered what images flashed on the screen of his mind. She wanted to enter his room, close the door behind her, and be alone with him.

This fantasy troubled her. The man didn't speak. He could hardly move. As the days passed, he remained under heavy sedation. Did she hope to heal him?

She had come to the institute needing a time out of time, a vacation from clients and quotidian routines, a period in which little would be demanded of her. She wanted to follow the gravitational force of her energies. Perhaps she would hike up and down the wooded mountainsides like the wild man, find a therapist on the staff and talk her way to a new vision of where she stood in her life, or write down her nightly dreams and use the daylight hours to tease out their meanings. She could sit on a bench in one of the lookouts that dotted the grounds and drift through the landscapes of her thoughts. Even boredom, if she wandered into that vast territory, struck her as meaningful and worth experiencing in its many varieties.

Her status at the institute could best be described as undefined. She possessed the degrees, accreditations, and experience to work as a facilitator and mentor to the individuals and groups who sought solace there. But her role as a resident didn't require any duties. If she simply needed to purify herself by breathing the clean air, wandering the vast forests, or resting her eyes on the mountains that stretched one after another into the distance, no one would interfere with her. Even the duration of the residency had been left open ended.

Thea wanted to be selfish, to be with herself and ignore the demands of others. Yet the wild man slipped in among her innermost feelings. As she contemplated the progression by which she had come to this place in her life, and to the institute, she would find herself distracted by the yellow walls of that room, the way the man's fatigued eyes stared at nothing, and her sudden fury at how the institute treated him. Anyone, even a wild man, deserved better.

3

Sitting on her straight-backed wooden desk chair, Thea looked through the open window as twilight darkened the lawn and walkways connecting the institute's buildings. Breezes flowed about her, a pleasant, light touching of her skin by the invisible hands of the air. She seemed not to be thinking anything, but beneath that emptiness she sensed the pressure of thoughts and images waiting to rise to her awareness. She resisted that pressure and focused on the fickle play of the air. In front of her was a white pad of blue-lined paper. She had placed it on the desk, with a gold-sheathed pen beside it, when she'd arrived seven days earlier. The pen challenged her to pick it up, but so far she had written nothing.

Irreconcilable—that was the truth. What she felt mattered not at all. There were others. She had loved. There were different kinds of love. The image of a child rose. "Let it go," she pleaded with herself, but the girl remained. Futile. Sadness, rage, the desire to start anew, to relive—all futile. Betrayal, rage, love, sadness—futile.

Take up the pen, she ordered herself. The command echoed in her head but failed in its journey from synapse to synapse down the chain of nerves leading to her hand. Instead of grasping the pen, her hand opened. Her palm turned up with fingers extended. This gesture was like a prayer. "Let something be given. Let me receive." She didn't dare say what should be received. "Let me accept what can't be changed."

At last, as if a message had arrived from a distant outpost, her hand swiveled and her fingers embraced the golden pen. The page looked unblemished; the blue lines, despite their straightness, felt reminiscent of waves. She didn't want to write. Yet her hand, animated by some brain in her palm or wrist, lifted the pen and slowly wrote a single word.

Forgive.

Thea stared at the word. Another word should follow, like one block placed beside another, but the brain governing her hand didn't offer another word.

Thea's eyes flickered across her room. On the top floor, the fifth floor, of Nile, her tiny room offered just enough space for a twin bed, a bureau, a closet, and the small wooden desk with its chair. The room was like a nun's cell, bare of anything that would distract from contemplation. Nothing decorated the pale green walls. Thea thought the tint might be called jade, a green that wasn't too dark and possessed luminosity. To use the bathroom or shower, she had to walk down the hallway and share the facilities with other guests whose furnishings were as meager as hers. That the founders decided on this configuration, the humble scale and the sharing, offered her a glimpse of the philosophy that brought the institute into being. Yet the mind could still distract itself. However good the intentions of the founders, they could do nothing about that.

Returning her gaze to the pad, she began to crosshatch between the blue lines beneath the word she had written. When she finished this mindless doodling, she considered whether to add other words after "forgive" or to begin fresh in the white space beneath the crosshatching.

After "forgive," she could add "me." But "forgive" was such a large word, open, welcoming, promising. To add "me" would shrink the word and blame her. She wasn't the only one who should be blamed. Anger heated her stomach and rose to her heart and her head. Beneath the crosshatching, her fingers resumed their dance with the golden pen.

You were her stepfather. If you couldn't respect her, did you despise me so much?

Why address him at all? It was like so many words she collected, rearranged, and ultimately let slip back into disorder. She couldn't find the magical sequence, the spell to undo the harm.

You were my husband. My husband.

That was just a cry of pain. "Husband" meant nothing, not now, after years had passed. If she could ever write this letter, to whom would she send it? "My husband." How could that mean nothing?

This construction of words would topple before its completion, as so many before it. It sounded like an email to be rushed over the internet, but it would never be sent. It was too late for outrage and pain. She had tried to take a reasonable path, but there was no reason. There could be no reason, not one she could understand. Yet words kept shaping in her mind, trying to solve a puzzle that couldn't be solved.

Delphina.

Her daughter's name was an incantation. Delphina. She had chosen that name with such joy, an unusual name. Surely her daughter would be an unusual child.

The ballet of fingers and pen ceased.

Her face warmed with shame. He had violated Delphina. He slipped into Delphina's small bed, an athletic man with a child of nine. He pressed against her. His hands touched her everywhere—

9

relentless, determined, possessed by an inexplicable hunger. He exposed himself to her, not once but who knew how many times. He would enter her bedroom abruptly and unannounced. He hovered about her. He spied on her. When Delphina finally told her mother, she said it began soon after Hugh arrived.

Hugh Eustis. His name sounded so promising. He'd seemed solid, caring, present. He didn't mind her divorce or her daughter who had just celebrated her ninth birthday. Hugh Eustis. The name resounded like a hunting cry or a drinking oath. Husband. Violator. She wanted to explain, to understand why he was what he was. But understanding is a prize for fools.

Barren, this endless winter. Bitter, this cold.

She chose each word with care. When she wrote the last word, her willingness to write was finished. It was enough for tonight. She had a sudden, violent desire to tear the paper to shreds, but her hands did nothing. As Hugh had once hovered near her daughter, now his spirit hovered near her—the aftermath of what he had done. Delphina, too, was always in her thoughts or just beneath the surface. Painful, changeless, never departing. How could she have failed to protect Delphina? Yes, failed. Not seen through him. Failed. A word of accusation. Her lament. Failed.

4

Returning from the mountain late the next morning, a hiking pole in each hand, Thea followed a bluestone walk through the wide lawn. Overhead, the sun peaked in the sky. The sundial, as she passed it, showed barely a shadow of time.

She paused in front of the administration building. Smoothing back a fallen strand of hair, she felt the perspiration on her forehead. Above her, engraved in ornate script on the massive stone lintel, the name Danube appeared over lines chiseled to represent water. That the founders used the names of the great rivers symbolized the flow of the world's wisdom to the institute's campus. So she meditated in the Hall of Mirrors in Nile, where she could climb the stairs to her small room, read mythology and psychology tomes in the library in Mississippi, visited the wild man on the third floor of Amazon, where she joined the staff and other visitors in the dining hall, and listened to lectures given in the auditorium in Yangtze.

Entering Danube, she glanced at the high ceilings and walls paneled in mahogany. This luxurious style dated to the previous century, when the institute had been planned and erected. A large map of the same period showed the course of the Danube River through Europe. Runners of Persian carpet made intricate channels along the wide-planked floor of the long hallway. Walking past a sitting room with aged couches and voluminous chairs, she could see the lawn through high windows. Opposite the windows, a sequence of doors like enormous dark dominoes gave entry to the various administrative offices.

"Good morning again," Thea said, smiling as she stopped at the desk of a red-haired young woman who was efficiently moving her fingers over the keyboard of her computer. Thea had come each morning in the hope of seeing Dr. Andreas Henniger, director of the institute.

"You're in luck," the woman answered. "He's back today."

"May I see him?"

Thea knew the director. In fact, he had probably played a role in her being invited as a resident. She had first met Andreas at another institute, the Center for Psychotherapeutic Training, where he'd both sat on the board of trustees and served on the faculty. A generation her senior, he'd taught seminars on subjects such as the symbolism of dreams and fantasies, mythology as a tool for understanding psyche, and the potentials of art therapy.

She wasn't certain if Andreas would see her without an appointment. After announcing Thea on the intercom, the woman rose and gestured to usher Thea to the imposing door.

"Come this way."

Inside, the office was spacious but bare. Thea expected bookshelves, but there were none. Behind the large man standing to greet her, windows opened to a striking view of the vast valley and the mountains beyond. For a moment, the light pouring through the windows made Thea blink. A bright halo glowed at the contours of Andreas's body, which seemed eclipsed in dark shadow. The effect lasted only a moment as Andreas, smiling, walked around his curved desk with his hand outstretched.

"Thea," he said, holding the vowels of her name on his tongue to savor the sound, "so you're here for a stay. It's been a long time. Please have a seat."

Andreas's features reminded Thea of the marble bust of an ancient Roman. The exercise of his facial muscles over a lifetime revealed determination and a high-mindedness seldom made so visible in others. He had always been handsome, but Thea compared him to the man whose lectures she enjoyed nearly two decades earlier. Then, she would let his flood of words wash over her, at times taking more energy than meaning from his crescendos on the intricacies of the human soul. Andreas today, while he still stood several inches over six feet, carried the gravitas of a ring of flesh around his middle. He was more wrinkled, his forehead cross-hatched by horizontal and diagonal creases, and his curly hair had thinned to a white fringe that floated about him like wisps of cloud.

His wide lips smiled in greeting to reveal a familiar flaw, an incisor that partially overlapped the adjacent tooth in the top row of his otherwise evenly shaped teeth. He wore dark-rimmed eyeglasses. His trousers were gray and his dress shirt black, which emphasized the whiteness of his face.

Releasing her hand from the soft envelopment of his, Andreas returned to his high-backed desk chair. Thea sat in one of the armchairs facing him. He studied her intently as if to see her anew.

"I'm delighted," he began, "to have you as a resident. Our visitors may benefit from their time here, but the institute benefits as well. The mix of new and old, the flux of change—it's refreshing, and now you're part of it. Welcome."

"I've stopped by every day since I arrived."

"I've been in the city. Board meetings, budgets, fundraising, side trips to court wealthy donors. Amazing what you have to go through to preserve a place like this."

Andreas had been one of the three faculty members on the panel when Thea defended her thesis. She'd argued that anyone's unconscious contains imagery and beliefs that transcend the person's particular culture and can be used in healing. The other two analysts vigorously attacked her. Strange as it might sound to someone outside the analytic community, these attacks weren't based on a fallacy in her thesis. Rather, they believed that she didn't fully understand why she had chosen to write a thesis on this topic. In their view, she needed to deepen her self-awareness. This failure, they argued, invalidated her thesis.

Throughout these attacks, Andreas interposed an occasional question related to her research. He seemed to sit on the fence, more like a spectator than a judge whose decision would help decide whether her years of work at the center would finally be complete. When the battering ended, she despaired of graduation. Yet a few weeks later, she was notified that she had successfully defended her thesis and would indeed be awarded a diploma. Clearly, Andreas had supported her.

"The hiking." Andreas gestured to the walking sticks she rested against her armchair. "You're enjoying it?"

"Yes."

"It's special country."

"Without a doubt," Thea agreed.

Andreas spoke of colleagues who had come from the city to rest for a weekend or even a week.

"You're unusual," he asserted, "a visitor who has no time limit."

"Everything has its limits," Thea parried.

"You'll have to resume your practice, isn't that right? Sooner or later?"

She didn't know. Some of her clients delighted her because of the way they discovered their own depths and moved forward with their lives. Others, entrenched in their complexes, made her dread the boredom of sitting in the same room with them. But it was this combination, the endless possibility of change, whether quick or ever so slow, that made her work rewarding. She had been frank with those who came to her for their weekly appointments. She was taking a leave of absence, like a sabbatical except that she couldn't say for how long or if she would ever return. Each person struggled in his or her way, especially because Thea couldn't be definite. Some saw her crisis as similar to crises in their own lives. Others struggled with feelings of abandonment, anger, and pain. To sacrifice these people and let them go, to let go of her career, whether for a while or forever—Thea was unsure where it would lead.

"I'll certainly have to resume something."

"After all," he added, "you have a gift."

"Thank you."

His words touched her. A sudden moistness in her eyes made her blink. Often, especially when he had been her teacher, she experienced Andreas as trying to close a distance between himself and others. He had mastered many subjects, some quite obscure. He could easily make himself invisible behind his store of knowledge. It might also have been his pose as a therapist. The therapist's personality and needs had to give way to make space for those in therapy. Yet she always felt warmth within his reserve.

His eyes connected with her, held to her with an unfaltering attention that she experienced as caring.

"Is there a special reason you're here?"

She hesitated. "It's a difficult time."

Andreas's gaze remained warm and unwavering. "Do you want to tell me about it?"

"Yes, but not today when you're just back in your office."

Andreas smiled. "You're very considerate of me. Are you as considerate of yourself? Whatever work I didn't do while I was gone can certainly wait a little longer."

"I want to speak about it," Thea said, her face flushing, "but I need a little more time."

"Come to me when you're ready," Andreas offered, rising behind his desk and adding, "My door is always open."

5

In Thea's exploration of the institute and its vast forested surroundings, she unerringly came to the yellow room to stare through the one-way mirror at the wild man within. The caregiver she most frequently found in the bright hallway outside the room was a blond youth whose accent she took for Swiss. As she returned day after day, sometimes coming in the morning and again in the afternoon, she introduced herself and found that his name was Moritz Manz. He was Austrian, not Swiss.

"I've seen you in the library," she said.

"Yes, I'm often there."

"You like to read?"

"It's a compulsion and a pleasure."

He looked no more than thirty. His slender physique radiated an energy that might move him in an instant. The energy gave a glow to his face, a brightness to his blue eyes.

"You're on staff?" she asked.

"I'm really a guest who forgot to leave." He smiled as he said this, his careful enunciation making each accented word like a picture in a frame. "I help if I'm asked."

"You work with the wild man?"

"Yes. I help feed him and clean him."

"Is that difficult?"

"Not really."

"He cooperates?" she asked.

"He doesn't resist."

"Is he ever . . . violent?"

"He's in another world." Moritz shook his head. "He's under sedation, of course."

"Does anyone else look after him?"

"There are several others, so someone is always in the room or here in the hallway. The hallway lights are kept bright and the lights in the room dimmer. That way we can look in, but he can't look out."

"He's locked in?" Thea asked.

"Yes, that's why someone always has to be here. We can let him out in an emergency."

"When did you arrive?" she asked.

"Almost four months ago."

"Are you a student?"

"Not a formal student, no," he said, adding, "I'm more of a traveler."

"Where do you travel?"

He shrugged nonchalantly. "To places like this one. Retreats, monasteries, ashrams, temples."

Moritz was a puzzle to her. If he was a spiritual seeker, why did he look after this wild man?

"Have you found what you're seeking?"

"No."

"But you stay here."

"Yes, for the moment I remain."

Thea positioned herself at the door and looked through the one-way mirror. The man wore only boxer shorts, pale blue and clean. Moritz dressed him this way, leaving the pants and shirts provided by the institute on a shelf in a storage room down the hallway. Facing the wall, the man lay without the least movement. To Thea he looked reduced, deprived of the freedom that makes one human. She saw from the corner of her eyes as Moritz seated himself, took a book from a small table between the two chairs, and began to read. The longer she looked at the man within the yellow room, the more she had a disquieting sense of something wrong. Wrong with the man? With his situation, the locked room? Or wrong that she and others looked at him when he couldn't know and had no way to look back?

6

Each visit with the wild man left Thea feeling she hadn't finished with him. More was necessary, but what she didn't exactly know. Visiting in the morning and again in the afternoon didn't seem enough. Several times after dinner she climbed the three flights of stairs to look through his door again. He puzzled her. She carried an image of him with her as she left Amazon and walked through the soft cling of the night air. The waist-high lanterns on either side of the walks looked antique and might as easily have been lit by candle or gas as electricity.

The bluestone walks all led to the sundial at the center of the lawn. It would have been far more direct to also have walkways from building to building. Unless she walked on the lawn, every excursion brought her to the sundial. In the twilight, the sundial became an ornament, a sculpture, rather than a tool for telling time. Thea considered whether to sit on one of the five stone benches positioned around it. Knowing she should go to her room, she came to the center only to leave again on a different walkway.

Standing in front of Nile, she studied the dark letters of the name, which seemed to be levitating above the curving lines of water incised in the stone lintel. She wondered about naming the quintet of buildings after the great rivers of the world. Perhaps this confluence of rivers implied a unity. The flow of consciousness, of inner development, could be found in everyone, whatever the continent of their birth.

She hesitated at the entrance to her room, reluctant to enter. Pushing open the door, she was reminded by the narrow space of the yellow room where the wild man was locked away. Crossing the room in a few strides, she sat at her desk. She didn't want to write, but she felt compelled and lifted her pen above the blue-lined paper.

What good could come of this?

The open window expanded the room. Was her interest in the wild man a distraction from this work she had come to do? She sensed inner presences. Writing would bring them forth from their concealment. Perhaps she would do better to leave these spirits from the past, and herself, in peace. Yet she knew she would have no peace until she did the work that must be done: the inner searching, the probing of depths, the construction of meaning, the unblinking stare at whatever she discovered to be the truth.

Quickly she read through her notes from prior nights. The pages were accumulating in a pile toward the back of the desk. She doodled, aware of her reluctance to begin. She lacked the power to direct her writing. Much as she preferred control, she set herself aside.

I am.

Each beginning was an incantation, a calling forth. Tonight, for whatever reason, she asserted her existence, her presence, her being. Her hand moved the pen to create a circle to contain the "I am." She added smaller circles to the outside of its circumference. Contained, it was protected. She was protected.

If she could be protected. Her mind held so many images of Delphina. Baby, little girl, adolescent, woman. Her child, the father gone before the baby learned to crawl. She raised her alone. When the girl was nine, Thea met Hugh. She needed a companion. She imagined her daughter needed a father.

What did she expect the pen to write when she felt so barren? Delphina had put that barrier between them. Her refusal to visit her mother. Her refusal to share. Of course, she knew the city where Delphina lived. Chicago. But it might as well have been Antarctica's snow-clad wastes.

Slowly, she began to write.

I look for your face among all the faces. In the faces of strangers. The endless faces.

She looked when she walked the streets of the city. She looked on the bluestone walkways of the institute. It was instinctive, ingrained. Two years had passed since Delphina's decision not to see her mother. At first, Thea hoped her daughter would return to her. She reached out again and again. Delphina rebuffed her, pleaded with her to stop. Stop the letters, the emails, the texts. Stop the effort to be loving. Respect her wish to be left alone, to be free of her mother.

Knowing I will not see you. Knowing you do not want to see me. I look for your face in the faces of strangers.

Thea tossed down the pen and leaned forward to rest her forehead on her palms. She had done as Delphina wanted. She had fallen silent. It wasn't only a silence with Delphina. It was larger. "I am." So many words could follow. "Not." "Less." "Sorry." "Hurt." "Hurting." "Silent."

Lifting her head, she scrutinized the small stack of books on the back of her desk. It was a relief to free her thoughts from Delphina. Several of the books were about the lives of men like Freud and Jung whose inquiries into the nature of the human moved them beyond the opinions of their time. At moments in her life, their journeys toward the edge, their transgressions of accepted beliefs, excited her and reassured her that her own journey made sense.

Sooner or later, she would have to forget what she inflicted on Delphina. It was impossible, but she had no choice. She could even imagine that her interest in the wild man was merely a way to distract herself from Delphina. But that couldn't be true. Wasn't her desire to help him, to heal him, the same impulse that made her choose therapy for her profession? She had brought her diploma with her only to hide it beneath the neatly folded clothing in the bureau. But if her intention was to escape the familiar for at least a little while, she may as well have left it on the wall of her office in the city.

Pulling the round handles, Thea opened the bureau's bottom drawer and felt the hard rectangle of wood and glass beneath the soft fabric of her clothes. How many times had she read the words of this diploma? Yet she sat on the bed to read them once again.

The Center for Psychotherapeutic Training

Theodora Lysandra Firth, having successfully completed the program requirements for the issuance of this diploma, swears a most solemn oath to seek the wellness and growth of clients, to hold information divulged by clients as confidential to the fullest extent allowed by law, to work for the betterment of community and profession, to avoid inappropriate behaviors or any appearance of such, to abhor discrimination, to serve psyche, and, above all else, to do no harm.

Among the three signatures to make this vow official was that of Andreas, illegible but bold, in dramatic strokes like Japanese calligraphy. It had taken her six years to earn the diploma, all the while working full time as a therapist. Four years had been devoted to courses she took in the evenings at the center; the final two years she worked on her thesis. With so much effort symbolized by this single piece of paper, she wondered that she felt so little. It seemed to her like an artifact, proof that in some distant past a person had struggled and at last completed a process. But did she believe the lofty aspirations enshrined by the center in its diploma?

She had been unable to heal her relationship with Delphina. It would have been easy enough to surrender her belief in healing, in its possibility. Delphina had locked their impasse as tightly as the door to that yellow room. Nothing could change because Thea couldn't even reach out to Delphina to reason, plead, or express her love. To offer whatever might help her daughter. The only possibility appeared to be to accept the unacceptable, to be separated, sundered, silenced. Thea opened her fingers in a gesture that might be plea or protest, then curled them closed to nestle in her palms.

Despite this, she remained a believer. Already certified to give counseling by her degree in social work, she had chosen the center because of its aspirations. If she despaired at times, such as when she found herself under attack in the defense of her thesis and feared she would never receive the diploma, she nonetheless believed in the hopeful view of human nature espoused by humanistic psychology. People could lift themselves by seeking their depths. This sustained her regardless of whether she could return to her work.

Thea searched the wall for a nail or a hook, but the pale green paint spread over the walls without a blemish. Picking up the pile of books from the desk, she moved them to the back of the bureau. It was like making a little shrine, a place of prayer for departed griefs and beloved presences. On top of this foundation, on the biographies of Freud, Jung, and the others, she carefully leaned her diploma against the wall.

7

Thea came after breakfast to sit cross-legged in the meditation hall. With walls of mirrors and dim light flickering from a single candle in a translucent holder of blue glass, the hall seemed a perfect place to let phantoms rise into awareness. Delphina, of course. Hugh. Thea watched the working of her mind. She would recognize each image that arose as a manifestation of her own thoughts and release it. Occasionally she would drift, without a separate sense of herself, in a space, a vastness, where her efforts were no longer needed—until the hungry images returned.

In these first days of visiting the meditation hall, her sessions inevitably ended in the triumph of the images over her power to release them. She would find herself pleading with Delphina. When had her daughter's eyes become bright and destroying? Or raging against Hugh, who had gone on with his life. When the images overpowered her, she would bow to her reflection in the mirror, rise, and end her session for the day.

About a week after her meeting with Andreas, she exited the meditation hall to find him sitting on one of the benches.

"Good morning," Andreas greeted her. "I've been waiting for you to visit me again."

This room was a transitional space between everyday activities and the meditation hall. It was square, easily crossed in five or six steps, and only a little smaller than the meditation hall itself. Oak benches lined every wall, and beneath each bench was a shelf where shoes or bags could be stored. Above the benches were hooks for coats.

"I did want to come," Thea said. "But I've been thinking. I'm not sure I'm ready to put it into words."

"So I've come to see how you're doing. Has it been two weeks yet?"

"Almost. I'm settling in."

Thea reached under a bench to retrieve her hiking shoes and sat beside him to lace them up.

"You come here every morning," Andreas observed.

"I like to start here."

"You had a good meditation?" he asked.

"Troubling."

"Any special reason?"

"Hard to keep my focus."

Thea expected him to ask what happened in her meditation, but he took a different tack.

"Yes, I know what you mean. It can be a struggle. Do you ever wonder about the mirrors in the meditation room?"

"Not really," she answered, "but why are they there?"

"The face is such an intimate aspect of our identity. The builders of the institute designed this hall to challenge us. They believed each person has the power to open the third eye." He tapped the center of his forehead just above his eyebrows. "Third eye has a quaint sound, but it's just another way to speak of transcending the physical. We're capable of seeing the greater realm in which the soul is journeying."

"Sounds a little overblown," Thea replied, wondering as she spoke the last word if Andreas might feel slighted.

"You think so?"

"Yes, I do. Isn't it enough to work on ourselves? At first, what the unconscious holds is invisible to us. Gradually, through dreams, fantasies, and inner searching, we receive gifts or messages from the unconscious. This, especially with the talking in therapy, allows us to discover new possibilities. But each person's discoveries are unique. There isn't a goal, only a process with an uncertain outcome. Certainly there's no one destination where we'll all arrive."

"The realm of the invisible," Andreas said confidently, like a chess master setting down a piece, "is usually death. Hades, the god of the underworld, is invisible. When people die, they enter that place where we no longer see them. Curious that the unconscious should be invisible too."

She had taken Andreas's course on mythology at the Center for Psychotherapeutic Training. The gods and goddesses of the Greeks offered excellent models for various theories, but personal pain could sear in ways that made irrelevant the distant lives of immortals on the heights of Olympus.

"The unconscious offers us insights," she rejoined. "It lets its contents escape in so many ways—dreams, slips of the tongue, desires that suddenly overtake us. Death isn't so generous. What it takes, it keeps."

Andreas smiled at her tone, her willingness to challenge him.

Thea hesitated. It would be painful to speak but more painful to be silent. He looked concerned. He had been her professor, her mentor. She had come here in part to encounter him again. For her not to speak made no sense. Yet she didn't have the words. She lacked the clarity, but here was her opportunity to confide. She had come to the institute for this. His coming to her had been intuitive and timely. She would never have the perfect words, the crystalline explanation that might save her discomfort. In a way that couldn't be true, she felt not to speak now would be irrevocable.

"My daughter. My ex-husband."

"What about them?"

"I'm estranged from my daughter."

The words reverberated in the small room.

"When did this happen?"

"The break came two years ago. She didn't want to see me. She'd just left for graduate school. She told me not to visit. I wrote to her, and she told me not to write." Unbidden, tears filled Thea's eyes, overflowed, and left glistening tracks on her cheeks. "Not to send emails. Not to text her. She wouldn't answer me. Finally, I realized I should stop. To show respect for her wishes, if nothing more. No matter the pain it causes me. I still want to reach out to her—that hasn't changed. But I don't."

"How old is she?"

"Twenty-two."

"Where is she now?"

"The University of Chicago."

"Studying?"

"Philosophy."

"What's her name?"

"Delphina."

"I like the name," Andreas said, nodding approvingly. "You named her after the ancient temple at Delphi?"

Thea smiled, touching her cheeks to dry them.

"You're one of the few people who would think that. I liked the name, but, yes, it did have to do with the temple too. And my ex-husband wasn't her father. He was her stepfather, my second husband. She was nine when I married him, seventeen when we divorced."

"And you're not with anyone now?"

Thea shook her head.

"You miss your daughter?"

"Very much."

Andreas considered this.

"Your ex-husband, what's his name?"

"Hugh."

"Hugh played a role in the estrangement." Andreas stated this as a fact.

"Yes."

"What role was that?"

How quickly Andreas brought the strands together. Thea felt she had touched fire and wanted to snatch her hand from the flames. She wanted to speak and be silent. She needed more time to prepare herself.

"It's so good that you came, but maybe I've had enough for today."

"I'm available for you," Andreas said, adding, "if you want, of course. You certainly don't have to tell me anything."

"It's just finding the words to speak. I need to listen to myself first."

"That I certainly understand."

"Shall we say," Thea asked, "to be continued?"

"Yes," Andreas agreed. "Let's definitely say that."

8

Often, Thea found the wild man curled on his mattress in a fetal ellipse with his arms embracing his knees.

He did have a private life of sorts. If she watched long enough through the one-way mirror, he might roll to the gray tiles, raise himself to his hands and knees, and finally stand up. Slowly, looking crumpled in on himself and leaning a shoulder against the wall, he would walk a few steps to use the toilet or sink. If he had truly become wild, he would have lost the ability to do this. But slowly, so slowly it could try her patience, he would relieve and clean himself. Then he would bend his knees to shuffle back to the mattress and awkwardly lower himself to rest on his side.

If Moritz entered the room during one of his walks, without a glance at Moritz, the wild man would return to his resting place on the mattress. From this, Thea gleaned his private life, his distinction between the many hours by himself and the far briefer periods when others joined him.

At times, she focused on the back of the wild man's skull. Directing her thoughts, she tried to create a beam of energy that would connect them. This was a futile fantasy. She could no more communicate with him by telepathy than she could speak with him in English. What penetrated her was his aloneness. With a sort of inner tumbling, she imagined herself as this lonely, imprisoned man. What hope could buoy her? Confinement in the yellow room kept her from the nurturance and warmth of other people. Even if she dared to think she could make a life without human contact, would she really want to return to her malnourished, furtive wanderings in the wilderness?

Visits to the wild man often proved to be visits with Moritz as well. He had been selected as the main attendant for the patient in the yellow room. Moritz read constantly, his startling blue eyes intent on the pages of one thick volume or another.

Thea would sit in one of the two chairs in the hallway, watching as Moritz continued his reading. Separated from him by the small, white-topped table, she experienced his hunger for information. Not just any information, but the insights of great minds that sought to explain the depths and processes of the human. "Do you miss home?" she asked.

He removed a bookmark from the back of the book, placed it where he had been reading, and closed the volume.

"I don't miss home," Moritz finally said, after waiting for a reply to come to him. "This is my home."

"The institute?"

"For the moment."

"But you came from somewhere," she said.

"Yes, I did come from that place." He smiled, the eyes brightening with a sudden sparkle of light.

"Vienna?" she asked, adding the German, "Wien?"

"A suburb, very old. Not like the suburbs here, all new and shiny."

"You don't go back?"

"I might visit, but it's not my home."

"But you aren't really here," she said. "You're just a visitor like I am. Sooner or later, you'll move on."

"And that will be home."

"How long are you here for?" she asked.

"Until there are no more books to read in the library."

Thea smiled. "Longer than I thought. Why this library and not some other?"

"Psychology, religion, mythology, cults, the occult, astrology—every book is about the path of the soul. There are different paths and obstacles, but the destination is the same."

His passion for the spiritual impressed her, but she wondered what caused such an intense yearning in him.

"And I have a job now," he added, pointing to the door of the room.

"Do you like the job?"

"Better if it didn't exist."

"You don't like it?"

"It's strange, a strange situation and a strange man."

"But you're helping him."

He considered this. "Perhaps you're right." He sounded doubtful. "But what of your home?"

"I have an apartment in Manhattan."

"That's where your practice is?"

"Yes."

"You can leave your work? How long are you here for?"

"I don't know."

Her office was a separate room in her apartment, and each month she paid the rent on that apartment. The payments were like the moving hand of a clock bringing closer the moment when her savings would be depleted and she would have no choice but to leave the institute.

"Your family lives with you?"

She shook her head.

"I live alone."

Twenty years her junior, Moritz showed no hesitation in asking these questions. What surprised Thea was his interest in knowing about her.

"Do you have children?"

"Yes, a daughter. She's studying philosophy in graduate school."

"So she's not following in your footsteps."

Thea smiled. "I never wanted her to."

"Aren't you the good parent," he jibed.

"I'm not sure 'good' and 'parent' go together in therapy."

"I wouldn't know."

"You've never been in therapy?"

"You're surprised."

"Your interests, what you read, you seem like the perfect candidate."

Moritz shrugged.

"You've lived in many places?" she asked.

He nodded.

"Where?"

"Too many to say, really. I started traveling after school."

"College?

"No, college wasn't for me."

"Where did you go?" she asked again.

"Holy places." He gave a quizzical tilt of his head lest his words sound pretentious. "In Greece, I lived beside the ancient healing shrine in Epidaurus. I visited the island of Delos, where neither death nor birth was allowed. In Turkey, in the city of Bergama, I spent several months near the Asklepion, the great healing center of antiquity. In Japan, I found a room close to the shrines of Ise."

"All ancient," she said.

"Or timeless."

"Christian sites?"

"Yes, I've been to the Holy Land, to Jerusalem, Nazareth, the river Jordan."

"Islam?"

"Mecca and Medina."

It was like pulling up blinds and discovering a view she hadn't imagined.

"You're self-taught?" she asked, thinking of his reading.

"Yes, but I search for masters."

"Do you find them?"

"Perhaps for others. I haven't found the one for me."

"Is there a master here?" she asked.

He shook his head.

"But you're planning to stay."

"I don't really have plans."

More inquiries trembled on her lips, but she kept silent. Moritz opened his book and began to read again. What shaped him, she wondered, and gave such force to his search for the spiritual?

9

Thea crossed her room in a few strides and sat by the open window. The sense of the space beyond expanded the room. She didn't need large quarters. In fact, the smallness and sparseness pleased her. They ordered and simplified. On the desk was the white pad. She picked up the pen and sat poised to write.

The images rose quickly. The first was of the cabin in the country she and Hugh used to rent for the summer. It had certainly looked like a retreat from the stresses of the city. It was reached by a long, dusty road and surrounded by overgrown fields transforming to thickets that would one day blend into the forest. A bubbling stream sang its winding way through the backyard. Large-girthed oak and maple trees shaded the small house.

Delphina was fifteen. The summer was bright, filled with the embraces of soft and yielding days. It happened late one afternoon, when Delphina came back from swimming and Thea was at work in the kitchen preparing dinner. Looking up from the desk, Thea shook her head, reluctant to write. This story, absurd and consequential, she especially disliked. And she hadn't directly witnessed it. She hadn't seen Hugh take the ladder from the shed or set it on the ground beside the window above the shower. Nor had she seen him climb up and look in at Delphina, covered in a foam of soap, beneath the spray from the shower head.

Thea had heard her daughter screaming. She ran to the bathroom and found Delphina, wrapped in a towel but soaking wet, on the seat of the toilet. Face in her hands, she wept and heaved as if she might vomit.

Thea shook her head. How many times would she have to replay this scene in her mind?

"He was looking at me."

Thea held her daughter.

"Through the window," Delphina added between her sobs.

"Who?" Thea asked numbly.

"Hugh. Hugh."

Thea glanced up to the window. It was unthinkable, but why would her daughter lie?

"I saw his face," Delphina sobbed. "He was looking in."

"Is everything okay?" Hugh called out as he entered the cabin.

"Go," Delphina said, pushing her mother toward the door of the bathroom. "Go. I don't want him to see me."

Thea left to meet her husband face-to-face. He was a slender, muscular man who could walk on his hands. He had a high forehead that Thea took as a sign of intellect, which indeed he possessed. That contrasted with a nose broken in a college boxing match. His dark hair curled about his head.

"Delphina . . ." she began.

"What?"

Absurd. Thea recalled shrinking within, shrinking back from what might have happened. To speak, she would have to allow that he might have done what Delphina said. Yet not to speak would be to fail Delphina.

"She says you watched her in the shower."

"I was checking the roof," he said, "to see if it needed any repairs."

You climbed the ladder.

She wrote and paused, then wrote again.

To repair the shingles.

Then, more fluidly and with a strong press of the ballpoint against the pad, she wrote.

A limb fell from the oak. It fell like a spear to pierce the roof of our summer home.

Thea had been married six years. From the first, when Delphina was only nine, her daughter avoided Hugh. She would barely speak to him. If Thea pressed her, Delphina would only say she didn't like him. Fear and loathing. Silence.

"I saw his face," Delphina said. "He was looking in."

Would she ever stop hearing that scream? Delphina saw Hugh's face. Hugh was looking in.

You took the ladder from the shed.

"I saw his face."

To make a repair.

Her arms around the towel-wrapped girl who wept, trembled, and heaved. The beads of water on her hair, her face, her shoulders, her arms, and her legs. Her daughter, her beloved child.

You climbed the ladder to repair the shingles. You went up and up and up. Then you came down.

Who to believe? How could she doubt her own daughter? What made her weigh the words of one against the other—to seek understanding when she needed the decisive violence of passion? No wonder she heard that scream again and again, shocking her to vigilance, though her daughter had long since slipped away.

41

10

After looking in on the wild man the next morning, Thea walked to the edge of the plateau behind the institute, where the mountain resumed its steep rise. Each time she left the wild man, she took his plight with her. After her incessant thoughts about Delphina and Hugh, she had to admit that thinking of the wild man gave her relief. Unlike her memories, his situation could change and evolve. Using her walking sticks for support, she speared the earth as she bent forward to ascend with legs akimbo.

She'd learned soon enough that the staff couldn't agree about anything regarding the wild man. Experienced therapists faced off on such issues as whether healing him was a real possibility, whether the room should have windows (even if barred), and the exact nature of the drug regimen to be imposed. Trying to understand these disputes, Thea learned more about him. Not only did he have a name, but he had been happily married. His wife had died, and in his grief he somehow came to wander the mountains with the bear. As for the sedatives, they were strong enough that Thea usually found him asleep on his mattress or staring off into space. If healing wasn't possible, the man presumably would be moved from the institute.

In fact, he had arrived by chance. If he had been captured nearer the city, he might have gone to a larger institution with established protocols for handling cases like his. That, Thea believed, meant he would have been incarcerated under psychiatric supervision for the rest of his life. But the deputies whose darts felled him belonged to the county constabulary and looked for a local solution. The Institute for Healing and Transformation certainly sounded like a place to bring such a case back to the more familiar territory of the human.

The more she thought of what she could only call his incarceration, the more the idyllic setting of the institute appeared a mirage. Looking down from above, the five buildings stood like a dam against the forest. Their rigid architecture held back the impetuous rush of saplings, bushes, and trees to grow wherever possible. The well-maintained lawn extended this sphere of artifice. On Monday mornings, a groundskeeper mowed it, sweeping back and forth in a small John Deere tractor with a bright green hood and a yellow seat. On the other days, irrigation nozzles looped long, gray snakes of water over the lawn.

In her imagination, she saw that, even if it took one hundred years or one thousand, someday the forest would reclaim this plateau. The deserted buildings would crumble into their foundations. The lawn would vanish in the dense embrace of the forest. The earth beneath the sundial would gape open and devour its useful measurements. The immeasurable time of nature would reign again.

Entering the forest, she felt a great relief in vanishing among the saplings and thick-trunked trees. She liked to start off at different angles and always seek new routes. The land rising underfoot, the vertical lifting of the trees, and the fluttering green flocks of leaves made her thoughtless, forgetful, complete in herself.

Although she followed no particular path, landmarks soon became familiar. An oak with a split trunk rose like a double tree. She put one hand on each of the sturdy trunks and let her fingers feel the irregular patterns of the bark. A large trunk, uprooted by the immense force of a hurricane or tornado, lay with dead roots opening skyward like branches. Farther on, she passed a depression, a circle where no trees grew and deeply piled leaves leveled the surface. The way the leaves closed on her ankles and calves made her think of a bog where ancient corpses with gaping wounds might rise from the soft silt. Outcroppings of gray, moss-covered stone jutted among the tree trunks. Large as the visible stones might be, she sensed how these were only the tips of enormous rock formations concealed beneath the earth. Where the rocks formed cliffs that blocked her, she studied the shadowed crevices, looking for a cave or even a cavity or cleft where the wild man might have sheltered himself. How could he have survived a winter out here? She had no idea, but her speculations made her feel closer to him. Here, at least, he had been free.

She constantly wanted to go higher. After walking for half an hour or a little more, she crested a ridge. This wasn't the top of the mountain, but the land beyond sloped down to a hollow. On the far side of that hollow, the mountain rose again to tower above her. Faced with the steepness of the descent, she turned to her left. Tracking through the trees and thick, clinging patches of blueberry bushes, she came at last to a carpeting of brown needles in a grove of pine trees.

Thea liked this quiet grove. Here, beneath a lofty roof of green-needled branches, she looked out to where the hollow widened as it followed the mountain's flank. Shifting breezes chased around her. High above, rising with spread wings on the thermals and descending in effortless glides, vultures and the occasional eagle circled over the landscape. Beneath the blue sky with its drifting banks of white clouds, turquoise mountains knitted themselves to the horizon, one after another.

A beating flurry of wings made her turn her head, but she couldn't see the bird that had taken flight from one limb to another. She wondered if the wild man with his sharpened instincts would have glimpsed the bird or found its new perch. No sooner did she think of him than she saw him in his windowless room.

Her sense of the injustice returned. But feeling so strongly about the wild man, she also felt regret for herself. She couldn't simply be alone, soothed by emptiness, void of rage, pleased for moments passing without expectation. She couldn't let go of her memories of Delphina, her sorrow to have failed Delphina. She couldn't let go of her outrage at the treatment of the wild man. She had to act, yet ever so strongly she didn't want to. She wanted to forget, to sink peacefully beneath the surface of thought. But whatever she wished for herself, it yielded before her desire to stand up for the wild man.

A wind, cooling and fragrant with the earthy scent of the fallen leaves, entered the pine grove and touched her. In that fleeting moment, she smiled wryly to realize she had not only brought the wild man with her but Andreas as well. She might want to sit with legs crossed on the soft cushion of pine needles, but in her mind Andreas and the wild man opposed one another. The wild man had been hunted down for his own good. Or was it for the good of those who didn't want any man to cross the boundary between civilized and wild?

She wondered how the lifting winds felt beneath the wings of the vultures drifting far above. They could scent the odor of carrion rising from beneath the leafy cover of the forest. Did that odor please them or merely attract them? Did they think of forest as separate from them? Or were vulture, hunger, carcass, mountain, and sky simply a whole in which they floated without knowing?

Some cultures in India, Iran, Tibet, and elsewhere in Asia disposed of their dead by offering the flesh to the flocking vultures. In this purification, this transformation of the body, the vultures served a sacred purpose. What was death, after all, but change? And the vultures, like gargoyles from ancient nightmares, played their role as guides of the souls spiraling up toward the heavens.

Aware of how her thoughts had taken flight, Thea returned to her wish to be at peace, to forget herself and blend with the forest, the breezes, the mountains stretching toward the horizon. If she could drift like the vultures, all instinct, no thoughts would agitate her. She would give up speaking words. She would give up thinking words. She would give up thoughts that leapt in one direction and then another, intertwining and engendering yet more thoughts. She would float in a silence like a thunderclap, full yet empty, eternal in each passing instant.

But she doubted that day would ever come. Looking to the sky, her eyes narrowing with the brightness, she saw the vultures like black dots against the radiance. How insignificant these drifting dots were before the powerful illumination of the sun. And the sun an insignificant star in its vast galaxy. And that galaxy a tiny droplet in the flooding infinity of galaxies without end. Such a familiar theme for Thea, this insignificance that reduced her to a speck, a vanishing point.

Yet she cared about the wild man and the world beyond. Even the inescapable pain in her love of Delphina was part of her caring. It made her insignificance fleeting, a realization of one moment that vanished in another. Taking a deep breath, she rose, turned her back to the vista of mountains, and started toward the institute. She didn't follow the path by which she had come but trusted the downward slopes to bring her to the quintet of buildings. When the descent steepened, her walking sticks helped secure her balance. She recognized landmarks: a cluster of white birches, a small meadow, a slender stream frothing with the rush of water over submerged rocks.

Coming from the forest to the monolithic buildings, she felt even more strongly that the institute made no effort to blend with its wild surroundings. It employed the architecture of cities. It would have been just as easy, perhaps easier, to build small structures of logs and nestle the campus into the forest. In the choice not to do this, she sensed that the founders viewed healing as possessing great power. Hadn't the advances of Freud, Jung, and their colleagues been simply one facet of modern progress, together with airplanes, penicillin, computers, and so much more? Just as the healing god Asklepios raised all the dead back to life, so the founders of the institute viewed their healing center as a force for progress.

But could that progress, with its sense of force, of its own grandeur, truly heal? The plight of the wild man made her see a contradiction. Wouldn't healing come from sensitivity, a willingness to endure the timeless flux of human nature, a receptivity that made no demands? The irony of the institute, as she saw it at that moment, was to bring those in need of the hush of nature to a speck of city dropped into the immensity of the wilderness.

11

Despite widespread publicity about the capture, the media and almost everyone else soon lost interest in the wild man. Miracles were newsworthy for a few days or a week at most, but newer stories quickly engaged the popular imagination. Caught up in the man's plight, Thea expected the staff quarrels to be resolved and a course of treatment mapped out to serve his best interest. He had been in the room for more than a month when she realized nothing more might be done. The man's image wouldn't leave her mind. Looking through the one-way mirror, she doubted healing or transformation could take place in that yellow room.

Finally, she took her concerns to Andreas.

"Thea, I'm glad you've come."

He greeted her warmly from behind his desk, gesturing for her to take a seat facing his. She had known Andreas before Delphina's birth, before her failed marriage to Delphina's father, and before her failed marriage to Hugh. He was a bridge to her early promise that found realization in her work as a therapist. Yet even with him, she couldn't easily speak of herself.

"Are you ready to continue our conversation?" he asked.

"Actually," she said, "I'm here about another resident."

"Ah." He raised his brows and nodded. "And who is that?"

"Our wild man."

"You're here for him?"

"Yes."

"And?"

"I've been stopping by to observe him."

Andreas raised an index finger. "Aren't you on a retreat?" He smiled as he admonished her. "Must you find a project to occupy you?"

She shook her head.

"In any event," he went on, "what is it about him?"

"I don't agree with his treatment."

"We've hardly begun to treat him."

"Why is he under such heavy sedation?

"He couldn't voluntarily commit himself, so we obtained a court order. We have the right to sedate him. Our treatment plan has been given to the agencies that have oversight. We've been careful to meet all the legal requirements, burdensome as they are."

"Isn't the room secure enough to hold him?"

Andreas surveyed her, his eyes lingering on her face as if comparing her to a memory from another time. At last, he nodded and pursed his lips.

"The room can certainly contain him, but can he contain himself? For example, can we be sure he won't harm himself?"

Thea didn't respond.

"Nine months in the wilderness and he came out alive. He'd be there still if he had his way. Now his life is in my hands." Andreas leaned forward, opening both palms. "But I have no idea what to do with him. As for what's best for him, who knows? I certainly don't. Nor does anyone, not really."

He surprised her. He not only made no claim to know the best course of treatment but openly admitted it.

"You're the director."

"Everyone has an opinion," he said sharply. "Which one is correct? Do you know?"

"I haven't even examined him," she replied. "How could I possibly know?"

He hesitated.

"I had a fantasy," he finally said.

"Yes?"

"That he vanished into the wilderness again." Andreas spoke the words softly, then shook his head at the impossible. "No one knew he was ever here. No one asked what became of him."

To hear this fantasy, this disclosure of hidden thoughts, made Thea feel closer to him.

"Is it true that you helped the police capture him?" Thea asked. Moritz had told her this.

"Tried to help," Andreas replied, "but it was a comedy of errors. We heard the man and the bear were heading toward the institute. I hid in a blind with two constables armed with tranquilizer darts. By a miracle, we actually saw them. The constables hit the bear with the darts. I kept yelling at them to shoot the man. But the bear was huge, terrifying. He charged right at us. We ran for our lives."

"You outran the bear?" Thea asked dubiously.

"No, none of us were capable of that. Once we started running, the bear simply stopped. Why he spared us—I have no idea. Then he and the man vanished in the wilderness again. We put posters on trees to let the man know he would be well cared for here."

"They did finally shoot him with darts."

"Months later, but he survived the winter with the bear. We don't know how he did that."

"Why did you want to capture him?" Thea asked.

"For his safety, his health."

"Now, what do you think? Would your fantasy be for the best?"

Andreas shrugged. "For him? Or for the institute?"

Thea didn't know. For the man, perhaps it would have been better if the tranquilizing darts had missed their target and he remained wild, the companion of bears, not subject to the learned judgments of those who might deem him psychotic or sane. But what purpose would be served if he vanished again into the wilderness? Hadn't he gone like an explorer who might return with secrets precious beyond imagining? Didn't she and everyone need whatever message from the unknown he might have, need it to shake them free from the tiresome and inadequate truths that kept their lives safely within bounds? Or was she fooling herself? Was her belief that the wild man had to return to himself a self-centered fantasy? Wouldn't life rush forward regardless of whether he appeared on the evening news or disappeared without a trace?

"For the institute," she answered, curious to hear his response.

"He isn't . . . right for the institute. He isn't in therapy. He doesn't seek a cure. If our goal is to develop the conscious life, his choice to live as an animal is the opposite. He's slipped into the vastness of the unconscious, the wild that we've struggled for millennia to escape."

"You're so certain. How can you know what's in his mind?"

"Clearly, he had a break with reality."

"You don't know that."

"It's obvious." Andreas moved his hand with a dismissive wave. "Who but a psychotic would attempt to live with bears?"

An angry warmth rose in her body. "If he'd died, maybe I'd agree with you. He didn't die. He did live with a bear. And what of his grief? His wife died a year earlier. If he had stayed, there would have been a celebration of her life."

"Many people grieve." Andreas shook his head. "But how many leave their homes and take up company with a wild animal, a dangerous animal? To say the least, it isn't normal."

"He isn't guilty of a crime," Thea snapped.

"Yet I imprison him," Andreas replied dramatically, straightening his neck so his head rose higher. This characteristic gesture allowed him a slightly higher vantage point. He raised his right hand to the edge of his eyeglasses and pressed to fit the frame more snugly on the arched bridge of his nose. "He's a strange case, unique really. There have been a few cases where monkeys or wolves have nurtured small children. Of those few, hardly any returned to human society. Language is difficult enough to master. More importantly, the cultural cues are lost. Those children became more wolf or monkey than human. But an adult? Honestly, I don't know what to make of him. How could a grown man become a feral throwback, a wild beast? And how did he find the bear? Or get the bear to accept him? How did he survive?"

"Have you asked him?"

"You say you've observed him," Andreas responded dryly, "so you know he doesn't speak."

"Hasn't spoken yet."

"Your fascination with this man," Andreas asked, "can you explain it? What of yourself do you see in him?"

He utilized the familiar tools of the analyst. In her feelings about someone else, what did she reveal about herself? What attributes that she gave the wild man truly belonged to her? How did her beliefs about the wild man, or anyone else, show her secret wounds, yearnings, fears, and reveal possibilities for growth that she might not otherwise be able to see? Every interaction offered an opportunity to explore herself.

"This isn't about me," she answered brusquely. "I want to discuss him, his situation and treatment."

Her determination made Andreas smile with a twist of the lips.

"I am responsible for him, for his well-being," Andreas responded. "It isn't a task that I take lightly. True, we fear that he might be violent or injure himself. But we also fear he might escape. His physical condition isn't good. How long would he survive without access to doctors, medicine, and the food we provide him? You've seen the patient. What would you recommend?"

"I can hardly recommend anything without an examination."

"He has been examined and examined."

"Give me his folder then."

"That's an excellent idea. I'd be interested in your opinion. But before you immerse yourself in our quarrels, why don't you visit him?"

"I've looked through the one-way mirror."

"He doesn't see you. Go into the room," Andreas suggested. "Spend time with him."

"Alone?"

"A staff member will accompany you."

"I want to help him," Thea replied quietly. "I have the desire and the energy to help him. To be honest, I don't know what 'help' means in this case. It isn't even a case. I don't come to it as a therapist or know if my training would be of any value. I don't know if his experience is a tragedy, a miraculous transformation, or something I can't begin to understand. I'm only certain that I want to offer him whatever I can."

"And your interest in him tells us nothing about you," Andreas replied, gently mocking her enthusiasm. "Soon, we have to talk about you."

She didn't answer him.

"I'll arrange it," Andreas said, rising to end the visit. "We'll see what's possible."

12

Thea followed Moritz into the yellow room. Although there was merely the opening and closing of a door, she sensed herself crossing a far larger boundary. She was no longer a passive observer. Instead, she might have a role to play in helping the man who lay facing the wall.

Moritz knelt with a knee on the mattress and put both hands on the man's shoulders to rock him gently back and forth.

"You don't have to wake him," Thea said.

Andreas chose Moritz, but Thea found him a curious choice for a guide. Who was he anyway? A foreigner, a young man, a visitor passing through the institute, a healer perhaps, judging by the way he touched the wild man with caring gentleness.

Moritz didn't answer but increased the force of the rocking until the man's eyelids parted. She crouched to see his eyes. Moritz raised him slowly and propped him against the wall. His dark eyes passed over Thea, but she might have been invisible for all he responded to her.

"I'm Thea."

His nose twitched. Was it involuntary? She couldn't tell. The room had a penetrating scent of disinfectant. The sedation didn't allow his features to cohere in a way she might make sense of. If inventoried one by one, his features might be called good-looking. But he lacked expression. More than this, she sensed an uncanny absence, or presence, that had nothing to do with sedation. She almost couldn't gather what she meant. Could a man walk out of himself and be left empty? Or receive a new life? A shadowy regrowth of hair darkened his shaved skull, but whatever thoughts and feelings lived within that skull eluded her.

"I'm Thea," she said again. Her heart rushed to be within this room and so close to him.

The stupefied man showed no sign of hearing her. His head lolled, his chin on his chest. Moritz supported his shoulders, so he didn't collapse forward.

"I hope you won't mind if I come to visit you."

Moritz released a hand and gently stroked the man's temple and scalp.

"He never speaks, right?" she asked Moritz.

Moritz raised a finger to his lips to silence her. Slowly he brought the man back to the mattress and positioned him to face the door. No sooner had Moritz released him than his eyes closed. After patting the man's arm, Moritz rose and gestured for Thea to follow him out.

Back in the hallway, Moritz locked the door and turned to Thea.

"You can't talk about him that way."

"What do you mean?" she asked.

"You can't act as if he isn't there."

"But . . ."

"He is there." Moritz nodded his head to affirm what he said. "But not the way we want him to be. We don't know what he perceives. But if we ignore him, how can we hope he will pay attention to us?"

"We didn't ignore him," she said, annoyed by the younger man. "We visited him. But how can you really visit when the sedation is overpowering?"

Moritz shrugged dismissively. "We're not the doctors in charge."

"If he could be housed differently. . . . He's like a prisoner."

"So I'm like a guard," Moritz said, his cheeks reddening.

"I didn't say that."

"Someone who just follows orders?" Moritz continued his train of thought. "That's what you meant."

"I'm talking about him," Thea said, perplexed by Moritz's reaction, "not you."

"He is what he is," Moritz said. "Why do you want to make him something else?"

"A year ago, he was a person like you or me," Thea insisted. "Why shouldn't he be that again?"

"You have no idea if he was like either of us. My guess is that he wasn't, but I don't really know. Why would you expect him, or anyone, to become what he used to be?"

"Not exactly, of course not, but not to be treated like this."

"It isn't pretty," Moritz conceded, lowering his voice, "but he's a patient, not a prisoner. Maybe it has to be this way."

"What if he doesn't need the sedatives? Or not the amount he's being given? Is it okay just because it's happening?"

His blue eyes searched Thea's face.

"It would definitely not be okay," Moritz responded carefully and clearly. "You tell me you want him to resume a normal life. You want him to be as free as you or anyone. But what if he isn't well enough to do that? What if a room like this, the safety of it, is what he really needs?"

"You've spent time with him. Are you sure that's what he needs?"

"I've spent no time with him. Near him, yes. No one can spend time with him."

"Yet you don't want me to speak about him in his presence."

"Because I don't know. I don't know what he hears, what he thinks, if he cares. I simply don't know."

13

It was easier to remember Hugh than Delphina. Easier to remember Hugh, whom she despised, than Delphina, whom she loved, when that love was unwanted and found no avenues for expression. Husband he might have been, but by the second year of their marriage, Thea had known Hugh wasn't the man she imagined. He could walk on his hands, but he couldn't stand on his two feet. He was well educated but not practical. He couldn't find the right work for himself. He couldn't provide in the way Thea had hoped. In her fantasies, she might have lightened her own schedule enough to be home when Delphina finished with school each day. That wasn't possible. Hugh earned what he could but didn't deal with the family's finances. At the end of each month, Thea sat down with the checkbook to make certain everything was paid.

You climbed the ladder.

Tiresome. Tiresome to repeat. Exhausting.

How could I not know?

The window was open to the night. In the dark of the forest, the wild dogwoods flowered with white blossoms, but Thea couldn't feel the spring. She tried breathing deeply from the breezes that were sweeping around the corners of the buildings and over the lawn, but her breathing didn't sweep away the images and thoughts. She hadn't known Delphina's suffering and pain.

My child. My daughter.

How could she try in any way to avoid responsibility? She failed to protect her child. She brought a predator into her home.

You craved power over a child.

Her rage always contained despair, self-accusation, and hope-lessness. She thought of people whose lives moved on. Delphina in grad school, Hugh close to remarrying. She'd heard it from a mutual acquaintance. He was marrying a woman named Justine. If that had been all, Thea could have let it pass. But Justine had a daughter the same age Delphina had been when Hugh entered their home. Thea couldn't accept that. No other daughter should suffer as Delphina had suffered. No other mother should feel the pain inhabiting Thea.

14

Thea quickly lost any fear or anxiety about being with the wild man. Arriving after her morning meditation and again in the afternoon after her hike, she would leave Moritz reading his book in the hallway and enter the yellow room by herself. Sometimes she would return in the evening to rest her hands on his bony shoulders, arms, or legs, or to gently smooth his temples with her palms. If the sedation caused his lack of response, as she believed it did, she wanted a better understanding of his situation before she went again to Andreas.

She kept returning to Andreas's fantasy. Yes, it would be much easier for him if the man simply vanished. As director, Andreas no doubt sought to stabilize the institute, to find adequate funding, effective staff, and appropriate guests. This wild man had entered like an unstable element, beyond the regulations and daily norms, outside the valued certainties that elevated introspection, meditation, growth, and transformation.

But she glimpsed something larger in what Andreas had said. The man came from the wilderness in much the same way that a dream, a fantasy, or a slip of the tongue might come from the unconscious. Her weakness, shared with much of humanity, was to prefer the familiar to the unknown. For her, change would always be a struggle. Yet this was the struggle at the heart of everything that gave meaning to her life. It was the struggle she embraced in the same way she allowed herself to hope this man would someday be free from the room and the regimen of drugs that now kept him under control. How easy it would be if he returned to the wild and left Andreas and everyone else in peace. But Thea had an urge to bring him closer, to bring the irrational and instinctual toward the center of their settled, civilized lives, and accept whatever might follow.

Years earlier, decades really, she had been a very different person. It had been true even when she wrote her thesis and made her defense before the committee on which Andreas sat. It wasn't that she wouldn't have welcomed the wild man at that time but that she would have had no idea how to take meaning from him, from the fact of his existence, from the innumerable ways in which he was not expected, understood, or desired. Visible as he was to her now, then he would have passed by her unseen.

Leaving the man resting on his mattress, she closed the door behind her and took the empty seat by the small table. Moritz glanced up from his reading.

"Good book?"

"Yes."

"Have you considered," Thea asked, "why we call him the wild man?"

"There isn't a good reason."

"Why don't we call him by his name?"

Moritz glanced down to insert a bookmark before closing the book. "Wouldn't that be strange?" he asked.

"Why?"

"He isn't whoever he once was. He almost needs a new name, but I can't think what that might be."

"He's not an animal," Thea said, "yet he's not quite a man either. That's what I'm hoping for him. That he'll be a man again, whether the way he was before or different. But he would have to speak or, at the least, show an awareness of us. The essence of being human is to connect with others."

"He did connect with the bear."

"Yes."

"So," Moritz suggested, "why don't we call him the bear man?"

Thea nodded in assent.

"Are you on a quest?" she asked.

Moritz smiled. "A quest sounds so grandiose."

"But you're looking for something."

"I don't deny it."

"You're like a spiritual tourist."

"Please, at least call me a traveler."

"Because?"

Moritz shrugged, setting the hardcover book on his lap to toss up his empty hands. "Must there be a because?"

"Yes," Thea answered, "always."

"Perhaps the answer is here," Moritz said, patting the dark cover of his book.

"Or in there," Thea parried, pointing to the door of the room. "When I came here, I certainly didn't expect him."

"No one could have expected him."

"What harm could come from lessening the sedation? I've seen him walk a little, but most of the time he's lifeless, asleep. Are we dealing with him or with the drugs?"

"Some of both," Moritz replied, "would be my guess."

"Do no harm. That's the healer's first rule."

"And a good rule," Moritz agreed.

"I'm going to speak to Andreas about our . . . bear man."

Even as she said the words, Thea didn't know what Andreas would say. His fantasy of the bear man vanishing back into the trackless forests had a dark beauty. Then the bear man's fate would be unknown, almost inconceivable, a life beyond the human. But if Andreas wanted the man to vanish, hadn't the regimen of drugs already achieved his wish?

15

Thea stopped abruptly. The orb of a spider's web, held by slender fibers to the trunks of saplings on her left and right, blocked her path. Near the center of the interlacing strands, the spider with its domed body moved dark limbs like needles to spin a silken shroud around prey that might have been a fly or a small moth. She leaned forward, her face a few inches from the web. The spider labored in its drama of life and death without any awareness of her presence. Leaving the web undisturbed, she stepped to the side and continued her ascent.

Through the covering of leaves and branches, the sunlight cast dark, dappled patterns. The shadow of a large bird with wings outspread rushed across the floor of the forest. Thea looked up to see whether it was an eagle or a vulture, but the bird had already vanished from the patches of blue sky.

Hiking on a sun-filled day like this one, Thea found herself occupied with her senses, the solid press of her feet into the leaves and twigs beneath her, the sensation of the breezes flowing around her, her shifting balance on the steep slope, the working of the muscles in her arms to impale the earth with her walking sticks, and the working of the muscles in her legs to propel her upward. Outdoors, with the brightness of the day filtering down through the canopy of branches and leaves, it was easy to put aside the preoccupations of her evenings. The figures of the past remained in the past, abstract and unable to touch her emotions while her limbs kept up their constant motion. If anything, she came closer to the bear man here. These forests had been his home. Hidden in these fastnesses was the bear who had been his companion. As she climbed, even that elusive bear seemed more present than the phantoms who filled her evenings.

Nearing the crest, she tested the smaller rocks with her weight before stepping higher. Balancing for a moment on a larger stone, the poles splayed for support, she looked down and noticed a wasp grasping the head of a grasshopper. The wasp, by moving its legs and occasionally fluttering its wings, dragged the much larger insect. Could its sting be paralyzing and allow the wasp to lay its eggs in the body of the grasshopper? Reaching a large stone, the wasp found a dark groove and, releasing the grasshopper, vanished into it.

Thea waited. The wasp didn't return. Her hamstrings and calf muscles burned from the long squat. She stood and carefully went back to where the wasp had let go of the grasshopper. Its gray-green body must have blended into the leaves and moss. She couldn't find it. She wanted to view the grasshopper as a vessel for new life. She wanted the death of the grasshopper to be a sacrifice that sustained the wasp and its species.

A process played through this interaction of death and life. But its end would remain inconclusive, as was so much in her life.

Thrusting her poles into the leaves and earth, Thea labored to the crest. On the flatness of the plateau, she walked more easily. The winds stunted the trees here. Oaks grew with multiple small trunks, like large bushes. The pines looked pressed down by an immense gravity. Raspberry bushes held their unripe berries in clustered husks on the thorny vines. Blueberry bushes grew in thick patches, the berries hard and green.

Ahead, the hollow sloped down to where the mountain rose again to tower above her. The sun above the peak filled her with its warmth. She slowed, surrounded by the coils of the rushing breezes. Stopping, she drifted in a thoughtless reverie. When she realized that she'd been standing like a statue, her next thought was relief at having forgotten herself. During that fragment of time, she had no concern for understanding or mysteries. She imagined that what she found inconclusive might be a completion she could not comprehend, a completion created of ceaseless, inexorable change.

Thea had vowed to use her phone as little as she could during her stay at the institute. When she hiked, she brought it with her in case of emergencies. Nonetheless, she unzipped the mesh pocket of her hiking belt, took out the phone, and turned her back to the sun so she could see the screen. She tapped the icon for the search engine, selected a bookmark, and in an instant reached her daughter's Facebook page.

In the large photo across the top of the screen, Delphina stood at the entrance to the Reg, the massive Regenstein Library at the University of Chicago. Slender, taller than her mother, she wore her dark hair in curls that fell to her shoulders. Silver pools of light reflected off the lens of her dark-framed eyeglasses. She smiled broadly, seeming to enjoy the presence of whoever took the photograph.

Thea had seen this photo before, but a smaller photo dated May 28 was new to her. Inset in a corner of the larger image of the library, it showed Delphina with her arm flung over a golden retriever. Both her daughter and the dog looked slightly off to the side of the camera lens. Delphina didn't smile, but she appeared content.

To look at this image of Delphina was at once painful and pleasurable. There was the separation that photographs always imply. Then there was the actual rift with Delphina. At one point, Thea had failed Delphina, but she had been with her for every phase of her growth. Now Delphina moved on her trajectory into the larger world. If there weren't a chasm between them, Thea would have been ever so proud of her daughter. She was proud, but her love and the pain of the separation could come together with an unbearable intensity.

Beware the dog that's friend to man. The happy toss of Delphina's arm around the golden retriever brought that fragment of poetry to mind. The dog would always be digging, rooting among memories, revealing what might otherwise be left untouched.

Thea turned in a circle to remind herself of her surroundings. A nearby birch had two slender trunks like white saplings. She wanted to put her phone away and be done with the world beyond the forest. Instead, she keyed in "wasp and grasshopper," then watched a blue line move beneath the rectangle for the search words. She only had to read a few brief entries before she realized how mistaken she had been. She saw a photo of a wasp and a grasshopper. The wasp looked exactly like the one that disappeared into the stone, but the grasshopper was smaller than the giant she had seen dragged across the forest floor.

"Wasps are omnivores," the website explained. "They will switch between hunting prey and eating nectar, tree sap, and fruit, depending on availability." She read further, at last coming to this detail: "A small handful of wasp species are large enough to take down, kill, and eat a grasshopper."

What of her notion that the wasp would lay eggs inside the grasshopper? She'd wanted to be present at the rite by which the sacrifice of old life brought forth the new. That's not what she had actually seen. No doubt the wasp would return to feast on the grasshopper. She pressed the switch to darken the screen and returned the phone to her hiking belt.

Still, it had been a small miracle to witness the grappling of wasp and grasshopper. She never imagined such a possibility. The bear man fell into that category as well. Except for the chance of her presence at the institute, she would have never imagined a man like him. If she entered "bear and man" in her search engine, would a website explain how a man crosses the boundary to the unthinkable?

16

The next morning, meditating in the Hall of Mirrors, Thea struggled to keep her eyes closed. The small, square room could be crossed in a half dozen strides. No one else meditated today, so she seated herself in the exact center. A candle in the glass globe illuminated the unnaturally silent room with dim, bluish light. She could see her shadowed reflection in the mirror ahead and, if she glanced left or right, in those mirrors as well.

The moment her eyelids closed, she faced the bear man. To break this connection, she opened her eyes. She reassured herself she was here, her weight pressing into the carpeting. Her image reflected back to her from the mirrors. But when her eyes closed, the bear man stood before her.

She released the thought, the image. She focused on nothing at all as her eyelids touched. The bear man returned, and she released him again and again until, finally, she drifted without thoughts. It might be a minute or two until he returned. Recognizing that her thoughts always came back to him, she gave up her attempts to escape and instead made him the focus of her concentration. Andreas

71

had given her three thick folders. In that dossier, she found not only the medical history of the man since his arrival at the institute but also the outlines of his earlier life.

Lucas Lamont. That had been the bear man's name before he entered the wild. Luke to his friends. He served as executive director of a small nonprofit that sought to bring urban youth to the outdoors, often by hiking or boating. He originated the idea and found wealthy donors to make it a reality. He had been married more than two decades when his wife was diagnosed with cancer. Juggling his schedule and often working from home, he spent five years caring for her as she gradually declined and finally died. He planned to celebrate her life on the first anniversary of her death. He invited relatives and friends, hired a caterer, wrote notes for a speech of love and praise that he never delivered. Instead, a few days before the celebration, he vanished.

That first anniversary fell in August. He and his wife had designed and overseen the building of a cabin in the mountains. He decided to spend all of August at the cabin, telling his friends how he hoped the beauty of fields and forests would be a balm for his grief. Toward the end of the month, on a Thursday, the housekeeper came for the weekly cleaning. She found his car parked in the driveway, but the cabin was empty. When she finished the cleaning and he still hadn't returned, she became alarmed and called the police. In the fields surrounding the house, close to a stone wall that marked the boundary with the forest, the police discovered a trench clawed into the earth. In the muddy bottom of the trench were the footprints of a man and the paw prints of a large bear. Next to the trench, neatly piled, were trousers, a shirt with short sleeves, underwear, and slippers. He didn't leave a note. He didn't text or take his cell phone. Looking at his computer gave no hint that he intended anything out of the ordinary. He must have just walked away, but no one could explain his disappearance.

Thea studied his medical records for clues. He belonged to a health club in his neighborhood and exercised regularly. He took a prescription drug for blood pressure. He had broken his right forearm slipping on ice a decade before. He and his wife had been childless, but the medical records offered no explanation for that. Basically, he had been in good health.

Thea hadn't been certain which tranquilizers were being used to calm the patient. Sifting through the multiple prescriptions, she was disturbed that lorazepam had been administered for thirty days. Not only was that the longest use permitted because of potential side effects, but the drug could cause anterograde amnesia. Quite simply, the man might not remember his life before he walked out of it, his life in the forest with the bear—some or all of both might vanish. Even if he began to speak, that personal history might be lost.

Opening her eyes, she had the disturbing idea that someone was watching her from behind the mirror. Who could this be? No one, of course. It was absurd. If she closed her eyes to escape this fantasy, the bear man waited.

"What do you want?" she asked the man.

In her psychoanalytic training she had been encouraged to think of a person in a dream or fantasy as a traveler from a distant and undiscovered region of her inner life. The challenge was to welcome such a guest and not be fearful or resistant.

He opened his mouth, his jaw quivering with inaudible words.

"What?" she asked. "What?"

His eyes, dark and imploring, held hers. His mouth gaped, gulping air in his effort to speak.

"Can't you tell me?"

Bowing his head, he broke the connection of their eyes.

At last, feeling stiff, she uncrossed her legs. On hands and knees, she lowered her head and shoulders toward the carpet, bowing, not to her reflection, but to the humbling immensity beyond her ken.

17

The day opened like a container unable to hold its boundless light. Andreas climbed ahead of Thea up the tiers of steps set into the mountainside. Breezes surging through the forest tossed the leaves skyward. In this windy shuffling, the undersides of the leaves looked a lighter green, almost silver, compared to the green of the leaves when still.

Andreas labored with each footfall, his bulk shifting side to side. Droplets of perspiration bubbled up on his forehead. After each dozen steps he stopped, leaned against the stone banister, and breathed deeply before continuing the ascent. He was dressed more casually than usual in khaki pants, a pale-blue short-sleeved shirt, and tan boots. To Thea's surprise, he had suggested this walk when she stopped by his office to make an appointment.

"You should be my guide," Andreas said over his shoulder. "I'd like to be more active."

"Maybe start with a short hike."

"Yes."

"Then you can build on that."

"Good idea."

Something in the way Andreas spoke, his not quite credible enthusiasm, made Thea doubt that he would make time to abandon his desk and enter the forest.

"I'm available if you want to go," Thea offered. "Just let me know."

"I certainly will."

Each of the five flights of twenty-five steps led to a patio with two stone benches facing the valley. Thea usually avoided these stairs, preferring to slip into the forest as soon as possible. Nearing the top, Andreas pulled a dark-blue handkerchief from his front pocket and wiped his forehead again. At last, on the fifth and final landing, they faced an obelisk thrusting up more than thirty feet. Mounted on a round base constructed of stone, the polished obelisk reflected light like a beacon high above the institute. The two benches, unlike those on the lower platforms, faced both toward the obelisk and away toward the valley below.

Andreas settled on a bench, his back to the obelisk. Thea sat beside him. The view encapsulated the incongruity of the institute, urban architecture surrounded by a vast wilderness.

"Quite a vista," Andreas said, opening his hand to the buildings, the forest, and the expansive blue of the sky. "It never ceases to amaze me. You hike every day, don't you?"

"I try to."

Above the valley, a vulture drifted on a thermal. The wind soughed through the forest. An orange butterfly looped in odd arcs, up and down and sideways, to vanish in a golden bush beside the patio.

"I've given a lot of thought to what you said," Andreas began. "To doubt whether therapy is the right career for you . . . it's understandable. To enter intimately into other people's lives, to witness their sorrows, joys, failings, and growth—it's demanding. At times, it feels unrelenting."

Thea wanted to speak of the bear man, not herself.

"It was the right choice when I made it," she replied, deciding to let Andreas guide the conversation.

"Yes. Considering your abilities, it was a wonderful choice. As someone who knew you when you studied to become a therapist, I would hate to see you leave the profession."

"Now," Thea said with a shrug, "I don't know."

"Is it good for you here?"

Thea started to speak about the bear man, but Andreas interrupted.

"No, I mean for you. Is it good for you?"

"I need this period, the space for myself. When I work with someone else, it's so easy to see that one issue or another will take time to resolve. It's not as easy to accept for myself."

"You're estranged from your daughter."

"Yes, she doesn't want to hear from me. She refuses to be in touch."

"Your former husband played a role in this."

She wanted to deny this unerring statement. The therapist would sometimes see what the patient resisted. To speak of it too quickly might strengthen the patient's resistance. Thea bristled and wanted to disagree, but she also wanted to relieve herself of the burden she carried. If she shared her story, then she and Andreas would carry the burden together. She would have a sense of being helped, of someone who cared, of working toward a possible solution. Andreas wasn't her therapist, but she thought of him in that way.

"When I married, my daughter was nine. I didn't know, but . . . my husband abused her. I didn't find out until she was fifteen."

That so many years had passed made tears pool in her eyes. Her chest constricted, and she breathed with difficulty.

"He touched her. He exposed himself to her." Thea rushed ahead, so Andreas couldn't interrupt. "And he spied on her. Once, when she was showering, she looked up and was terrified to see his face in the window above the shower. She was fifteen. Finally, she told me what had been happening since the marriage began. What he did disgusts me, and I feel such sorrow for my daughter. But what I did and failed to do also disgusts me."

"You think you should have known?"

Thea nodded her head miserably. "I was her mother. I had to protect her."

"Yes."

He spoke that one word gently, with concern and affirmation. Yes, she was Delphina's mother. Yes, she should have protected her. It was no longer a secret. She no longer had to struggle alone with her endless dialogue of blame and excuses. She used her palms to wipe the tears from her cheeks.

"But that isn't all."

He nodded to show he listened. His body was turned toward her on the bench. His eyes focused on her face made her feel nothing could distract him.

"I wanted to have a loving family," Thea continued, "but Delphina disliked and avoided him as much as possible. Now I understand it was because of the abuse."

"She didn't tell you?"

"How could she? I wanted her to love her stepfather. I couldn't fathom her refusal, her obvious aversion. At times, she enraged me. I struck her, more than once, feeling she wanted to sabotage my marriage."

"You hit her," Andreas said, to make certain he understood.

"Yes."

Thea remembered the flesh of Delphina's cheek. The loving mother had swung her open palm hard against her daughter's small cheek.

Reassured that Andreas had heard her confession and still listened, she went on.

"After I knew, I didn't divorce him."

"Why not?"

She shook her head. "I simply couldn't."

"Did you seek any help?"

"No."

That she, a therapist, hadn't sought help in therapy . . . let him judge her, if that's what he wanted.

"What happened?"

"My daughter went away to finish school. Hugh went to a therapist."

"He went and not you."

"Yes. And he never admitted to her that he abused Delphina."

"How do you know that?"

"After his so-called analysis ended, he told me. When it was over and he was leaving."

"Did he admit to you what happened?

"No. I knew. I insisted he go to therapy." She shook her head. "It sounds crazy. He never admitted what he did. I knew and sent him to therapy. He never told the therapist. I don't know what I hoped to achieve."

"You're a believer in therapy," Andreas said. "You must have hoped the therapist would help him."

"Foolish hope."

"But a hope nonetheless," Andreas replied, nodding his head slowly.

"And I was his partner in the abuse. I took his side. I struck my daughter."

"His unknowing partner," Andreas interjected. "You only learned of the abuse when Delphina was fifteen."

"I was confused," Thea said. "I wasn't happy in the marriage, but for some reason I couldn't simply end it. Now, now it's so clear that I should have. What was I thinking?"

Tears returned to her eyes.

"It must have been so very painful not to speak of what happened."

"I spoke to Delphina, but . . . it was too much. Too much of a failure. I ended up inside myself. Trapped."

"Why couldn't it end?" Andreas asked gently, "Why didn't you leave the marriage?"

Why hadn't she gone to therapy instead of sending Hugh? She had wanted to right it all, but what would that have meant? What would the correctives have been?

"I made a mistake," Thea answered, "a terrible mistake."

"We all make mistakes," Andreas offered. "We are, all of us, imperfect. We can only try to understand and forgive. Forgive ourselves, if we can, as well as forgive others."

He held her with his eyes and the warmth of his compassion. He hadn't denied anything she said. He hadn't interpreted her story to make it easier for him to hear or for her to tell. He hadn't judged her. Although nothing had changed in her situation with Delphina, Thea sensed a small lightening of her burden. He would be there when she was ready to confide in him again.

"I do want to speak with you about something else."

"What is that?"

"I've been visiting our patient every day."

"Yes, I know. Moritz gives me updates."

"And . . . our patient has been visiting me."

Andreas raised his eyebrows at this.

"Meaning?"

80

"When I meditate . . ."

"In the mornings," Andreas supplied.

"Every morning, without fail, he appears during my meditation. In fact, he refuses to leave."

"What does he do?"

"Sometimes he tries to speak."

"Tries?"

"He hasn't spoken yet."

"But if he could," Andreas went on, "what would he say?"

Thea smiled. Andreas wanted her to use the technique of active imagination. After all, the bear man had been an image in her mind, a fantasy of her creating, so she could equally well imagine what he might say.

"He wants the drugs stopped," she answered, adding, "and so do I. This isn't helping him. He isn't a danger."

Andreas lowered his eyes. Thea wished she could see the thoughts moving on the complex pathways of his mind. She had trusted in speaking honestly to him, about herself and the bear man. It was out of her control now.

"You know what I've always liked about you?"

He surprised her. Thea hadn't the faintest idea.

"What?"

"You hold your own. It was true when you were my student. It's true now in the way you question my treatment of our wild man. When you were a student, I encouraged you and fought for you. I persuaded the other analysts on your thesis panel to pass you. I did it because you deserved to graduate."

It could be taken as praise, but Thea took it as observation.

"Your application for a residency surprised me. I hadn't seen you for so many years. I imagined you happily settled in your work. Once I realized you might come, I wanted you here."

"Why?"

"The institute is like an experiment. There's a formula, and the result is always the same. Maybe the result is good, but at some point," he said, straightening on the bench and gesturing with an open hand, "it's also familiar, even boring. A new ingredient is needed to bring the element of surprise."

Thea had to smile.

"That's why I was invited?" she asked. "For surprise?"

"You were an excellent candidate." Andreas kept his eyes on hers. "You had all the qualifications. But for me, yes, surprise played a role."

"Who approved my stay here?"

"There's always a committee. But I advocated for you."

She didn't resent him for telling her of this debt she owed him, if he thought of it as a debt.

"Thank you," she said.

"Not at all. I did what I wanted. There's more." He paused, shifting his gaze to the expanse of the valley before looking at her again. "I felt I had helped you. That I had been your mentor. Not your only mentor—I don't want to claim too much. Perhaps one among many. I wanted to see you again, to see one of my students who possessed such promise. What had you achieved? What had you become?"

"And have I been surprising enough?"

"Far more than enough," Andreas said, bringing out his handkerchief again to touch against his brow and above his lips.

"More?"

"It's curious how events fall together. Suddenly, two things are joined that have nothing in common. I'm thinking of your arrival and that of our wild man."

"He must have been quite a surprise."

"I wanted a modest amount of surprise, just enough to make the days more . . . piquant. But the best-planned experiments have their dangers. I think my need brought the wild man out of the forest."

The absurdity of this was apparent. The constables shot innumerable darts at the fugitive fleeing through the forest. It was a miracle that any of them found their target. But the darts brought down the man. Despite this obvious cause and effect, Thea agreed with Andreas. Chance might play its role in daily life but not in the realm of the soul.

"I've thought about your fantasy," Thea said. "Do you still wish he'd vanish back into the forest?"

Andreas shrugged and pursed his lips.

"No," he replied. "It's strange how I've become . . . attached. A man resting on a mattress, barely able to move, unable to talk. If I'd never seen him, I am not sure what I would feel about his story. But to see him, it's made an impact on me. I care what happens to him."

"You don't go inside?"

"No. I stand at the door. I almost can't believe he's here. Then I see him again. People don't just walk away from their lives. They don't keep company with wild animals. His case stretches the boundaries. Despite all that, I feel a connection to him. It's hard to explain. If he could ask me for something, anything, I would want to give it to him. He's a lost soul, that's for sure."

"Maybe not forever."

"So," Andreas elongated the word, "yes."

"Yes?"

Surprise, and a sudden joy, jostled within her.

"We should reduce the drug regimen."

"Reduce?"

The word made her wary.

"We can't simply stop the drugs. He's going to go through withdrawal. It will be hard on him. He's at risk for seizures. We'll have someone in the room with him around the clock. We'll taper the drugs and see how he does."

"But you want him free of all these drugs?"

"I do," Andreas agreed. "Let's follow your direction. If it goes well, he'll be drug-free in three or four weeks. If it doesn't go well, we'll make the necessary adjustments. One way or another, he'll come through this."

After Andreas left to return to his office, Thea had the curious sensation of being out of her depth. She had thought of Andreas as director of the institute, but that view was insufficient. He was the director but also a mentor, a confidante, a friend. She felt like a woman treading water with no idea whether her feet were a few inches from the bottom or whether she floated on fathomless depths. This mystery of depth was like so many others. How many times had she heard the whir of wings and wondered what bird possessed the gray, blue, or red feathers vanishing among the leaves? And what explained those things that never moved—the stones, the trunks of the trees, the earth spread over the steep rising slopes? If Andreas had eluded her full understanding, who exactly was he? Was his mystery different from that of a bird vanishing in flight or a stone anchored in the earth? Would he continue to help her and, through her, the bear man?

18

June passed in a procession of sparkling days, each longer than the last, as the summer solstice neared. Sitting by her windowsill, Thea recalled the dark speck of an eagle floating effortlessly beneath an avalanche of clouds. Her thoughts drifted like that, lifted by a wind that carried her without a destination, shifting from the bear man to Andreas, from Delphina to Hugh. Slowly the sunlight faded from the lawn, and the buildings darkened. The lanterns beside the walks cast their glow against the descending dome of night.

She knew she should slide the chair beneath her desk and write, but she didn't want to. The bear man's medications had been reduced the day after her meeting with Andreas and again a week later. The bear man still appeared in her morning meditations, but he no longer tried to speak. In fact, she often pictured him walking free in the forest. Sometimes she even imagined the large and wild presence of the bear moving close beside him. As for Delphina, Thea began to imagine a life lived without her. Her desire to be with Delphina was like the light—visible, comforting, and known. The possibility she would remain alone, unconnected to her daughter, felt as vast and unknowable as the boundless dark. She didn't like this, but she could at least contemplate it.

Finally, she turned to the desk.

Picking up her pen, she twirled the cylinder end over end.

Love . . .

That single word exhausted her willingness to write. It was hard to love in the face of Delphina's rejection. Painful, unrewarding. Inevitable. She thought how curious love was. It could be one thing or so many others. Sexuality was a kind of love. As was the decency of the everyday, the making of a home, the raising of a child. Or the hope for the well-being, the prosperity, the happiness of the beloved. But could love embrace separation? Could two people joined in many ways grow apart and still love? Could a form of love be like looking up at the night sky and appreciating the glow of the stars? Appreciating that someone existed on her own terms, not tethered to or anchored by another? Could Thea find joy in Delphina whether or not they remained in contact? That struck Thea as impossible, yet wouldn't it be best?

The image of the bear man in his yellow cell floated into her mind. She could feel the pull he exerted on her. The withdrawal hadn't been easy, but he was becoming more alert.

She had been twirling the pen like a small baton. Poising its point above the blue-lined pad, she continued beneath the word "love."

can be larger

Her thoughts came in small clumps of words.

than I imagine.

It sounded like a greeting card. She had an impulse to cross out all the words. Yet she couldn't.

What of painful love? When the pain honored her daughter's desire for separation?

What of the love that does nothing?

The love that is but only waits?

She wrote but had no answer to her questions.

"Why couldn't it end?" Andreas asked her that question when she admitted her shame at not having left Hugh. As much as she turned the question in her mind, first one way and then another, she didn't have an answer. It had to do with Hugh. Of that, she was certain. It wasn't that he was strong, fine, or impossible to leave behind. It was more elusive. She felt it on the tip of her tongue. If only she could blurt it out, but the words became phantoms. They lacked shape. No matter her incantation, they refused to rise. This frustrated her. There was an answer. If she returned enough times to Andreas's question, she felt sure that one day she would know that answer. After all, she had been unhappy with Hugh before that terrible day when Delphina, soaked from the shower, sat sobbing on the toilet's white seat.

She shook her head for relief from these oft-repeated thoughts.

At last, moving down a line, she continued.

You, my able child, in the world, able to live without me. Can that be enough for me? Simply knowing you exist?

"Why couldn't it end?"

How quickly the banished question returned with even greater force. She grappled with it again but without hope of success. If she had ended the marriage the moment she found out, everything might have been different. Why had she sent him to therapy? Why didn't she side with her daughter and throw him out, without worrying what became of him? The damage to Delphina would still have been done, but she wouldn't have been complicit. She wouldn't have sent her daughter away to school and stayed with a predator in a marriage that was already unfulfilling. Predator. She had trouble using that word.

Predator.

Predator.

PREDATOR.

Looking at the last words she had written, she wondered at herself. She didn't like the word. He sounded like a beast that devoured. Did she not like the truth? He was a beast. He did devour. The love Delphina had for her. He devoured it. Did she want to find a better therapy for Hugh, so he could go to session after session and still never admit what he had done? What was wrong with her?

She could have kept Delphina close and sent Hugh away. In thinking back on Hugh, he seemed a pale ghost, gliding through walls and floating up to look through windows. But before he became a ghost, when she first met him and he was alive for her, he married the vigor of an athlete with the refinement of a poet. He seemed such a considerate man.

It might be a flaw in the very concept of analysis to search for depths instead of accepting surfaces, to feel there was always more, more to be understood, more to be discovered. As for Andreas's question, Thea believed it could be answered. If she was fearless and probed more deeply, one day she would have the answer.

"Why couldn't it end?"

19

The bear man sat on his mattress, his legs stretched out and his back against the yellow wall. Beads of sweat covered his forehead and his scalp. Settling beside him on the mattress, Thea could feel his body trembling. She placed her hand on his chest. The rushing beat of his heart matched his quick and shallow breathing. Thea visited each day, after her morning meditation, before hiking, and again after dinner.

"It's going to be all right," she said quietly.

He didn't look at her.

"You'll be all right," she said again, despite his showing no sign of listening. Nor had he spoken yet. Nonetheless, she repeated her assurances to him. She touched him in the hope that he would feel less lonely. Of course, Moritz and the other caretakers were a continuous presence in the room.

"You've been on medication," she continued. "They're starting to take you off it."

She had given him this explanation on each visit. If he absorbed nothing from the words, her tone at least conveyed her concern. He probably had no idea who she meant by "they," but she did the best she could to comfort him.

The pulsing of his heart vibrated against her palm and fingers. She slipped her other arm around his shoulders and gently held him. Heat radiated from his skin. There was no loosening of his wiry muscles, but he remained for a minute or so in her embrace. Then he rolled his back along the wall to move away. Reaching for the edge of the mattress, he rose slowly with his knees bent and his shoulders hunched. Moritz moved beside him, put an arm around his waist, and walked slowly with him about the perimeter of the room. Thea watched their orbit, one time around and past her on the bed, another time around and past her again. The perspiration poured from the bear man's scalp and face. She could see a tremor in both his hands. His gait looked broken, each step requiring its own will. But it was his will that impressed her. He made the choice to begin moving, to keep moving.

At last, she rose to intercept him. He stopped but gave no sign of seeing her. Bending her knees, she looked into his eyes. How to describe them? If he were listening to an almost imperceptible sound, his eyes might have that look of immense distance. Quickly he averted his face.

She stepped aside. Moritz helped him finish a final circumnavigation of the room and brought him back to the mattress. Again he sat up, propped against the wall. Thea stepped into the hallway, and Moritz rose and joined her.

"He has more energy," she said.

"Yes. He's walking more and more."

"And sitting up."

"But he hardly sleeps," Moritz said.

Thea looked into the room again. The man had the palm of his right hand on his right thigh. Slowly, watching carefully, he turned the hand so the palm faced upward. Then turned it down again and up again. Did he understand this was his hand, that he made it move? She wanted to ask Moritz if the bear man would be all right, but did Moritz really know?

She had treated many people struggling with adversity. Some, perhaps all, searched for the particular inner sense that would give direction and hope to their lives. If Thea had a creed, it would certainly be this quest for a life of meaning. Any struggles, including her own, could be addressed by a therapist and a willing patient. That she believed this and hadn't sought therapy as her marriage collapsed was perplexing. She had sent Hugh to therapy, but of course, Hugh hadn't been a willing patient.

Nor was the bear man a willing patient. Wasn't he more a prisoner? What did she really have to offer him? She would feel her way and try to shape the best treatment, but the magnitude of the responsibility weighed on her. Without sedatives, wouldn't he want to roam in the vastness of the forest? What if her efforts to cure him yielded nothing? Andreas said the bear man had experienced a break with reality. If he inhabited a world of his own imagining, schizophrenic and perhaps paranoid, what hope could she have to free him from the yellow room?

What if he injured himself?

Was she really acting as a therapist? Could the bear man be called her client? She didn't think so. Her relationship with him eluded the norms of therapy. A force of attraction brought her to the bear man. She wasn't paid. As for the bear man himself, who could say whether he wanted or needed therapy and, for that matter, wanted or needed her presence? But without having him speak, she couldn't imagine gaining insight into cause and effect, into the life before and the life after.

She certainly couldn't promise a cure. No therapy was perfect, but her patients in the city moved through their daily lives. Many she'd helped. When she failed, when the patient drifted and was unable to find a better way forward, she tried to accept that each person's process moved at its own pace. And she might not have been the best therapist for that particular person.

Thea wanted the bear man to walk out of the room. She wanted his life to flow forward. If that wasn't his fate, if he would be institutionalized indefinitely, could she accept that outcome? A sliver of a dream came to mind. In the languor between sleep and waking, she had recalled the whole dream, but now most of it was forgotten. It didn't seem so much about the bear man as about herself. What she recalled was the insistence of the dream that forgiveness, even in a dream, is real.

20

Wrapping the leather loops of her hiking poles around her hands, Thea moved up the slope behind the institute and slipped into the forest. The solstice had passed. Each of the lingering days was shorter than the last. Today, rain clouds filtered the light and humidity weighted the air. The shadows, usually sharp and dark, blurred and softened.

She stopped in a small clearing to sip from her water flask. Above her, a stone's throw away, a peregrine falcon perched on a thick branch. It looked like a lord of the valley, its eyes imperious as it surveyed the domains over which it could so easily soar. Beneath its dark hooked beak was a white bib of feathers and then the light and dark striations of its lower body. Watching, her head tilted upward, Thea felt the cool traces of the water slipping into her depths. After a few minutes, she realized her expectation that the bird would take flight made no sense. To the falcon, she was no more than a bush or a rock—earthbound, a slave of gravity.

Weaving among the trees, she ascended and followed the crest to the pine grove. She settled herself in the cloister of evergreens, her legs crossed and the needles soft beneath her. She breathed deeply until the air stretched her lungs. As she tried to empty her mind, she couldn't help but think of the bear man. He had left everything behind. He was no longer the executive director of a nonprofit. His friends, his habits, and the life he had known, he had abandoned for the wild.

She had done much the same. She had left her practice. Her friends were like a footnote to the life she lived now.

The wind coursed through the boughs of the pines. She wanted that wind to clear her mind. She spent so much mental energy weaving thoughts of the bear man, Delphina, Hugh, and even Andreas. It was like making equations that hinted at a solution. The proper proportions, the correct configuration, the optimal order . . .

Think as she might, there were areas where she could not go. Not yet. She imagined the process like diving in a submersible, down mile after mile into the great trenches of the ocean. There, in the bright and artificial lights of that self-contained craft, she would discover inconceivable, multitudinous life forms thriving in the darkness of the abyss. She had already probed beneath the surface, but those depths six and seven miles down eluded her. She lacked the will. She lacked the heart. She couldn't face the waters closing above her, the fading of the light as she made her lengthy descent, and the uncertainty of return.

The shadows deepened around her. Looking up, she saw the clouds had darkened as well. The moist thickness of the air crowded against her. Placing a hand on the textured carpet of pine needles, she pushed herself to standing and started back along the crest. A gentle rumbling of thunder rolled over the mountains and faded away. When she passed the branch where the falcon had perched, she looked up to the empty limb and saw the clouds transfigured to thunderheads. Striding down the slopes, she hurried on until the buildings of the institute rose ahead. She trotted up the steps of

Mississippi and entered the library. It filled the entire ground floor. Mahogany bookcases holding esoteric volumes stood in rows that opened to arrangements of oak tables and leather armchairs. In the dark basement below this floor, the stacks contained metal shelves with books that could only be perused by request.

Seating herself before one of the computer monitors, she entered "capture wild man" in the search engine. Quickly she found the article that she remembered. It recounted the hunt in the mountains and the hail of darts that brought down the bear man, interviewed the hunter who had feigned not seeing him in the gloomy recesses of the cave, and included a photograph taken by the infrared motion-detecting camera that the ten-year-old boy left in the wild for his science project. She printed a copy of the article. Borrowing scissors from the librarian's desk, she carefully cut free the photograph and discarded the rest.

The bear stood upright in a small clearing. Beside him, the man, bearded and naked, crouched with his face tilted downward. The bear's gaze was away from the man, whose crouch looked like he might be falling to all fours. Studying the man, Thea compared him to the person in the yellow room. Both had narrow faces and wiry, lean figures, but the man in the photograph might have been almost anyone of that general description. What was unique about him was not his face or physique but the suspended instant of fluid motion that would bring him to all fours like an animal. Could he really have shed millennia of human culture and development to return to this wild state?

She slipped the photograph inside her blouse as she exited Mississippi. A light rain feathered the lawns and walks. She crossed her arms to protect the clipping and hurried past the darkened sundial. Reaching her room, she used the browser on her cell phone to search "infrared photography how." She had imagined a bright flash illuminating the night, but that wasn't at all what happened.

Instead, the camera captured images with a light invisible to the human eye. "How is it possible to take a photograph with invisible light?" one website asked. "And, if the light is invisible, what does it look like?"

Thea sat on her bed, facing her bureau where the small stack of books supported her diploma. To see with invisible light impressed her as very much like therapy. She sought to help her clients discover the unseen light of the unconscious and let its images take shape and become intelligible, so she studied her own dreams, her fantasies that came of their own volition, and her spontaneous thoughts and reactions.

Crossing the room, Thea placed the photograph of the dark, formidable bear and the crouching man against the pile of books on her bureau. Interpreting her tiny shrine, she imagined that the diploma with its promise to seek the wellness of her clients took power from the lives and ideas of Jung, Freud, and their disciples. She didn't know how long she sat on the bed staring at the diploma, the books, and the photograph. In the end, she wondered why one human being decided to take responsibility for another. Maybe "decided" wasn't the right word.

She suddenly felt that if she was going to stay very much longer in her small, bare room, it would need more decoration. Even a monk would want to see a crucifix or a diminutive statue of the Buddha. Personally, she would have enjoyed a framed artwork, however small, its surface built of a thick impasto of greens and blues that brought the forest and sky into the room. A flash of lightning opened a bright canyon in the darkness. Thunder followed without a pause, clap upon violent clap that shook the floor and made Thea's heart tremble. Hurrying to the window, she saw small lakes forming on the lawn. In weather like this, where would the bear man have sheltered? For that matter, how had he survived the winter?

21

Rectangular tables, each draped by a white tablecloth and surrounded by ten chairs, filled the dining hall with its lofty ceiling. When completely full, the hall could seat several hundred people, but many of the staff had left for the weekend, and the influx of visitors barely filled half the hall. Spying Andreas sitting alone at the head of a table, Thea made her way to settle beside him.

Andreas smiled to greet her. "Hello. How is our friend today?"

Thea felt relief that he treated her in the same way he had before she shared her secrets about Delphina. She moved her dishes to the table and put her tray aside. "He's more alert, more present."

"Yes, the drugs are leaving his system. How often do you visit him?"

"Morning and afternoon. Usually after dinner too." As she began to eat, she said, "I have a question for you."

Andreas rested back in his chair, his dishes empty and pushed off to one side. "What?"

"You've encouraged me to return and continue my practice in the city. I appreciate that, but you also had a practice. Why did you stop? Your patients must have found it painful to end their work."

"For me to give up what I had done for so long surprised them, but I was also surprised. You've experienced the intimacy of the engagement. The trust that grows. The work to discover the unknown, even when it's distasteful. The way in which lives can be transformed, lived more deeply and fully. Some people were distressed. Some felt at a loss to be on their own. Certainly, some felt betrayed. Although the relationships were professional, I also felt many of my patients to be friends. I wouldn't meet them socially, of course, but friends nonetheless."

"Why would you stop?" Thea asked again.

Andreas blinked a few times, straightening in his chair and lifting his neck as if to gain a better vantage point.

"It isn't easy to explain. I enjoyed listening to the stories of their lives, puzzling out mysteries and ambiguities. I believed I could help. If I didn't have the solutions"—he smiled—"at least I had the questions, an inexhaustible parade of questions. My patients and I were partners, adventurers on a quest of discovery. I trusted in the process. I fancied myself a very useful guide."

"And?"

"It ran its course."

"Why?" Thea asked.

"It was simply over. I can't explain why, but I felt it. It was a fact, a truth to be ignored at my own peril. After decades of being a therapist, I didn't want to listen to people dissecting their lives. I couldn't bear to hear my own voice dispensing tidbits of wisdom."

"Did you get counseling?"

"If I could have found someone to help me go forward, I certainly would have. My analysis was completed a long time ago. There, and in my training, I learned analytic processes. I became fluent in the foreign language that the unconscious speaks in dreams. I also came to understand that the unconscious isn't always benign. I didn't have a goal, a post I wanted, even an idea of what might be best."

"How did you decide what to do next?"

"I heard the institute was looking for a director. I had attended conferences here, so I knew the place. To my surprise, I very much wanted the position. I had never been an administrator, but I trusted my desire. When I received an offer, I accepted."

"How long have you been here?"

"Four years in December."

"How old were you when you came?"

"I had just turned seventy. Here, the board values age."

"You live here, right?"

"Yes, just like everyone else who comes for a retreat. The director is given an apartment in Danube. I'm on the second floor."

"Has it been what you hoped?"

"I admire the institute. My private practice was about compassion, the desire to help and serve the people who came to me. The institute also allows me to be of service. It offers an escape from everyday life. It nourishes in silence. What mattered to the institute's creators transcended culture. Computers, cell phones, and the like—these are marvelous tools, but the institute focuses on the potential of the human. Each person who comes here is given the time, and the quiet, to find the new within. That was the dream of the creators. That's why so much is kept unchanged."

"Don't you miss the city?"

"I go back from time to time. For the institute or myself. But truthfully, I'm used to the life here. I don't need more."

He leaned forward, his large stomach tabled on his thighs, his hands on his knees.

"Wait," Thea said, seized by an intuition.

Andreas straightened but remained in the chair.

"Is there something else you want to tell me?" she asked.

Andreas paused, then shook his head. "Not tonight."

"I have more time," Thea offered.

Andreas's eyes held an inward focus toward a distant vanishing point. Thea sensed an absence in him. Was the absence painful? About sorrow? Did Andreas even feel it, or was this fugitive feeling conjured by her imagination, floating on air, shapeless and unreal?

"This," he said, waving a hand toward the stragglers still dining at the other tables, "is too public. I appreciate your willingness to listen. It needs more time and a certain kind of space. One evening I'll invite you to my apartment."

To go to his apartment struck Thea as a new step in their relationship. She couldn't imagine what he might want to say.

"Are you excited about the progress he's making?" she asked, changing to the topic of the bear man.

"We still have a distance to go," Andreas said, holding her eyes with his, "but, yes, I'm pleased."

"I want to make some changes. His furnishings. I . . ."

"By all means, do what you think best. I've trusted you with his care."

"It's okay to give him books?"

"Yes, although I doubt if he'll read any."

"And art supplies?"

Andreas raised a hand to impede the flow of her questions. "For everyone else, this wild man is an aberration, an intrusion into the smooth working of the organism that is the institute. We weren't prepared for him. We were doing the work we chose to do, and it had nothing to do with him. But you"—he opened his hand toward Thea—"you had no history, no expectations, no routine to be broken. You weren't forced to treat this unexpected case. You wanted to. He woke something in you that made you care. Without that caring, he will never be cured. So, yes, change his furniture. Give him books and art supplies. Do what you think is best."

22

"Doesn't the Danube run through Vienna?"

Thea settled across the small table from Moritz, who tilted his chair so only the two back legs touched the polished tiles of the floor. Each day, for more than a month, the sedatives given the bear man had been reduced until, in the last few days, the regimen entirely ended.

"Not through the center," Moritz replied. "It's more on the outskirts."

"Did you travel on it?"

"I took some day trips. Like a tourist really. It isn't far to Budapest or Bratislava."

"Curious that your room is in Danube."

"Yes, it's a little strange," he responded, bringing his chair forward so all the legs rested on the tiles. "But what's stranger is to name a building after a river. A building is nothing like a river. It's rigid. It doesn't flow. Water has nothing to do with it. In fact, buildings resist water. The ideal building is waterproof."

"What would have been better?" Thea asked.

Moritz rose, placing his hands on the back of his waist and stretching with a backward arch of his spine. In the architecture of his face, the high cheekbones above the hollows of his cheeks, she found a microcosm of the architecture of his entire body. His lean and muscular torso floated the width of his shoulders high above the narrowness of his waist.

"If not rivers, then what?" Thea repeated.

"Why not the names of mountains? At least mountains are solid and keep their shape."

"So Danube could be Fuji."

"Exactly." Moritz smiled. "Or Everest."

"Mountain names would have a different feeling," Thea said. "More about ascending spiritual heights than the vast flowing of life. Are you disappointed?"

"Disappointed?"

"With the institute."

"It's much as I expected."

"But less than you hoped," Thea supplied.

Moritz shrugged and didn't answer.

"This quest of yours," Thea went on, "the seeking of spiritual places, the searching for a master, what made it begin? There must be a reason, a history."

"A family history, is that what you mean?"

"It could be that."

"It's more than that, but that too."

"So?"

Moritz made a circle of his arms in front of his chest, then lifted his hands up the center line of his body to float above his head. Pushing his palms away until his arms were fully extended to his sides, he circled his arms forward a half dozen times and then backward. With a deep inhalation, he sat on the far side of the small, white-topped table and sighed.

"It's history within history. The large history of nations and the small history of people. How the large affects the small."

"How did it affect you?"

"My father's father was a guard in a concentration camp. If there had been no war, no doubt he would have lived an ordinary life. But there was a war. He never spoke about what happened in the camp. That legacy, that indelible experience, touched all of us. My father was a child during the war. He was overcome by the guilt and shame my grandfather never admitted to feeling. My father's life, the very air he breathed, was sucked out of him."

"But you were born long after the war."

"As I grew up, I could see that my father lived without enthusiasm. He tried to be a good man, but he was like a performer on a stage. He couldn't hide from me that he was joyless, lifeless. Once I understood, I vowed to live my life differently from his. I believe the history of a nation, or a family, can be changed. Because there is a way the present affects the past."

"What do you mean?" Thea asked.

"There is so much sentiment in history, so many grievances and endless struggles rooted in ancient wrongs and retaliations. But a man or woman can decide to let those grievances go. Focus on his or her own purification. Use prayer to live a life not governed by the past. When the power of the past is attenuated in this way, the past itself is changed. It loses the force it once had to control the future."

Moritz, leaning forward toward Thea, nodded emphatically.

"You asked about my quest. I want to change what happened to my father. I even want to change what happened to my grandfather. Not that I could prevent him from going to the camp or doing what he did, but I could refuse to let his actions control how I live my life. In the same way, my freedom could redeem a piece of my father's life."

"He still lives in Vienna?"

"No, he died more than twenty years ago. What amazes me is how life can be unfair and simply end. There's no justification or tallying of accounts. A person suffers and continues to suffer. After suffering for however long, the person dies or is killed. There's no reversal of fortune." Moritz nodded to confirm his sense of this injustice. "Anyway, to go back to your question, I'm not disappointed in the institute. On the other hand, it may not be the right place for me."

"Do you think of leaving?"

"I think of staying too. But, yes, I do think of leaving."

"Where would you go?"

"It's not so much where I go," he answered, "but where I'm taken."

"I think about him so much," Thea said, turning up her palm to gesture toward the bear man's door. "Aren't you curious about what will happen? He's not sedated anymore. You've been here to help him through this. How could you think of leaving now?"

"It doesn't depend on me—what happens to him."

"Even if I'm not thinking about him," Thea replied, "he's just below the surface. You don't think about him that much, do you?"

"Honestly, no. He simply is."

"Not for me," she said. "For me, it's the way he changed. The man in this room is a kind of fossil, a record of what happened in the past. I want to know the process that made him what he is, that made him change."

"He's still alive," Moritz protested. "Not a very good fossil."

"What brought him from there to here?"

"Where was there? For that matter, where is here?"

Thea didn't answer. *Here* was somewhere inside the bear man.

"If he ever talks," Moritz added.

"You think he won't?"

"I don't know. How could I possibly know?"

104

Thea didn't know either. She'd never been so uncertain what she could offer a person. Yet she wasn't deterred from her desire to offer what she could.

She rose without responding and passed Moritz on her way to the bear man's door. As she looked through the window, she found herself face-to-face with the bear man. She stepped back in shock.

"He's looking out," she said.

"It's a one-way mirror," Moritz replied. "He can't look out. He's looking at himself."

"Are you sure he can't see out? He's so close to the glass."

Moritz took her place at the window. "No, he's looking at himself."

Moritz stepped away. Looking again at the bear man, Thea realized Moritz was right. The intense focus of the man staring at her, really at himself, was beyond her ken. Not only did she not have a clue as to what he might be thinking, his facial expression was strange in a way that she could only describe as lacking the human. Even as he studied himself, his eyes were furtive and his ears twitched to listen for a barely audible sound. His head inclined forward slightly. His mouth moved like a man murmuring to himself. She watched his lips for a sign of meaning but could make out nothing. Was he merely vigilant from his time in the wild? Was this a symptom of withdrawal from the drugs? Or was she looking at the face of a madman?

"I've never seen him like this," Thea said.

"It just started today. I believe he recognizes his face in the mirror. I don't think he knows what to make of himself."

"Has he tried to speak?"

"Not at all."

"Let's go in," she said.

Moritz turned the bolt and opened the door slowly to allow the bear man to move away. Thea entered, glancing back when she heard the door close to make sure Moritz remained with her. The bear man retreated to rest against the wall and turned until his forehead touched the smooth surface. Each day, as the sedation tapered and finally ended, the bear man had become more animated. Thea preferred to see him walking the perimeter of the room instead of resting listlessly on the mattress or leaning against the walls, but he still refused to interact either with her or Moritz. Thea could take him in her arms, and Moritz might clean him or give him food, but he didn't acknowledge their presence. If Thea's eyes met his, he quickly shifted his gaze. To all appearances, he inhabited a world of his own. She had felt his absence when the sedatives sapped him, but he was no more with her now.

"Hello."

She spoke in a low voice. The bear man appeared not to hear her.

"Hello," she said again, no louder than the first time. "How are you?"

She didn't expect an answer and received none.

"Could you bring in a chair?" she asked Moritz.

Moritz opened the door. Would the bear man follow him, whether from curiosity or an urge to escape? But he remained with his forehead against the wall, denying the presence of his visitors. She seated herself facing him. She wanted answers, but the bear man wouldn't even offer her words. She breathed into her depths. Moritz sat beside her. She could hear the shifting of his chair. It reminded her of someone entering the Hall of Mirrors while she meditated. If that person settled noisily on the carpet or expelled a breath with too much force, her concentration would break and her thoughts chase away in untold directions.

In the Hall of Mirrors, the bear man had refused to leave her, his image returning again and again. That man she invented lacked the power to speak. But unlike the actual bear man standing before her, the bear man she imagined sought her out. Half-closing her eyelids, she could see the real man before her and also the image of the bear man she carried within. She had hoped for too much from ending the sedatives. The process of recuperation would take many more steps. Each would require trust. She wanted him free of this windowless room.

She tried to let go of her thoughts. She breathed in and out with a deliberate, rhythmic flow. She saw herself, from a vantage point up toward the ceiling, sitting in her chair, Moritz beside her, the bear man leaning against the wall. She watched her chest fill and fall. It had wonder, the gape of the lungs, the feeding of air through flesh to the brightness of rushing blood. Only she wanted even this witness to withdraw. She wanted to be empty, vanished, unremembered. But this wanting held her in the container of her desire. To let go completely, in a way that would allow her to escape herself, even for an instant . . . she couldn't.

Was there meaning in the movement of the bear man's lips? Studying the busy, apparently involuntary movements of his mouth, she found it more like a tic or a trembling than an effort to speak.

Thea appreciated Moritz's stillness, his watchful presence. Since the bear man turned away from them, she closed her eyes to summon the bear man within. How did he differ from the man before her? He wanted a connection with her. He longed to be met, to belong, and to occupy a place given him by another person.

But the actual man showed no sign of wanting anything. He cared nothing for therapists, had no interest in companions. He didn't seek a cure that would make him anything like what he once had been. Did he know that he had arrived at a sanctuary of sorts? Or did he think it a prison, an asylum? What had she or anyone done to make him aware that his healing was their goal? Why would he long for anything but the wilderness from which he had been plucked like a fruit before it ripened? If left there, alone in the wild, what would he have become? Unanswerable. And where, Thea wondered, was the bear? Why had the man been alone?

"Why?" she asked the man within her. When he didn't answer, she went on, "Why did you come here? Why seek me out?"

Of course, the bear man hadn't come there by choice. Certainly, he didn't seek her out. How useless facts and reasoning could be! They had been brought together for a purpose. They had been brought together by a force larger than reason, a force able to make a union between apparently unrelated events. If an observer could be sufficiently empty to witness the working of this force, he or she could tease out the hidden meanings of its magnetism.

Thea began to hum. The resonance rose from her throat to fill the room. Looking at the man pressed to the yellow wall, Thea saw no response. But the bear man within her listened with rapt attention, the transport in his moist eyes such that she raised her voice and brought words to the melody.

He's got the whole world in his hands.
He's got the whole world in his hands.
He's got the whole wide world in his hands.
He's got the whole world in his hands.

The sweetness of the sound, its fullness, surprised her. She could have continued with more verses, but she let the silence return. The bear man remained as he had been. If the singing failed to touch him, it gave her warmth and a sense of connection to him. Feeling she had done enough for today, she stood, picked up her chair, and led the way to the door. Moritz closed the door behind them, turned the bolt in the lock, and placed his chair on the opposite side of the small table from hers.

"I didn't know you could sing." Moritz said, slipping into his chair. "But why that song?"

108

"It was an impulse," she replied. "Especially today, I wanted to reach him. I hoped he would respond."

"He's much more alert," Moritz responded. "If not today, maybe sometime soon."

"He didn't seem to hear me."

"In a way, of course he heard you."

"In a way?" Thea echoed.

"He only appears to be with us. Words, songs, art—nothing can mean for him what it means for us."

If she believed Moritz, how could she comfort the man? Suddenly she pictured him in a very different room. A large window offered the dramatic panorama of the forested valley that Thea had first seen from Andreas's office. Breezes swayed branches, and volumes of air rushed through the open window to freshen the large room. Standing utterly still, the bear man gazed out at the wilderness that had been his home. The sun made him luminous in front, shadowed in back. He didn't flinch from the brightness.

Beside him, a desk with a rolling, high-backed chair faced the window. On the opposite wall, a blue couch was surrounded by a coffee table and end tables. Through a doorway at the far end of the room, she could see a sleigh bed framed in the warm russet of cherry wood with side tables of the same hue and grain. A bookcase of a darker wood, mahogany, covered the wall next to this doorway. Books, upright or piled one on top of another, filled some shelves while stacks of art paper protruded from others. A profusion of books covered the coffee table. On the desk were boxes of drawing pencils, a tin of watercolors, upright brushes with wooden handles gathered in a green jar, a sketchbook, and large pads of varying sizes.

Moritz stood and stretched with his arms above his head. His movement interrupted her thoughts.

"Are you going?" he asked.

"Not yet," Thea replied. "I'll stay a little longer."

"Good. My shift isn't over. It's nice to have company."

In that vividly imagined apartment, had the door to the hallway been locked? Or could the bear man turn a handle and walk free?

Moritz brought his eyes to the one-way window again.

"Any change?" she asked.

"No."

Moritz continued to stare into the room. After a minute or more passed, she asked, "What's he doing now?"

"Still the same."

She didn't question him again. Letting the silence lengthen, she recollected looking through the one-way mirror and seeing the bear man stare at his reflection with such strange intensity.

"Thanks for singing. By the way," Moritz added casually, still looking toward the bear man, "the waters of the Danube aren't blue."

23

"We will make you a golden woman."

She heard the voice in her dream, but whose voice?

"I care nothing for gold," she replied.

The first light infiltrated around the edges of the window shade. Awake, certain she wouldn't fall back to sleep, Thea rose. There had been a struggle in the dream, but who struggled or why she couldn't say. After dressing and walking downstairs, she still hadn't escaped the upset of the dream.

A gray mist hovered over the lawn and shrouded the buildings. Condensation darkened the walkways and benches. Stalks of grass shone with tiny silver spheres of dew. Thea made her way to the round terrace at the center of the lawn. Sitting on the cold stone of one of the benches positioned around the sundial, she could see where the shadow of the dial's gold-colored, upright arm would fall on the face with its ornate Roman numerals.

A circular table, also of stone, held the face of the sundial. On the side of this platform, just below its top, dark, chiseled letters declared, A LUMINE MOTIS. Thea had found the meaning of this motto on the internet: "Moved by the light." But in the mist, no sunlight cast a shadow to point to the passage of minutes and hours.

The dream eluded her. Trying to recall it was like sealing an entrance. If she made no effort, perhaps images from the dream would suddenly come to mind. But to think directly of a dream invariably made it vanish. As for the little she remembered, what could it mean to be a golden woman?

Gold had long been the most prized of metals. Just as a golden age reflected the highest achievements, a golden woman would be virtuous, wise, and just.

But those qualities couldn't be given. And why did the voice say "we"? Did more than one person wish Thea to be golden?

Not people, she thought, but parts of herself. Hidden perhaps, visible only in a dream, in a voice in a dream, but real nonetheless.

"I care nothing for gold." Nothing? Did she mean that? Her choice of career meant the material rewards would be modest. But gold as a symbol of the spiritual process, the alchemic transformation of baser matter into what was superior and finest—did she not want that?

The rising sun glowed through the slowly evaporating mist. The buildings emerged, Danube's rigid outline resisting the liquid luminescence curling about its edges. Thea watched the delicate tints of dawn give precedence to a deepening blue. Could sight be so unreliable that shapes and colors constantly transmuted? Or was she simply witness to the power of nature to transform? Looking at the sundial, she thought it only a matter of time until everything altered. Continents flowing on tectonic plates, men and women growing old, stars bursting into novas of inexpressible energy, branches shuddering with every breeze, each movement of their leaves unique and never to be repeated.

What did it matter if she forgot parts of dreams or failed to remember dreams at all? Wasn't almost all day-to-day life forgotten as well?

And yet . . . she recalled the photograph of Delphina on Facebook. She had brought along a photo of Delphina at the age of four. It was in the same drawer, at the bottom of the bureau, where she had kept her diploma.

If she thought about it, she knew she left that photo in the drawer because it was like a pentimento, an abandoned image only just visible through the top layer of a painting. It showed a dark-haired girl whose face was still plump with baby fat, a Delphina smiling without restraint, light pouring from her dark eyes. Thea wanted to enclose that small, soft bundle of a child in her arms again, but her nostalgia, her yearning, always led back to Delphina's renunciation. Her daughter was no longer that bundle of light. The girl of four no longer existed—not in the world, not even in Delphina. That infant could be remembered but never again touched or wrapped in a loving parent's arms.

The growing light drew people from the buildings. Some, following the walks, greeted her in passing. On any other day, she would have gone about her usual activities. She would meditate, eat in the dining hall, hike, visit the bear man, and so on. Today, she had no desire to meditate. She didn't want to hike. She didn't even feel like eating.

What would her future be? She had arrived at this desolate place like a familiar crossroads. To know she had moved through it many times before gave her a small comfort.

Slowly, in much the way the mist had lifted earlier in the morning, her spirits lightened. She considered the bear man and the gifts she had brought him—books, paintbrushes, colored pencils, paper. She had a new bed, a desk, and a chair placed in his room along with a bookcase where she carefully arranged everything.

Gently, she would bring him to sit in the chair and open a sketch pad on the drawing board set at a slant on the desk. He kept his eyes from meeting hers, but he didn't resist when she slipped a pencil between his fingers and then moved his hand. What a difference windows would make. But she didn't feel ready to ask Andreas to move him to another room.

Her thoughts drifted back to the dream. The impossible is so easy to accept in a dream. Running like the wind and leaping into flight. Conversing with loved ones long deceased. The dream had a vantage point so different from hers. Yet the dream was hers, a corrective to her waking thoughts.

Another fragment of the dream returned to her. Thea had something important to say to a woman, but she didn't know who the woman was or what she wanted to say.

She realized the woman could only be Justine.

No doubt Justine believed Hugh would be a good stepfather for her young daughter. Justine nurtured the same innocent hope that had once possessed Thea. Suddenly, the upset of the dream made sense to her. If Hugh was a serial predator, she had to speak before Justine's life and her daughter's exploded into fragments that could never be pieced together.

But what if Hugh wasn't a serial predator? Violently, she brought her fist down on her thigh. What made her want to protect Hugh? Why shouldn't Hugh's wife-to-be know what he had done to a child he should have nurtured and loved?

If only Delphina would visit, join Thea in the meditation hall and on her hikes. Sleep in one of the small rooms. If she could share in the rhythms of Thea's life, even for a little while, she would understand Thea's love and her grieving.

What would a golden woman do?

She thought of the bear man. *A lumine motus.* Until she opened him to the light, she would not have done all she could. As it stood, dimmed fluorescent lights flickered with unnatural light on his yellow walls. If he had windows, he might be filled with the warmth of natural sunlight and views of the forest spreading in all directions. And what of his inner light? That unseen light could bring understanding and a largeness of being that defied his present circumstances.

She wanted that for him, but what kept her at the institute was something different. Made of gold. Moved by the light. A vast gravity seemed to hold her to the earth from which the buildings of the institute rose. She could wander the forest, but the gravity would not let her leave. Not now. She was held here, contained, until . . . she didn't know when. She didn't know the outcome or even the process.

Sunlight sparkled off the sundial's golden gnomon, which cast a long, slender shadow on the face's numerals. That shadow, in its very darkness, was moved by light through the minutes and hours. This was time of a sort, but Thea wanted a different time. She might call it timeless time, the fathomless flow of being that was indifferent to the accretion of seconds into minutes. It might be a current of thought, a meditation, the footfalls of hiking when the mind is elsewhere, or a daydream. It was the time in which she imagined the bear man lived, time beyond counting, boundless time.

24

In the corners of the yellow room, standing fans swept back and forth to stir the air. The moment the fans turned away, the stifling heat of mid-July returned. Thea sat beside the bear man at his drawing board. He touched his slender brush to the deckled cotton paper to apply one color and then another. She no longer needed to guide his hand. Instead, she rested a hand lightly on his back. This touch, to her at least, was a communication. It brought her closer to the silent man absorbed in placing shapes and colors on the page.

In the few weeks since she had given him pencils, brushes, and paints, he had gone from needing the prompting of her hand to sitting for hours poised above the drawing board. He quickly used up the first pads, and she purchased more.

Only six weeks earlier, he could barely rise to his feet. Each corner of the yellow room presented an obstacle that halted him before he found a direction in which to continue. After shuffling awkwardly around the perimeter, he would collapse again onto the mattress. To watch his limping gait had been painful to Thea. Couldn't she see his progress? Instead of sleeping through the day, he now worked on his art for hours at a time. Walking, he looked lithe and wary. At times, his ears or nose twitched. Was he hearing or smelling what she could not?

If she could question him, she would be in familiar territory. Thea was accustomed to the back-and-forth of therapy with its challenges and opportunities to probe more deeply in search of insights, whether rich, painful, or both.

She wanted him brought close to her. What would bring his eyes to hers? What would prod his tongue into the acrobatics of speech? She placed an arm across his shoulder or took his hand in hers, but what would enable him to do the same? What would give him the desire to connect with her? Or if not with her, with others, with people? What would bring him back from the wild? Because that was where she felt he remained.

She rubbed the center of his spine.

"Good, good," she said encouragingly.

"What is this?" she asked, not expecting an answer.

The man simply continued. His absorption was like an addiction, a compulsion. The tranquilizers might have deadened and concealed this need for constant movement. She doubted he could be still. To be still would force him to look at her, to look at what surrounded him.

"Do you want to rest?"

What mattered to her was not the meanings of her words but the way in which she spoke. She hoped her warmth and concern would touch him.

"Maybe when you finish this page," she suggested. "You can always continue later."

But when he finished that page, he went on to the next.

She pressed her left hand against his breastbone and her right hand between his shoulder blades. His chest expanded and fell between her palms. The moments passed slowly.

Her thoughts drifted to fields filled with sunflowers, their brown faces following the fiery orb of the sun. This was a memory of the south of France on her honeymoon with Hugh. As she and Hugh took turns driving the small Renault with its stick shift, Thea kept thinking how intently the sunflowers gazed toward the sky. Delphina had been safely at home with Thea's mother. Now, remembering, Thea imagined the flowers as witnesses to an inexpressible reality.

They turned off the road to stop at a small inn for lunch. On the front lawn, a wedding party of two dozen people posed in a half circle for a photographer. The bride wore a vintage wedding gown. The bridesmaids dressed in lavender with lilies in their hair. Thea still remembered the magic of coming suddenly upon that scene, especially on their honeymoon. Once the photographer took the photo, everyone burst into movement, with the bride and groom at the center of attention and the little children running on the outskirts.

Later, after lunch, they drove to a hotel in a small town nearby. Walking up four or five flights to their room, they found themselves looking down on the town square. There was a small park and, across the square, a church with a white steeple. Thea thought how strange memory was. She remembered the wedding party made them happy, but she had no recollection of what they said. They had stopped at an inn for lunch, but she didn't remember what they had eaten. It was quite possible that after carrying their suitcases up the stairs to their hotel room she and Hugh had made love, but she couldn't bring to mind whether or not that had happened.

What she remembered with absolute certainty was the next morning. Hugh slept in the bed, entangled in the sheets and blankets he had pulled off Thea. It was characteristic that in his fitful sleep he would manage to cocoon himself that way. The sunrise brought an expanding light that seemed to stretch the walls of the small room apart. Thea rose to sit by the open window, where the breezes rushed at her first from one direction and then another.

She should have been joyous. Her husband slept in their bed. He was a well-proportioned man, lean and muscular. She could run her hand over his body and feel its firmness: the calves, the thighs, the clearly delineated rectangles of the abdominal muscles, the biceps that could bring a tennis racquet overhead with such grace and force. Receding slightly at the temples, his dark hair curled about his head. That recession emphasized the rise of his forehead, which promised fineness of thought. His nose, broken in a college boxing match, hadn't been set exactly back on center. This gave him a ruggedness matched by the dark stubble of his cheeks that no amount of shaving could subdue. His strong jaw was the foundation to all this, the face of a forceful and determined man.

Except that he wasn't.

So many possibilities might have carried Thea into the future. Hugh had been only one, but she made him her choice. Now, looking out at the empty square in the early morning light, she doubted that decision. It was more than doubt. She was certain of her mistake. The certainty didn't have words. It was an unease, a worry, and a sense that she didn't know the man she'd married.

Looking to where Hugh rested, wrapped in the bedding, Thea wondered at their chance encounter with the wedding party. It should have been an affirmation of the honeymoon that brought them to Provence. During the first moments of that encounter, she found herself joyous, lifted up. But the feeling passed quickly enough. That morning, the happy wedding party struck her as a contradiction of her own marriage. She wasn't a tourist in Provence but a wanderer searching to complete the ceremony by which she took Hugh to be her lawfully wedded husband. Searching for a way forward.

The church bell began to toll. The sound was insistent, solemn, beseeching worshippers to leave their homes for morning prayers. If she could float on air, Thea might drift through the window to the nave of the church.

The bell tolled on and on. She couldn't quiet her doubt. Hugh slept soundly no more than a handful of footsteps from her, but the solitude immersed her with its volume and density.

To be on her honeymoon—how was that possible? Those irretrievable vows she had taken. . . . As she sat by the window that morning, the realization that she lived a lie entered her with a force too great to exit.

25

Returning her attention at last to the yellow room, she smoothed the bear man's shoulders and rose. Moritz had been sitting behind her on the new mattress, which was supported by a box spring and metal frame. He stood and followed her out of the room.

"What is he thinking?" Thea asked the question of herself, but Moritz replied.

"Maybe"—Moritz stressed the word—"he's been taken over by God."

"But . . ." Thea started to protest, thought the better of it, then protested anyway. "He doesn't speak. He certainly isn't normal. How can you possibly know what's happening with him?"

"In India, I saw people who were intoxicated by God. Their thoughts were always with God. To you or me, they might appear lost, out of their minds. They lived in poverty, on the fringes. Their clothes were ragged and often filthy. Some didn't even wear clothes but walked naked in the streets."

Thea frowned. She'd read about these sadhus but had her doubts. It didn't seem possible. Yet she trusted Moritz.

"You met people like these?"

"I was in their presence. They don't 'meet' someone in the way you or I would. They are absorbed by God."

"How can that happen?" Thea asked.

"Just thinking of God makes some people lose balance. Others seek a spiritual life, but a crisis carries them off from the everyday. Sometimes an encounter with a teacher sweeps away what had been firm footing. The intoxication of God is like a flood. It transforms the ground on which they stand."

Thea sank into one of the chairs by the small table where she and Moritz often chatted. He sat opposite her.

"How do they live?" she asked.

"In one way or another. They depend on the goodness of others. Some have a begging bowl, some ask for alms, some do nothing at all. Their vulnerability sparks compassion. One may be cared for by a family, another by a shopkeeper. Those who wander knock on the doors of strangers or stop at temples."

"It seems so uncertain."

"You and I are uncertain," Moritz replied. "Their love of God is a constant joy that never leaves them. They appear lost, but they are consumed by a bliss that makes the world around them vanish. They understand us no more than we understand them."

A sudden exhaustion sapped Thea. She was uncertain in many ways, but there were also ways in which she was quite certain. Her choice to be at the institute, her desire to help the bear man—these were certainties.

"But are you sure?" she asked.

"I can't say I know," Moritz replied with a slight shrug of his shoulders. "I don't know."

If the bear man lived in bliss, why did she waste her time on his healing?

She couldn't agree with Moritz. The yellow room was a cell, but the bear man was also trapped in himself. If he was no longer quite human, neither was he truly wild. He was an oddity, unique, alone. What he felt, she was sure, was not bliss but pain. For Thea to touch his hand, his shoulder blades, or curl an arm around his back was her effort to comfort him.

Of course, the pain might be hers and not the bear man's. The comfort she imagined she conveyed by her touch might in fact be comfort she gained from his closeness. By the same reasoning, the bliss that Moritz believed was the bear man's might be Moritz's yearning to brush against the divine.

"If you could be like the bear man, would you?"

Moritz opened his mouth but didn't speak.

"Well?" Thea prompted.

"It's not a choice I can make."

"Just as a fantasy," she said to encourage his reply.

He shook his head. "I can't choose."

"Any normal person would want to remain normal."

"You're sure?" he countered with a smile. "I've heard of teachers who work with those intoxicated by God."

"In what way?"

"The intoxicated ones only want to be with God. The teacher tries to deepen their bliss by bringing the clarity of consciousness. With this clarity comes a more expansive love and a more creative response."

"Creative?" Thea asked.

"Perhaps to help others," Moritz replied. "So many people are in need of spiritual help. Who better to guide them than those already merged with God?"

26

Thea walked with long strides through the blueberry bushes. Pausing, she leaned her hiking poles against her waist and lifted her water bottle to her lips. The cool liquid made her shiver. Above her, the canopy of branches and leaves broke the force of the July sun. Nonetheless, she perspired and took a handful of water to pat against her face.

She studied the trees around her. Some were saplings, others thick trunked and far older. Of the trees she might climb, none had branches she could reach. If she needed to scramble to safety, she would have nothing to grasp. What would she need to escape? Looking through the forest and the outcroppings of stone, she saw nothing. Except for birds, squirrels, and an occasional deer, she never saw anything living in the forest. Where did the bears vanish to during the day? And the coyotes? The foxes? Life surrounded her, but it was wild, wary, cautious, adept in its concealment.

What if, now, the bear came charging toward her—on all fours like a dark engine hurtling down the slope? Of course, she should raise her hiking poles, bang them together, and appear fearless and large. But in her terror she would probably be unable to think. She might turn and race like the wind, though she could never outrun the bear. Even if she could shinny up the rough bark and grasp a limb, the bear could climb too. Its claws and strength made the heights no obstacle. It could tear her from whatever perch she might find. On the ground, bleeding, perhaps half-conscious, she might mimic death. If she did, would the bear paw at her a few times and at last leave her bruised but alive?

She drank again, twisted the bottle's top back on, and replaced it in its holder on her belt. Peering into the forest, she saw no more than she had seen before. Where did the animals hide? Or was that the wrong question? She couldn't assess how well a bear might hear or discern scents carried on a breeze. Her most silent steps might crash on a wild ear. Perhaps, by sound and scent, she unknowingly announced her presence in the forest. As she moved, maybe the bear simply moved to keep at a distance from her. It was like a dance, the partners unseen yet moving as a pair.

Taking a deep breath, she tried to exhale away these thoughts. To fear the invisible was like playing a game with herself. Her anxieties were arbitrary, phantoms, nonessential. How many times had she fearlessly hiked this same terrain? Gripping her poles, she reached the crest. Ahead, the land dropped sharply only to rise again as the mountain completed its ascent in a massive peak.

At the opening of a small meadow, she lifted her face to the warmth of the sun. Shutting her eyes and stretching out her arms, she felt like a morning glory opening to the light.

She moved through another wide patch of blueberry bushes until she came to pendulous, thorny shoots laden with raspberries. Bending, careful to avoid the thorns, she plucked the hollow, scarlet berries. The tartness of the first one broke over her tongue. Picking two or three at a time, she filled her mouth again and again. Occasionally, she knelt by the lower bushes to select among the clusters of blueberries. When she had eight or a dozen of the tiny spheres, she cupped her hand to her lips to savor their sweetness. With her palms stained red and blue, she kept on until her appetite was sated, although the berries still tempted her.

She sat on a flat ledge of rock. Her concentration on the berries gave way to the subterranean river of her earlier thoughts. If she was at the center of a circle and the bear was her partner in a dance that kept him on the circumference, how far away was he? She reminded herself she only described a possibility, not a fact. The bear wasn't really five hundred or a thousand feet away. He might be anywhere in the forest. In any event, he could keep his distance from her or anyone.

He might as well be invisible.

Invisibility brought to mind the first night she'd spent with Hugh. As was so often the case, she didn't recall the words they had spoken. But she remembered the maroon blouse she had worn, with a pattern of white and pink orchids. As he watched, she deliberately removed each garment, draping blouse, slacks, bra, and panties over the armrest of a chair. Standing before him, wearing nothing, she felt certain of herself, sufficiently beautiful, embodied and present. But Hugh hesitated. Only for a few moments, but enough for her to sense his reluctance. When he finally rose and brought his hands to his buckle to unfasten his belt, she saw his lips briefly tighten with distaste. It took years for her to understand that he wanted to remain hidden. He didn't want to shed his clothes and stand before her with nothing to shield him. If he had been offered a choice, she had no doubt he would have chosen to be invisible.

Sitting on her rock in the midst of the raspberries and blueberries, Thea shivered with an odd sensation like a slender snake uncoiling up her spine. Her eyes watered and brimmed over. She didn't dab at her cheeks but filled her lungs with the freshness of the woodland air until her lower ribs expanded. Slowly, she released her breath.

Standing, she wiped her cheeks and eyes with the soft backs of her forearms. She turned, her gaze sweeping over tall grass and boulders strewn by a giant hand, to the shaded darkness among the trees. Could the bear be near her?

Picking up her hiking poles, she moved quickly back the way she had come. On the downward slope, she slipped a short distance on the carpet of brown, withered leaves before spiking the sharp tips of her poles into the earth to arrest her descent. Nearby an enormous, toppled oak held among its roots raised perpendicular to the ground a large rectangle of stone. Hurrying forward, Thea used her poles to help her as she slid down the leaves that covered the steep incline. When she reached more level ground, she strode quickly among the large trees.

As she neared the institute, she suddenly recalled the statue in front of the white church in Provence. Before the worshippers entered through the tall wooden doors, they passed beneath the gaze of a dark Virgin Mary cradling the baby Jesus. The blackness of the Madonna's skin surprised Thea. The Madonna's face shone with the purity of her love for the baby in her arms and for the congregants on their way to prayer. For Thea, this radiance made the virgin's love more complex and, in its darkness, profound.

27

"You asked me why it couldn't end," Thea said. She'd accepted Andreas's invitation to talk in the refuge of his apartment.

"It wasn't a straightforward decision for you."

"I waited too long."

"It's easy to accuse yourself now," Andreas offered, "but not true to the moment when you had to decide, when you had to choose whether to separate from Hugh or let him stay."

"I had no doubt that Delphina was telling the truth. And there were other ways the marriage just didn't work. I knew what I had to do," Thea said uncomfortably. "And I didn't do it. I didn't tell him to go."

"Do you know why?"

Thea shook her head. "I still don't know. I've certainly thought about it enough."

"If only everything had a neat explanation. But that wouldn't be living."

"And I hit her, a defenseless child." Thea touched her fingers below her eyes where tears had begun to flow. "I loved her, but I wanted her to love her stepfather. It blinded me. How could hitting her have made her love? All to serve the dream of a happy family."

Andreas didn't reply. He relaxed in the armchair across from Thea, who sat on the end of the couch. He held a brandy snifter loosely in his hand. Touching the rim of the rounded goblet to his lips, he inhaled slowly to fill his nostrils with the bouquet before sipping the brandy.

Gathering herself, Thea added, "It's strange to think so much about the past. All the people are static—simply what they were."

"Yes," Andreas agreed, "those old images won't change, but you can change your understanding of who those people were and why your life was as it was."

"I have so much time now, but it feels wasteful to think back. And not pleasant. I especially don't like my situation with Delphina. It's painful, unendurable really."

"You don't know the future."

Was this meant to give her hope?

"That's true. The bear man is actually a relief. At least he's here. He's real. He has changed and could change more."

"Yet you say he doesn't interact with you."

"Or with anyone."

Thea scanned the apartment. Andreas, as director, had a small kitchen and a separate bedroom. He even had a bathroom of his own with two doors, so it could be reached from the entrance hall or his bedroom. The living room had two pairs of windows, one looking over the valley and the other opening to the mountains to the west. Earlier, when Thea arrived, a rosy light on the mountain rims anchored the darkening sky. With the fall of night, the valley and mountains slipped from view, breezes chased one another haphazardly through the open windows, and the panes of glass in the upper sashes became mirrors of the life within the apartment.

"What made you finally decide to leave Hugh?"

Thea's face warmed. She touched the rounded sides of the brandy snifter Andreas had placed on the coffee table for her. She hadn't drunk. For her, the landscape, the bear man, even these questions by which Andreas sought to understand her life made her feel an intensity to which brandy would add nothing.

"I never left him."

"I don't understand."

"I had an affair."

Andreas frowned. "I assumed you left him," he said.

"It would have made sense. That I finally came to myself. But instead I was myself—unable to act, paralyzed in some way. The action I took . . . at least it led to an ending."

"Having an affair ended your marriage?"

Thea smiled ruefully. "Looking back, it seems ridiculous. I had an affair. To me it seemed an opportunity . . ."

"For what?"

"To begin a dialogue with Hugh about our relationship, the way it wasn't working, the fact that he never admitted what he had done to Delphina, the way he so often seemed a bystander. He had been in therapy nearly two years, but I saw no change in him. I wanted to have a conversation."

"You couldn't just speak to him?" Andreas asked.

"Believe me, I tried. He's never admitted what happened with Delphina. If I said our relationship was troubled, he would become quiet."

"Close down."

"Yes, as if he couldn't hear and certainly wouldn't speak. When I told him about the affair, I believed he would open up. He'd be upset. There's generosity in being upset or angry, brimming over with emotion. That's not the person he was."

"So you told him."

"Fool that I was. Not that I was a fool to tell, but a fool to expect he would react in a different way. He said, very calmly, that he couldn't believe I had broken our marriage vows. My behavior was unacceptable. I thought he'd at least be jealous, but he was like someone reading from a book of rules. If I had violated this rule, then it was impossible to remain together. He couldn't look at why I had lost faith in our marriage and in him, why I was desperate for change. There was no exploration of what drove me to an affair. No consideration of Delphina, of her absence, of how he hurt me and pulled my daughter away from me."

Thea lifted a hand to brush at tears gathering in her eyes.

"I'm crying too much," she said, slender rivulets shining on her cheeks. "He disappeared. Then I wished I had never met him. My first husband, Delphina's father, was an alcoholic. When I met him, I didn't recognize what his drinking would lead to. Unworkable and terrible as that marriage was, I never felt he betrayed me. He simply was what he was. Hugh betrayed me."

Andreas looked at her. She expected him to speak, but he didn't. She met his gaze. When he still didn't say anything, she let her eyes flicker across the living room. It was spacious enough, but the furnishing lacked any charm. The coffee table, low and square, was manufactured with particle board and finished with a grainy brown stain. The arms and legs of the two armchairs facing the couch looked like the same standard issue, with gray cushioned backs and seats that might originally have been closer to white. The rectangular dining table by the windows had folding legs and a surface of shiny maroon laminate. The two bookshelves, catty-corner to the windows facing the valley, were built of knotty pine stained brown. Nothing hung on the walls. Thea felt a thirst for a bright stroke of yellow or red, a print of Monet's water lilies or Hokusai's wave, but the same green that covered the walls of her room had been used here. No personal touch made the place belong to Andreas. Even more peculiar, each bookcase had five empty shelves.

"I feel," Thea finally said, "like those odd creatures you used to teach us about. One had the body of a snake and the head of a jaguar. The snake could penetrate the earth and the jaguar leap to heaven."

"So you're neither serpent nor jaguar?"

"That's right. Not entirely either."

She could see Andreas calculating, his eyes veiled with inner considerations and yet also focused intently on her. Thea felt he was looking at her depths. At last, he nodded with approval. But for what?

"You're talking about psyche," Andreas said quietly, "not wholly this or that but blended, complex, in flux, unfolding. We fail ourselves and try to understand why. In that way, failure may become self-knowledge."

"I wanted to live that life of discovery," Thea responded, "the inner life, and be whatever I had to be. But I feel sidetracked. I'm so far off course."

"You're in a process. That's why you're here. You can't know the outcome."

Andreas lifted his glass again. He savored the brandy on his tongue. The institute didn't serve wine or liquor with the meals in the dining hall.

"When I invited you to visit," Andreas said, "I wasn't completely certain if I dared to say what I wanted. Listening to you, I realize I was right to invite you. Would you like to spend the night?"

Andreas's words were unmistakable, but Thea faltered at their incongruity. What in their back-and-forth had brought them to this?

"Would you like me to spend the night?" she temporized.

"Yes."

"Where would I sleep?"

"With me."

135

She couldn't imagine him as a sexual partner. He was a generation older than she. Although his face was handsome enough, she disliked his bulk. And it was more than that. She had always known him in a role. He had been her professor. Now he was the director of the institute. She didn't want to change this.

"For sex?" she asked, without concealing her disbelief and instinctive distaste.

Andreas smiled, seeming not in the least disturbed. "No, actually not."

Had she misunderstood him? Strange as it felt for him to want her as a sexual partner, without a prelude or feeling of attraction, to want her to stay for any other reason was far stranger.

"But you want me to stay?"

He straightened up, vertebra by vertebra. From this higher vantage, his head tilting to his left, he surveyed her again.

"I invited you. For me, it couldn't be about sex. I'm not, how shall I say. . . ." He searched for the mot juste. "Able."

Andreas appeared untroubled by this admission. Hearing him, a curious freedom rooted in Thea. If the night with Andreas was not to be about sex, its possibilities enlarged. That his invitation was odd, even bizarre, gave her an exciting sense of crossing a boundary into the unknown.

"In that case," she replied, "how can I say no?"

"Yes?"

"Yes."

"Good. Wonderful."

Andreas made no effort to rise from his armchair.

"If it's not about sex, what is it about?"

Thea didn't press him with the question but asked with genuine curiosity.

"When I recollect sex," Andreas said, smiling at his formulation, "I recall a way of being with others that was at best always incomplete. The problem, if I can put it this way, is that the body is an inadequate portrayal of the spirit we each possess. The joining of bodies is meant to join the spirits, but it can't. And that's only part of the problem."

"And the rest?"

"I believe our spirits are individual, our own, and yet I also believe we are part of a unity. If you ask me to be more precise, I can't be. But in some parallel way, our bodies are part of a unity as well. We are subordinate to the natural laws that make survival and perpetuation of the race the highest goal. My individual passions, the feats of any of my bouts of lovemaking, are only mine in a way. In another way, they belong to the longing of the race to exist, to persist, to survive long enough to achieve some inscrutable purpose."

"Ours and yet not ours."

"That's what I believe. But you didn't ask me about sex. You asked what my invitation is about if not sex. For me, it's about the slender bonds of intimacy that join us. Even if we aren't aware of precisely what makes someone a companion, a friend."

Thea waited, but he didn't continue.

"Tell me," she asked, finally breaking the silence, "why don't you have books in your bookcases? Or art on the walls? All this furniture looks like it belongs to the institute."

"You're quite right. It does."

"Didn't you want to decorate a little bit?"

"No."

"No?"

"What I love, I keep out of sight."

"Why?"

"The few precious things I own I want to keep unfamiliar. I don't want my sense of them dulled by repetition. Art on a wall, a book in a bookcase, a photograph in a frame—soon I don't see them at all."

"The apartment feels bare, unlived in."

"Yet I live here happily enough." Andreas leaned forward to slip his hand around the brandy snifter, then released the glass without drinking and rested back in the chair. "We're so good at producing things. Innumerable things everywhere. They compete for our attention, for our affection. I don't want something I love surrounded and lost in what's ordinary. I've tried to shed belongings. For the few objects I treasure, I want each encounter to be like a first meeting, fresh, eyes open and able to see."

He used his hands to push himself up from the armchair.

"Please, come with me."

Walking ahead of Thea, he opened the bedroom door, turned on the overhead light, and stopped in front of his bureau. She took in the room with a glance. It was as bare as the living room. The empty tops of the bureau and side tables shone in the light. No art hung on the green walls.

"Have a seat." Andreas gestured toward the queen-size bed.

Thea perched on the edge of the mattress. Above the bureau, another pair of open windows brought breezes spiraling through the room. Andreas bent over the top drawer and removed a small rectangle wrapped in a white cloth. Thea thought of how she had concealed her diploma and how she still kept her photograph of Delphina as a little girl out of sight.

He settled beside her, his weight shifting hers. Placing the bundle on his lap, his carefully measured movements made the unveiling like an oft-repeated ritual. First he lifted the cloth flaps at the ends out to the left and right, then moved the cloth folded over the top up and the cloth folded over the bottom down.

"Here."

She heard the pleasure in his voice. He held out an oil painting no more than ten inches in width and five inches in height. Thea put a hand on each side of the plain black frame and studied the image. It was a seascape, with the vast wash of waves and, above the horizon line, the delicate brightness of orange, yellow, and pink tones blending in a spectacular sunrise. In the hands of a lesser artist, the scene would have been unremarkable and passed over with a glance. But Thea studied the image until she could sense the thick layering of the paints and how the brushstrokes gave texture to the surface. The more she looked, the more the image of sea and radiant sky gave way before the materials. A radiance remained, but it was the radiance of pigment that by its otherness from the pictorial gave a spiritual dimension to the art.

"How long have you had this?" she asked.

"It was painted by one of my first patients, so"—he paused, calculating—"nearly fifty years."

"You've kept it hidden away?"

"Actually, at first, I hung it on the wall in my waiting room. One day, I realized that I hadn't seen the painting in a long time. It was still hanging on the wall. I saw it in the sense that I passed by it every day. But I wasn't looking deeply. I wasn't really seeing it. This painting was the first of the few things that I put out of sight. In all the time since then, I haven't shown it to more than five or six people."

"So only you possess it."

"Possess isn't the right word. My intention isn't to keep it away from others. It's to make certain I appreciate it as fully as I can."

"Thanks." Thea handed the painting back to him, then watched as Andreas carefully enfolded it in the cloth. At last, he stood, returned the wrapped painting to its resting place, and closed the top drawer.

"Shall I turn out the lights?" he asked.

"Yes," Thea agreed. "I'll just use the bathroom."

Emerging from the bathroom, Thea stopped to let her eyes adjust. Andreas had shut off the lights in the living room as well as the bedroom. Gradually, she saw his dark form in the dimness. He lay on the side of the bed nearer the windows. Sitting on the opposite side, Thea gripped the heel of each shoe and set them side by side on the floor. Lowering to rest on her back, she tucked a pillow under her head. It was strange to be in bed fully dressed, to have the bed not be her own, and to have the large shape of Andreas so close by.

"Are you comfortable?"

"Yes," she replied.

The open door to the bedroom made a passage for the breezes. In the darkness, much had vanished that in the light had solidity. What remained was transformed, shadowed, difficult to discern.

"In your bureau," Thea said, speaking to the darkened room rather than to Andreas whose face she couldn't see, "do you keep any photos, scrapbooks, or old letters?"

"I never made scrapbooks. Photos, I've kept some. Letters too, but not many."

"How do you decide what to keep?"

"It's hard to describe"—Andreas paused—"but I tremble in a way. You might call it wonder or awe. I feel myself like an instrument set vibrating, brought to sound, when I'm touched this way."

"That's what the painting makes you feel?"

"Each time I take it from that drawer and open the cloth, yes."

In the brief silence that followed, Thea considered closing her eyes and drifting to sleep.

"Also," Andreas added, "there's a risk in sharing what I find precious."

"A risk?"

"What if the person doesn't value it as I do?"

"Why would you care?"

"There are a few objects, only a few, I want to enjoy without a thought as to whether others are moved as I am."

"Can't you do that, no matter what anyone says?"

140

"Perhaps I could train myself, but there's more. It's really about something else."

Thea wanted to see his face, to understand whether some visual cues might explain his words.

"What do you mean?"

"Imagine it's not a painting, a photograph, or an object at all. Imagine it's a memory of an experience. The experience, or I should say the memory of the experience, is very important to you. It changed your view of life and, well, transcended death. You're not sure anyone else ever had an experience like yours. But you don't dare speak to anyone about what happened."

"Why wouldn't you?"

"Because words aren't adequate to describe what happened. It doesn't matter how carefully you choose them. Even worse, the more you describe, the more you replace what happened with the inadequacy of the words. The words shape a new memory. The experience drifts away until only the words remain. You may not even know what you've lost."

"What are you talking about?" Thea turned her head but couldn't make out the expression on his darkened face. "What transcended death? Did this happen to you?"

"Yes."

"But you don't want to speak about it."

"Tonight, to you, I want to speak. I invited you to stay so I could speak."

Thea waited. As she had dared tell Andreas a secret she believed unspeakable, now he wanted to confide in her. In the darkness, Andreas's voice was disembodied.

"Once," he began, "through this window, I heard the song of a whippoorwill. The sound made me want to rush into the forest and chase those indelible notes. I looked out, but the light was failing with the dusk. A whippoorwill usually repeats its song quickly again and again. This bird sang once."

"They're nocturnal, aren't they?" Thea responded. "I've heard them in the dark. Strange the bird didn't keep singing."

"Long after the vibrations had vanished, absorbed into wood and earth or vanished in the farthest reaches of air, I waited and listened. My ears hungered for the song. What mystery of creation could bring from a diminutive throat such a melody? I searched out recordings of whippoorwills, but their trilling came nowhere near the resonant beauty I heard that night."

"You never heard that song again?"

"I didn't," Andreas replied, "and I don't think I ever will. I doubt anyone will."

"But why? Surely the bird continued to sing. Perhaps lower in the valley or farther away in the forest."

"That would be logical, but I don't think so. Maybe I'm wrong. In any case, that it would only happen once for me gave it special meaning. Nothing I say will bring that melody to your ears. You have to decide whether to believe me. It's up to you."

"Why wouldn't I believe you?"

"Simply because you didn't hear. You weren't with me that night. Only I heard."

"Of course I believe you," Thea said.

"Good, I'm glad." Andreas paused before he went on. "But what if I were to tell you something far more incredible?"

"I'd have to hear it."

"What if I said"—he paused again—"I can float on the air and move faster than the speed of light? Would you believe me?"

Thea turned her head to look in his direction. She could barely make out his form. Was the moon a crescent, a sliver of silver gleaming high above? A short walk across the lawn would bring her to her room. Wouldn't she be more comfortable in her own bed?

"What if life is far different from what we imagine? What if the boundaries we believe in aren't the real boundaries?"

"What if, what if," she echoed. "It's like a song."

"Think how much possibility we close off. What if we're wrong? Maybe what we believe is impossible isn't impossible at all. Even if you have one experience outside the boundaries of what you believe possible, that's all you know. You can't know whether your other certainties are right or wrong. And you'll only believe if you have the experience. You won't believe me if I tell you about an experience I had."

"Try me," Thea offered.

"What I want to tell you about . . . it only happened once. I've shared this with very few people, but each telling has the danger of the experience feeling less real for me. If you, or whoever I'm talking to, doesn't believe the story, why should I talk about it at all?"

Thea didn't attempt an answer.

"It begins," Andreas continued, "with meeting a woman. It was soon after the end of my first marriage and long before the beginning of my second. I was confused, in pain, sad about the old but eager for the new. I attended a daylong program about the mystery cults of antiquity. There were thirty or forty people in the audience, mostly women. When the lecturers asked for questions, this woman began to speak. I had noticed her before. She spoke of her heart, touching her palm to her breastbone. She said she was a sensitive."

"A psychic?"

"Yes. She was exotic, not foreign but different. From the jumble of what she said, sentences and thoughts in collision, I wondered about her sanity. She spoke of a lover who had been murdered, her terrible pain at his recent death, and her certainty that he had gone home."

"Home?"

"That he was more spirit than flesh. He wasn't meant to live in a body subject to hunger, gravity, desire, and all the rest. Within months of her meeting this soul mate, he was gone. I realized I was listening to someone on the edge of a precipice. What I accepted as firm ground had little meaning for her. I felt challenged and stirred by her. When the session broke, I had to speak to her."

"What was her name?"

"Her name isn't really important. I don't mean to conceal who she was, but for me, she was larger than a name. I can't explain how she came to be who she was. Her father made a fortune in Hollywood, but he was incredibly stingy. Her mother died when she was very young. As an infant, she suffered painful physical abuse from the woman hired to care for her. All her life, she ran very high temperatures. She loved the taste of food, but for food to pass through her was a painful struggle. She wasn't, as she said, well suited to the physical. In a lighter mood, she might say the material world gave her indigestion. She called our universe sensational, by which she meant ruled by sensations. To her, our lives were experiments.

"When I say she was a psychic, I don't mean a fortune teller. She was psychological. She wanted to understand why we are who we are. She was highly intuitive. She thought of herself as a seer, one who sees. She wore a necklace with a golden moonstone framed in silver. The silver made the outline of an eye with the moonstone as the iris. Her own eyes were gray, penetrating. Her right eye had a keyhole, the roundness of her pupil touched by a small, dark rectangle. She had been born this way and claimed it gave her greater sight. In her sessions, she would look over a person's left shoulder. That was where she saw the soul, the deepest dimension of the other. She was fluid, receptive, a medium for conveying what rose from sources beyond her. At least, that's what she said.

"As a psychic, she had the power that comes from knowing. But she was also fearful. In part, she felt she didn't belong here. She believed she might have come from another dimension. She might be a walk-in, an alien living in the body of a human. What frustrated her sometimes was not being able to remember. If there had been another place, a previous life, it was recollected in fragments like a dream. People could frighten her. Sometimes by the pain she perceived, whether or not the person was aware. Sometimes by the capacity for violence she might feel in someone, even if I looked at the same person and saw no danger at all. I frightened her. She felt the child she had been still lived inside her. So, she said, the boy I had been lived within me. While she didn't fear me as an adult, she said my child was bullying and made her fearful. Having been abused by her nanny and starved for love by her father, she had to protect her child.

"After a session, she would draw a hot bath with lavender bath salts. Lighting a candle, she soaked in the water to cleanse herself of the energies of those who visited her. That impulse for cleansing led her to retreats and visits to healers of every imaginable kind.

"She believed herself a teacher of young men. I was forty, not so young, and she was fifty. But I have to agree. She was my teacher. Difficult, very difficult at times, but I wasn't always the best of students. I could go on, but I've said enough to give you a sense of her."

Andreas stopped speaking. The silence hovered like a vibration, an anti-sound. Unable to see him, Thea imagined his essence escaped his flesh and floated above them. As her ears adjusted, she could hear the whistling of Andreas's inhalations in the shallows of his chest. For a moment she wondered if he had fallen asleep, but then he resumed.

"It happened the first night we spent together. It was so long ago, I don't remember our lovemaking. After separating, I fell into a deep sleep. Suddenly, I was awake in utter darkness. In my confusion, barely aware of where or who I was, I realized someone else was inside me. The person in me was as confused and disoriented as I was. By what I can only call telepathy, I understood the woman sleeping beside me had somehow slipped from her body into mine. She, this spirit, was lost and shocked to have returned to my body instead of hers.

"If I had been awake, I don't think she could have entered me. I can't explain why sleep allowed it. And only on that night. Perhaps our sexual joining opened us in some way. The sensation of having her in me was exquisite. I believe she flew into the cavity of my chest and reached the root of my spine. What was she? Energy, thought, a powerful whirling, sparks—so hard to describe. She was the woman asleep beside me, but in another dimension. Stripped of the need for flesh, spirit only, a traveler in cosmic spaces. While I might say she entered the wrong body, in an unerring way I don't understand—nor did she consciously—she had made the correct choice. She wanted a union. She withdrew from me quickly enough, but I had been penetrated. If I heard such a story, if it hadn't happened to me, I wouldn't believe it. Nonetheless, it's true."

Thea had no idea whether Andreas told her the truth. She had never had such an experience. Nor had any client of hers offered a narrative like his. But as improbable as the experience might be, why would he construct so elaborate a lie? He didn't pressure her to say she believed him.

"I never met anyone else like her."

"Why tell me now, especially if you didn't want to speak about it?"

"She's gone," he replied quietly.

"I'm sorry," Thea said, adding ten years to Andreas's age to find the woman would have been in her mid-eighties.

"I wanted to speak to someone about her. I wanted you to know of her."

"When did she die?"

"Only a few weeks ago."

"What did she die of?"

"A rare cancer. It was in the tissue in front of her intestines. It made me think of all her digestive problems. As much as she loved the realm of spirit, she had a painful departure from the physical world. I had been certain death was the final end. That first night with her changed what I believe. Knowing some part of us can leave the body, why wouldn't it leave at death to travel on? I had the briefest glimpse of a universe far different from what I imagined. I don't know its laws or the details of its magic."

"But you haven't been with her for a long time."

"She believed I was the one for her, the one to share her journeys between worlds and be her life companion. She saw a future for us together that I couldn't imagine. If I wasn't going to be with her, she found an occasional meeting too painful. We kept in touch. Long distance. Occasionally, we exchanged a letter or an email. We remembered each other's birthdays. Now that she's gone . . . the world is poorer without her."

Andreas stopped speaking. Aware that she had stayed awake far later than usual, Thea drifted. A coolness settled in her. Her thoughts glanced one way and then another. In the darkness, what time showed on the sundial's Roman numerals? Could the subtle moonlight also cast shadows across the dial? Her head and limbs felt heavy with the gravity of a far larger planet. She wanted to turn on her right side where she always began her sleep.

"I would rest beside her," Andreas said, his voice bringing Thea back from the dissolve of sleep, "just as you and I are side by side now. One night, she began to chant aloud while she slept. The voice was far larger than her own, deep and resonant, drawn from her entirety.

147

'Om, om, om,' again and again, and I could feel a stirring in the air. On many nights, I felt the vibration of her leaving her body. Where she went, I can't say. When I asked her, she remembered traveling but not the details of those other planes. One night, while I slept across the city from her, she appeared like a silver dervish whirling by my bedside. I felt her as a dynamo generating the energy for her travels.

"I began to have inexplicable experiences. Sometimes when I slept, a wave would gather at the base of my spine and slowly flow up through my vertebrae. The feeling of this was exquisite. I might wake and lie in a joyous paralysis until it ended. Or I might remember the experience like a dream. I learned not to think about what was happening because that would make it stop. After, I could feel the energy on my skin, a radiance like a buoyancy and a cleansing. It would happen from time to time, even when I was no longer with her."

Thea wanted to ask a question. If the trees spoke by their swaying, what did they say? Did each tree have its own voice, its own thoughts? Or was there a single voice for the forest? She tried to lift herself from the powerful undertow of sleep. Strange to have Andreas beside her. Strange to have heard his story and not know whether she believed him. It would be easier to say he lied, but she couldn't dismiss him so easily. The woman of whom he spoke seemed mystifying, even bizarre, but fantastically real. Thea did have a question. If what he said were true, what beliefs would she have to discard? Transform? Her thoughts skipped like a stone across the rushing surface of a stream. As the stone slipped beneath the surface and sank in the depths, she slept.

She was wakened by the growing light of early morning. Disoriented for a few moments in the strange room, she pieced together her memories of the evening with Andreas. Turning her head to the side, she saw he was gone. She sat up, pressing her feet to the floor and hurrying to the bathroom.

"Thea?"

She finished washing her face, used her hands to shape her hair as best she could, and tried to brush the wrinkles from her clothes.

"Good morning," he said when she came back to the bedroom.

He stood in the doorway between the bedroom and living room. He had changed into freshly ironed charcoal trousers and a blue shirt, but the half circles beneath his eyes were puffy and dark.

"Did you sleep well?" he asked.

"Yes."

"Thanks for staying and listening."

"Not at all."

"I want to give you something."

Andreas pushed off the doorframe and went to the side of the bed away from Thea. Opening the top drawer of the bureau, he lifted out a small rectangle wrapped in a white cloth. Holding the small bundle at the level of his heart, his fingers curled beneath and his thumbs above, he offered it to Thea.

"She made this."

Thea wanted to protest his giving it to her, but she took it from him. It was thicker and a bit heavier than the painting.

"She took off for a month to study sacred arts in Japan. I came for her graduation, and we traveled together. It's a small book, or maybe album is a better description. It's about her time at the school and our travels."

The woman had been like a fiction, an architecture of words. But the book was tangible, proof of at least some of what Andreas had said. Thea left the book wrapped in its protective cloth.

"Thanks, I'll take good care of it. I'll give it back soon."

149

28

"Are you afraid of the woods?" Thea asked.

"No, why should I be?"

"You never hike."

"That's true," Moritz agreed.

"Why not?"

"I'm too busy."

"Would you like to?"

"If things were different, maybe."

They walked side by side up the slope of the lawn behind the library and passed through a zone of trees before reaching a wide path that made an arc through the forest above the institute. The path connected a sequence of clearings with benches for solitude seekers.

"So you don't know."

"What?"

"The forest, how empty it is."

"It's not empty," Moritz said. "You don't have to hike to know that."

"But it seems empty. Once in a great while, I glimpse a deer leaping away."

"What else would you expect to see?"

"Have you heard the coyotes at night?"

"Howling? Sure. More in the spring than now."

"I've never seen a coyote in the woods."

"They're nocturnal. You don't hike at night."

"Or raccoons?"

"Why would you expect to see them? They avoid people. If you see one, it's probably rabid."

More than a week had passed since her night with Andreas, but in a way those hours with him continued. Consciously, Thea found Andreas's story difficult to believe, but taking a sidelong glance at Moritz, she entertained the possibility that he too might contain a subtle energy that could move him beyond the ordinary. Andreas told her how those vibrations entered him, an ecstasy rising upward from the root of his spine. If this happened to Andreas, couldn't it happen to Moritz, to her, to anyone?

"How can something seem empty," Thea asked, "when it's actually full? Full of life, everywhere around you, unseen. Isn't that strange?"

"The animals avoid us for good reason."

"They're like a thought you don't want to think."

"A thought?" Moritz echoed.

"The unconscious is filled to the brim with thoughts, feelings, ideas that aren't in our consciousness. It's like the animals filling the forest. They're there, but we're not aware of them. Once in a while, a wild turkey ambles by, followed by a dozen chicks so small you think they couldn't grow up to be turkeys. For the most part, though, you never see the wildlife."

They reached a clearing where a carefully positioned bench faced the valley and the rise of the mountains beyond. Seating herself,

Thea watched Moritz sit down at the far end, with an empty space between them. The July heat had peaked earlier in the afternoon, but the humidity remained. Thea touched the back of her hand to the moistness on her forehead.

The call of a bird came from not too far away, but Thea couldn't summon an image of which bird made that call. They sat awhile in silence.

"Are you thinking about him?"

Thea considered Moritz's question. The bear man almost never left her mind. He lived a new routine now, with his drawing and painting, but it was as much a routine as her morning meditations, hikes, and visits to the yellow room. It frustrated her that his life lacked variability and the surprise of the new, but that wasn't why she'd sought out Moritz.

"Actually," she answered, "about you."

"Really?"

"You're surprised?"

Moritz smiled but didn't reply.

"Life can be unfair and simply end," Thea said, quoting his exact words. "It's such a harsh view."

Moritz didn't answer immediately. His brow tightened. His head rocked forward and back in small arcs.

"You spoke of a legacy," Thea prompted. "What your grandfather did during the war affected your father and your family."

"There's so much suffering," he replied.

He rose and began pacing in front of the bench.

"We never seem to learn." Moritz raised his hands as he spoke. "I'm sure the guards at the camps took pride in doing their jobs well. We make our contributions, meager though they are in the larger scale of things. We earn what we need to feed and house those who depend on us, to raise children or care for parents. We make our place in the community. And then someone says, 'But what you did is wrong. You were merciless. You incarcerated. You murdered.' What is the response of any ordinary soul? What would that be like, the moment when you—or I—realize that everything we labored for was immoral? That by doing what we did, or doing nothing, we colluded in the unspeakable? What happens then?"

"You think that happened to your grandfather?"

"It must have happened. Why else would he have been silent?"

"Do you remember him?"

Moritz sat again and spoke more quietly.

"I was a small child, maybe three, when he died. I have a few memories of him when he was a very old man. Once, I was playing with my toys on the floor. He sat in an armchair and watched me. Although we were alone in the same room, he seemed very far away. It wasn't just physical distance but something else. As far as I recall, he never spoke to me."

"Was there anything special about him?" Thea asked. "Did he stand out?"

"Not to me. He seemed an ordinary man."

"Ordinary in what way?"

"At the least, not an angry or violent man. If the war never happened, I'm sure he would have been . . . better. But the war did happen. My father said he spared us by not speaking about it, but that kind of silence . . . it would have been best if he spoke."

"Why?"

"If you imagine the worst horrors, your imagination will fall short of what actually took place at Mauthausen-Gusen."

"That was the camp where your grandfather . . ."

"Yes. I don't want to speak of it. Call it hiding if you like, but it's not hidden from me. I see it plainly, and feel it, despite it happening before I was born."

"You blame him."

"I blame him for what he did there. Even though he was insignificant, a nobody who followed orders. And I blame him for what he did after the war when he resumed his ordinary life. That he couldn't speak, that my father knew yet didn't know. My father knew the silence held events too terrible to describe, but he couldn't know exactly what his father had done. Later, he learned what happened at the camp but not his father's role in it. He could have spoken to his father then, questioned him, but he didn't."

"His father was silent," Thea observed, "and so was he."

"My father did what he could."

Close by, a bird chirped repeatedly. Farther away, a crow cawed. From the direction of the cawing, but closer, came a twittering whistle. Higher and even closer, a double call echoed like a high pitch on a tuning fork. Then a throaty "jug jug" sounded nearly a dozen times from the branches behind them. Thea listened to the chorus of the unseen birds. The callings didn't compete but blended into a larger song, a dialogue of creation, that rose and fell without the baton of a conductor.

"Shall we walk some more?" Thea asked.

Moritz rose in response. The paths circling the institute were wide and well cleared. In some places, a century of footsteps had worn away the earth and left an uneven surface of stones. Thea preferred to hike farther up the slopes, where she had to find her own way through the trees and underbrush. While crossing one of the white patios on the marble staircase rising up to the spear of the obelisk, Thea glanced at the miniature tableau of the buildings and lawn below. If the staircase continued its downward cascade, it would slice in half the rigid, rectangular bulk of Nile where she had her small room. Beyond the staircase, the path curved, the trees thickened, and nothing could be seen to either side except trunks and leaves. Reaching another small clearing, Thea settled herself on the bench and again Moritz sat with a space between them.

"When you say the forests are empty, you know what I think of?" he asked.

"What?"

"The first Europeans to arrive in the Americas. They found thriving communities. But thirty or forty years later, those towns had vanished. Everywhere in North and South America uncountable numbers of people died. Smallpox, measles, diseases that don't have a name. The Europeans brought the diseases, but the diseases rushed ahead. When the explorers and conquerors came to a new place and found few signs of habitation, they had no way to recognize the destructive paths of their own diseases. They didn't see the people dying. They didn't know the vanished cultures. How could they imagine these lands had ever been populous? My question is, how can so many lives vanish?"

He paused, but Thea didn't reply.

"The ancient Greeks had an answer," Moritz went on. "When they built their healing centers, like Epidaurus and Delos, no one was allowed to give birth or die in those sanctuaries."

Thea knew this from her courses with Andreas.

"As if they could stop nature itself," she said.

"Life is so bountiful," Moritz said, "and always vanishing. The only way to stop death is to stop birth. Doesn't it seem unfair?"

"The Europeans didn't intentionally bring the diseases."

"I am not blaming the Europeans, not for that. But it's better for some than others. Always."

"My daughter," Thea said, suddenly overcome by the thought of Moritz's youth and how close he was in age to her daughter, "won't see me. She doesn't speak to me."

Moisture slicked her eyes. Having spoken to Andreas of her failings, she could speak now to others. She hadn't intended to confide in Moritz, but she didn't apologize for deflecting their conversation.

156

She wanted Delphina. The wanting was visceral, a squeezing of her heart, a breathlessness, and a desire in her arms to reach and enfold.

Moritz pressed his palm on the knob of her shoulder.

"I'm sorry," he said, "sorry to hear that."

The flow of her tears subsided. As the silence lengthened, Moritz withdrew his hand from her shoulder.

"You hear the birds?" Thea finally asked.

"Of course."

"But do you see them?"

"Rarely."

"Yet they're there."

Moritz slowly smiled, his blue eyes questioning.

Thea hesitated before continuing.

"When I'm alone in the forest, sometimes I'm afraid."

"Of what?"

"The bear."

"What bear?"

"His bear," she replied softly, referring to the bear man.

"You'll never meet that bear," Moritz said, leaning forward with an intent stare.

"You sound so certain."

"It left him behind. It's not coming back."

"How can you know?"

"If the bear had been with him," Moritz responded, "would they have shot tranquilizer darts at it or bullets?"

"If it was so dangerous, why was the bear with him at all? And not just for a day or two but for months? What could the bear have gained?"

"It's one of those things we'll never know."

29

Balancing on the front edge of her desk chair, Thea looked at the neat pile of books on her bureau. Her diploma remained on top of the books; the newspaper photo of the standing bear and the crouching man was propped against the stack. Closer to the front of the bureau she had left untouched the small package given to her by Andreas. Nearly two weeks had passed. Tonight, she should finally fold back the white cloth and look at what was so precious to him.

The woman who created the book was dead. Could that explain Thea's reluctance to open the pages? She thought back over the night she spent with Andreas. Had that conversation drifting through the dark hours been unpleasant in some way? Strange to lack certainty, but she didn't think so. In memory, the night rose like an island, a jut of gleaming black stone ringed by fathomless depths. Why hadn't he invited her again? Why did she feel no eagerness to return? She couldn't reason her way to an explanation.

Papers sedimented her desktop. To her right were blank pages. To her left was what she had written. She should read over what she had put to paper, but there was no center from which to start.

What she wrote was more like an unearthing and releasing than a linear essay.

She is a child.

Delphina stood in front of the open grave, a green bucket on the ground beside her. She was four, a tiny gatekeeper for the line of adults moving toward her. The gleaming coffin holding the remains of Thea's father had been lowered into the rectangular hole. It was early in May, a day with the sun bright and the shadows dark.

The shuffling adults passed between the brown earth heaped at the foot of the grave and the little girl offering yellow daffodils lifted from the bucket. When the adults nodded and thanked her, she smiled with pleasure. Each passerby clasped a handful of soil to toss into the pit with the lush yellow flowers.

Flowers of spring. Yellow as the sun.

So much of what Thea wrote was incomplete, fragments she knew would never be knit to make a whole. Why one memory arose and not another, who could explain?

Uncountable times, Thea had recalled a terrifying moment coming home from the park when Delphina was ten. Her daughter rode a silver scooter. Thrusting a foot against the pavement, she flew forward in a smiling rapture. Stopping when they reached the wide avenue, they waited side by side until the light changed from red to green. Then Delphina pushed strongly ahead across three empty lanes to where two rows of cars had stopped for the light.

With a chilling fear, Thea saw that the farthest lane, where normally cars would be parked, was open. Because the crosswalk was in the middle of the block, a driver unfamiliar with the area could speed along the parking lane and go right through the light. Just as she thought this, she saw a dark sedan accelerating in that lane. Its speed was too great to halt for the light. She had to stop Delphina, but she couldn't catch up to her. She couldn't reach out to restrain her. In a moment Delphina would enter that lane, and this dark, speeding car would smash her and her little scooter into oblivion.

"Delphina!" She screamed her daughter's name, uncertain whether the girl would heedlessly continue or hesitate at the sound of her voice.

Delphina turned to look back at her mother. The car rushed past her and through the light. In another moment, Thea and Delphina were safely on the sidewalk. Strangely, Delphina seemed unaware there had been any danger.

This event, this death that never happened, was seared in Thea's mind. She would relive it with terror for what might have been, the unbearable loss, the moment of collision when this daughter whom she loved beyond all else was taken from her.

You were safe. By a miracle too quick for prayer and too strange for words, you were spared.

Against that survival, nothing mattered. If she chose to live her life without her mother, painful as that might be, at least she lived.

I was blind. The blind trying to lead the blind.

But there were different kinds of blindness. Sight, of course. Moral vision. Seeing into another. The last had so much to do with therapy.

Her thoughts led nowhere. Memories like fragments of a shattered mosaic. This was enough. She wanted to turn her thoughts elsewhere.

Moving the newest sheet of paper to the pile on the left, she put down her pen and studied her small room. Except for the books, the diploma, and the photo on her bureau, she had still done nothing to personalize this home of hers. Her room was as sparse as Andreas's apartment. And he made a point of minimizing his belongings. Her furniture, all property of the institute, was no better than his. Only, he had lived here so much longer than she. He had no plans to leave, while she would certainly be going soon.

She stood and crossed to the bureau. Carefully gripping the small package with both hands, she seated herself on the bed and unfolded the wrapping of white cloth. What she held in her hands was neither a book nor an album. It had a cushioned cover finished in fabric. Flocks of white cranes with long necks and wings outstretched flew above the bright scarlet of a sunset. Small golden arcs of mountaintops showed how the cranes transcended even the highest peaks below. A blank strip ran down the left side. Here, in black block letters, was printed, "To Andreas with love and joy from Japan."

Holding the front cover in her left hand and the back cover in her right, Thea moved her hands apart and saw that the inside of the book was a folded, continuous sheet. A photo on one page would be balanced on the facing page by a few lines of poetry in a flowing script with generous loops in the letters. If she wanted, she could hold open an entire half of the book and scan across the accordion of images and words. Most of the photos showed the woman learning the sacred arts. She held a pen for calligraphy, carefully arranged white-petaled flowers in a large turquoise vase, gripped the handle of a wooden sword, swirled a bamboo whisk for the tea ceremony, and stood firmly planted for her role in a Noh play.

But in the very first photo, the woman and a much younger Andreas knelt side by side on tatami mats. They wore light cotton robes with black-and-white patterns, his with striations like waves and hers with pictograms that might be Japanese letters. Andreas, with a full head of dark hair curling over his ears, showed no sign of the weight he carried now. He smiled, his mouth an upcurving bow. The flash of the camera reflected in small pools off his forehead, cheek, and the tip of his nose. It reflected from hers as well. At first, studying her, Thea thought the woman's smile like that of Andreas. Looking longer, she discerned a difference in their eyes. Andreas was watchful, calculating, while the brightness of the woman's eyes brought her forward to engage. She had enthusiasm, eagerness to meet what lay before her. The woman's hair was russet, pulled away from her face and falling to her shoulders. Thea could see the decade's difference in their ages. It wasn't so much that the woman's face was more lined, although small vertical lines rose from the inside of each eyebrow, but rather that Andreas, while middle aged, had a boyish look. Written on the facing page was a brief poem:

Above the rooted pine,
the eagle
soars.

At first, she didn't understand what connected the poem to the photo. Studying the man and woman, Thea began to see the rootedness of Andreas and his companion's readiness to soar.

Turning to the final page, Thea saw Andreas standing in front of stone blocks that formed one side of a platform supporting a giant Buddha. Andreas, visible from his feet on the pavement to his head, reached almost to the surface of the platform. The Buddha filled the sky, dwarfing the man. Sitting in meditation, head bent forward, large lobes of ears like pendulous jewels, hands in lap with fingers carefully positioned—this shape was formed for eternity.

The same couldn't be said for the smiling man standing below. Andreas wore khaki pants and a pink short-sleeved shirt that blended to pale orange on the chest and collar. Looking at the hands in the Buddha's lap, Thea realized the significance of the finger positions. Because of the upward angle of the photo, she could only see how the tip of the Buddha's thumb sealed to the tip of his second finger to complete a circuit. The Buddha's eyelids hung shut like heavy gates, but the circuits of energy opened the third eye, which gazed intently into realms far beyond this passing world.

Strangely, the tilt of the Buddha's head seemed to concentrate his attention on the man standing below. Had the woman positioned Andreas before she snapped the photo? The statue might have been made of stone or sheathed in metal. Whichever was true, the man looked tentative in comparison, small and perishable in contrast to the massive bulk filling the sky. On the opposite page, in the loose flow of her script, she had written:

He does not see with eyes,
seeker of the boundless Love
within.

30

Sitting beside the bear man, Thea watched him bend over the drawing board, his intensity conveyed by the tilt of his head, the focus of his eyes, and the energy in his wiry frame. His right shoulder hunched slightly downward. His delicate, dexterous fingers used the side of the pencil's tip as a brush to create a zone of the darkest blue.

On the lower corner of the drawing board, she had placed a bowl holding raspberries and tiny blueberries. Thea had worked up a sweat, crouched among the blueberry bushes, just to fill the small container halfway. The scarlet raspberries she had carefully plucked from the thorny branches.

August had brought one humid day after another. A week passed, and still the temperatures peaked in the mid-nineties. On Thea's daily hikes, perspiration poured from her face, beaded on the nape of her neck, dripped down her sides, and gathered in the small of her back. Her blouse would first dampen, then become a sodden burden to carry. Beneath a hazy sun, the breezes lacked force and leaves hung limp. The rich darkness of the surrounding green had faded to a shade that hinted at transformations to come. One day, from noon to nightfall, thick-clustered drops of rain leapt from the walkways and inundated the lawns. It seemed like the miracle that would give relief, but no sooner did the rain cease than the heat and humidity returned.

Thea blamed the weather for her lassitude. She went on with her routines, her morning meditations, and her visits with the bear man. She intended to return the photo album to Andreas, but it rested, in its white cloth, on her bureau. She didn't feel her usual enthusiasm. She wasn't as deeply involved, as intensely present. She tried drinking more water, but it wasn't dehydration.

The bear man left the berries untouched. The fans swept back and forth across the room, but he appeared unfazed by the heat. In fact, he seemed unaware of the heat. The way his hand gripped the pencil and the precision with which the colored tip moved on the paper showed a mind busily at work. But working at what? Wouldn't anyone, no matter how inspired, hesitate, if only to formulate an image or daydream for a moment or two? But he could go for an hour without stopping. Did more than tiny muscles animate the gymnastics of his fingers and palm?

Glancing over her shoulder, she saw that Moritz hadn't even looked up from his book. He sat cross-legged on the bear man's bed, a thick volume open on his lap.

"I brought you berries," she said quietly to the bear man.

She wanted to blame him, but what had he done? Of course he didn't speak. He had sought out the wilderness. Shooting him with tranquilizers hadn't changed that choice. By refusing to meet her eyes, or speak, he remained in the forest. What happened to the man he had been before? Was he imprisoned within this patient, ready to come forth, even awestruck by the strangeness of his current circumstances? It frustrated her to have so many questions.

Picking up a raspberry, she placed her fingers against the softness of his lips. Finding no resistance, she slipped the berry into his mouth. He chewed and swallowed. She followed with a blueberry, pressing until he accepted it. Slowly, piece by piece, she fed him. The red and blue juices stained his lips and her fingers.

His hand didn't stop its movement. Nor did he glance up to see whose face and body might be connected to the fingers touching his lips. Finally, Thea picked up the empty container. She leaned forward, pressing her feet to the floor and readying to rise.

Halfway to standing, she realized his head was slowly rotating. His eyes grazed hers, but he didn't look away as he always had in the past. His head continued to move until he looked toward the container in her hand. Slowly, not wanting to startle him, she settled down again on her chair. She trembled, a coolness lacing her spine. Did the wild berries nourish him in a way she couldn't understand? His look had a penetrating strangeness. Did he see her? Or, like an X-ray, did he see into her? Or beyond? Slowly reaching out, she rested her hand on his shoulder. He trembled ever so slightly but let her hand remain.

"Let's all go for a walk."

Thea spoke on an impulse. The bear man hadn't left the confines of the room since his arrival at the institute. Moritz pointed to the door, slid forward on the mattress to stand, and walked past Thea to the hallway. She watched the bear man a moment longer, then followed Moritz and closed the door behind her.

"Is that a good idea?" he asked.

"How long has he been working at his desk?"

"Maybe two hours or a little more."

"Without getting up?"

"That's how he is."

"We should take him out."

"I haven't been instructed to do that." Moritz looked down as he spoke.

167

Thea didn't know if she had the right to give him orders. Andreas had put her in charge, but he hadn't detailed what she could and couldn't do.

"We'll just take a short walk and sit on a bench."

Thea wanted Moritz to want this with her. She had her own doubts about taking the bear man outside.

"It's not a good idea."

"You're afraid he'll escape?" she asked.

"Not that."

"Go out of control?"

Moritz shook his head. "No, not out of control."

"You say you haven't been instructed. Even if you had been told what to do, couldn't you say no?"

"It isn't as simple as yes or no," he replied, his blue eyes glittering like sunlight on ice.

Without saying more, he opened the door and didn't close it as he entered the yellow room. He slipped his arm through the bear man's and brought him to his feet. Moving with careful, halting steps, he walked him to the door, where he stepped ahead and then took the man's hand to guide him over the threshold.

Thea feared the bear man's reaction, but he accepted the hallway as he accepted the room. He gazed ahead without a sharp focus as he followed Moritz's lead. In the stairwell, Moritz held one of his arms and Thea took the other. Without looking where they led him, he unhesitatingly stepped into air and let his feet fall to the steps beneath.

"Let's go to one of the lookouts," Thea said when they exited Amazon. The bear man hadn't been in sunlight since his capture. She wanted to shelter him from the penetrating brightness.

They moved ahead, the bear man stumbling from time to time on the rising ground. As they entered the woods, the bear man seemed to be in a reverie. They might hold his arms, but he, in his essence, escaped their grasp. His nostrils twitched. Thea breathed deeply but smelled only the familiar scents of vegetation and earth. Entering the edge of the forest, shaded by the canopy of leaves, she could feel his muscles tighten. Yet he walked forward with the same eccentric steps, more challenged by the uphill gradient than he had been by the downward drop of the staircase. Reaching a bench on the path behind the institute, she and Moritz turned the man and gently pressed down on his shoulders until his knees folded and he sat. His ears lifted with an uncanny alertness. Thea listened. In the distance, she heard the faint drone of an airplane. Closer, the birds were silent.

Thea looked around the man to where Moritz sat on his other side. "We're outside," she said, marveling to have taken him from the yellow room.

Moritz patted the man's forearm.

"At least there's some shade," she added. "It's hard to get your breath."

"The heat goes on and on," Moritz replied.

Reaching in her pocket, she brought out a handkerchief to press against the moisture on her forehead.

The bear man sat like a statue. Thea ran her hand up and down his arm. She reached to loosen the muscles between his shoulder blades. He was no longer emaciated as he had been when the darts brought him down, but he was lean and leathery to the press of her fingers. She imagined he could be stronger than an ordinary man of his size and unusually quick. She studied his face. He didn't avert his eyes, but he didn't connect to her. Taken one by one, his features might be called handsome. His prominent forehead promised a world of extravagant fancies. His deep-set eyes looked like chalices brimming with icy fire. The circular flare of his nostrils lent interest to the linear architecture of his nose. His wide-set cheekbones were elevations from which the inward slope of his cheeks gave an angularity to his face. His lips were thin, precise as if his every word would be exact. Taken together, his features promised refinement, but refinement required a shared culture, an understood vocabulary of facial expressions, a common ground of agreement about what is civilized. He offered none of these. His features didn't cohere. They left his sense of himself, his knowledge of others, even his inner life to the imagination of Thea or whoever else might behold him.

What was her hope? If he couldn't return to the human, what did she want for him? This question, or the absence of a certain answer, discouraged her. The humid air pinned her to the bench. Realizing how strongly her hand tightened on the bear man's shoulder, she released him. Why had she taken him from his room? There, at least, he was safe.

"There is a safety like death." The sentence came complete, spoken in her mind. She had no idea of its source, but like an exclamation mark, its energy revived her. There was a reason she had brought him to the wild. She smiled—the well-trodden path with its clearings and benches was hardly wild at all. But she had brought him closer to the vast forest where he had roamed free. It lifted her spirits to have him there, unconfined, the yellow room an insubstantial memory for at least a little while.

31

The old man's hands on the wooden handles made the jump rope blur with speed. Midsized, muscular, he had a full head of wavy white hair and a smile brightening his determined face. This was Glenn Eustis, Hugh's father. No sooner did Thea meet him than Glenn bundled everyone out of the living room and into the fenced backyard. Thea, Delphina, Hugh, and Hugh's sister Sally gathered about this man in his mid-seventies who moved one foot forward and then the other in an easy dance. Glenn had been a gymnast, and Hugh had learned to somersault, cartwheel, and backflip with ease and precision. He could jump rope like his father too, one foot and then the other jabbing forward, keeping pace with the whirring rope.

Thea reached the ridge and turned to start along its crest. She picked her way among the squat trees and the tumbled rocks. Her thoughts flitted like birds moving from branch to branch. She recalled Delphina standing by the grave, the yellow flowers in her hands. Her smallness, the kindness of offering a daffodil to each passing adult. Hard to fathom what moved her, what shaped anyone to be what he or she became. She glimpsed her office in the city, light streaming over the two black leather chairs set to face each other. Between the bookshelves crowded with volumes, a small painting showed a dancing woman dressed in a flowing tunic that looked ancient, Grecian. Her feet and arms were bare, and she appeared in midstride, with legs apart and arms tossed up. The strangeness of the painting was that her right foot and arm were white while her left foot and arm were brown. Thea understood the painting to portray the light and the dark, the conscious and the unconscious with its hidden territories.

It was midmorning, the heat of the day stirring like a giant not fully awake. The pines began as the ground sloped away. Protected from the winds on the plateau, several dozen large pines formed a circular grove. Thea came to its center, where the brightness was filtered and subdued by curtains of green needles. Pine scent filled the air. As the forest was a further retreat from the retreat of the institute, so this pine grove was a retreat from the forest.

Resting her hiking poles on the ground, she knelt to place her palms on the brown carpeting of needles and slowly sank to sit with her legs crossed. She should meet with Andreas. She had to return the album he had lent her. More importantly, she had to ask for new lodging for the bear man. She and Moritz took him for a walk once a day and sometimes twice, going out again in the twilight when the grip of the heat eased. In her opinion, he needed windows, views of nature, sunlight on his face, the chance to open out of himself and return to the world.

Thea filled her lungs and tried to release these images with her exhalation. Her conscious desire to be free of thought contended with the power of the unconscious to generate image after image. Seeing Glenn in the center of the whirling rope, Thea recalled feeling an uncomfortable distance from the older man. To have a father who demanded the spotlight, how had that affected Hugh?

172

Or Sally, who was a few years younger than Hugh and Thea? Sally had a strong jaw and thick, dark brows that lent intensity to her eyes. She always spoke quietly, slowly, with a precision that disturbed Thea. Often she looked down while speaking and seemed to search the floor for what was lost. Her demeanor conveyed her desire to be caring, but she seemed encased in a substance that separated her from others. As she watched her white-haired father whose masterful hands controlled the rope, Sally raised the edges of her lips, but this expression never completed itself to become a grimace or a smile.

Again, Thea breathed until the bottom of her rib cage expanded. Telling herself to give up these ricocheting thoughts, she focused on the sensation of her breath flowing out of her body. The air returned to fill her lungs and course out of her again. She saw the young Andreas standing in his pink and orange shirt beneath the eternal gaze of the enormous Buddha. Contemplating the statue and the human longing and aspiration that caused its construction, she floated in the ingress and outflow of the air. Breathing was like the ocean tides, the rush of waves against the beach and the long undertow pulling away from the shore. Moments passed when nothing moved on her inner horizons. She was drifting, floating in a measureless nothingness in which she was nothing too, unaware of herself, beyond relationships or responsibilities. When she returned to herself, she retained a sense of the largeness and otherness of the place where she had been.

"He loves animals."

Sally said that on the day they met. They couldn't have been her first words, but Thea didn't recall what she might have said before them.

"When I was little," Sally continued with her slow, careful linkages of words, "we lived on a bluff above a river. My father had enough land to keep animals. Goats. There were always chickens in the yard. We'd get fresh eggs from the coop in the morning.

Cats. He especially loved dogs. He loved to pet them and take them walking along the riverbank. The dogs loved him too."

Why did her thoughts keep returning here? Glenn loved his dogs. But why, when Sally spoke, did she seem both proud and deferential? Her last visit with Sally had been after Delphina broke away. She didn't want to injure Sally by saying what Hugh had done to Delphina, but she loved and trusted Sally. She wanted to understand how Glenn could be as he was, how Hugh became who he became. What Thea learned was deeply disturbing. When that visit came to mind, she turned her thoughts away.

The image of the old man jumping rope might help her understand. He had strength, quickness, coordination, and an agility surprising in a man his age. But that wasn't the meaning she sought. It might be in his determination to be the center around which everyone else gathered. That he performed for his middle-aged son and daughter. Or was it in his need to hold his audience captive?

32

"This is where we bring him," Thea said, settling herself on the bench. She wore a waist pack where she carried the collection of photos and poetry to return to Andreas.

Andreas sat slowly and rested his bulk against the slats.

"He's doing well?"

"So far, very well. We've come here almost every day this week. There haven't been any problems."

Andreas tilted back his head, opened his lips, and drank deeply from the pure air rushing over the leaves. The humidity had been swept aside by a cold front from the north. The day hinted of fall. Having invited Andreas to meet her, Thea should have initiated conversation. Instead, she let a hush enter between them. The longer the quiet lasted, the more she found it restful. She expected Andreas to ask why she took the bear man from his room. On whose authority? But he simply looked into the trees, sighing occasionally in accompaniment to the soughing of the breezes.

It surprised Thea that he didn't ask why she wanted to meet. Today, he didn't seem subject to the clock, his work, his appointments. The sundial brought time to the center of the institute, but it was an ancient, slow-moving time that required the sun to rise in the east and settle later behind the western mountains. It lacked the precise vehemence of digital time that vaulted forward in darkness as well as light.

Their shared night had brought them together differently. It had an afterglow, peaceful, emptied, and intimate. Andreas had chosen her to listen to his love story. One not fully lived, but a love story nonetheless. Once Andreas put aside his role as director of the institute to tell that story, he became different to her.

Thea restrained her desire to speak. She had questions, observations, demands. She could easily fill the space between them, but she wanted to give Andreas, this new Andreas, a chance to come forward.

"When are you going back to the city?" he asked.

"I don't know," Thea answered, surprised and not ready to speak about herself.

"Isn't that where your life is?"

She wanted to temporize by questioning why he asked her this, but she didn't.

"It's here now. It's here until I move on."

"In the city, you had your practice, the patients you helped. Here, you have the wild man."

"I'm not ready to go back."

"I'm glad to hear that," Andreas replied with a smile. "I'd be disappointed if you left. But is it the wild man who keeps you here?"

She felt misgiving each time Andreas called him that.

"If he hadn't been captured, I don't know how long I would have stayed. Probably much less."

There was more that didn't lend itself to words. She could feel she was involved in a process. She didn't know all its elements or how those elements made a whole. It wasn't only the bear man, but she could neither speed nor escape what kept her here.

"He still doesn't speak?"

"No," Thea replied. "Really, he doesn't interact. I'm not sure what might make that possible. Maybe getting out of his room, being stimulated by new sights and sounds. That's why I've been taking him for walks."

Andreas nodded.

"Even if he doesn't speak, you can feel how he might change," she said, "how he might return to health."

"He's one of those cases that attracts us," Andreas replied. "It happens when a person has so much that might be possible. You can see it, even if he can't. Or, if he has any sense of it, he can't achieve it. You feel it with such certainty. You see the beauty of what could be. The attraction of the healer to the person who can be healed is powerful. It's about potential, the way he might go in one direction or another. How different the outcomes might be."

"He's been through a lot," she said.

"That's undeniable, but who lives a perfect life? You only have to sit in that room for a little while," Andreas said, referring to the room where analyst met patient, "to know that everyone fails, suffers, goes on."

"If I'm to do my utmost for him, he should be moved from where he is."

"Your utmost," Andreas echoed, smiling and speaking with a light but approving mockery.

"It should have windows. No locks. It should be like anyone else's room."

Andreas considered this. "He'd still need round-the-clock coverage."

"For now, yes."

Andreas settled back, his elbows propped on the back of the wooden bench.

"Healing is a dream, really," he said, watching the treetops as a breeze tumbled the branches and tossed up the leaves. "An impossible dream. It's like the fountain of youth. Or El Dorado, the land of gold. We're driven to pursue the impossible. We follow the dream for the betterment of others. Often we fail, but we give what we're able."

With that, he looked at Thea and continued.

"The healing doesn't reside in us. We may coax it forth, but it lives in the other. Whoever comes to us comes with the seed of healing."

It was like hearing a familiar story with a different inflection. The dream of healing depended not on the healer but on those who sought to be healed. Did the bear man possess such a seed, or was her fate to fail him? She championed weaning him from the drugs. Their walks took him from the imprisonment of the yellow room. But was her desire to heal him a way to deny his essence? Did he have possibilities unacceptable to her? Possibilities that, if realized, would make him appear to her to be anything but healed? What if he wanted to remain as he was? She could only picture healing as a return to the human. If he regained the ability to speak, he would be so much more a man. How could she want less for him?

"Would it be possible for him to have a bedroom?" Thea pushed ahead. "He isn't like a visitor staying a few nights and then going. We don't know how long this may be his home."

"I'll see which units are available."

She kept expecting him to say no.

"When can you do that?" she asked. "I'd like him to move as soon as possible."

"I should have an answer by tomorrow."

"What I find strange," Thea said, moving to a new topic, "is how the mind constantly returns to certain images, certain memories."

"They must be significant."

Thea shrugged. "Maybe they are, but I want to resist them. Part of me presents the images, and part of me resists looking at them. I don't see any meaning in them."

"We're always at war with ourselves," Andreas observed calmly, "sometimes more, sometimes less. The unconscious has its own volition. It brings the images forward."

"Yes, but I don't find an answer."

"It can be a slow process, the buoyant rising of what the unconscious offers. May I ask what these images are?"

"It's about my former sister-in-law, Hugh's sister. She has a sweetness, a concern for people, but she's withdrawn and very private. I could never understand why. I should have asked her more about her life, but I don't think she would have told me the truth. I didn't go to her when I found out Hugh was abusing Delphina. I waited until Delphina broke off with me, after Hugh was already gone. I wanted to understand why. Why it happened the way it did."

"Was she helpful?"

"She was truthful. Because I told her what Hugh did to Delphina, she was able to speak. Her mother died when she was six. It began after that, the sexual abuse by her father. She said she hadn't told anyone except her husband."

Andreas nodded. "It comes down the generations," he said.

"She says Hugh didn't know."

"But something was wrong in their home. It must have been deeply disturbing to him. Maybe he didn't want to know or didn't consciously know," Andreas said. "But there's a way to know without knowing."

"Now we're speculating," Thea said, uncomfortable with what he had said.

"We resist what we can't accept," Andreas replied. "When that happens, we may not be able to understand. Then we're stuck and can't move forward."

She wanted to contradict him. "Stuck" was such an inelegant word. To feel unable to move forward, restrained by an invisible force. Why challenge him when she should challenge herself? Instead, she removed her waist pack and brought out the wrapped collection of photos and poems.

"Thanks for this."

With both hands, he accepted the album and brought it to rest in his lap.

"I should have returned it sooner."

Andreas gave a slight shake of his head.

"She looks immersed in being a student. There were so many art forms. I didn't expect swords."

"The sword fighting was like dance, choreography," Andreas replied. "I arrived just before the students performed and exhibited for their graduation. Each art required such attention to detail. To see what they showed, the surface, was easy enough. But in the rituals were mysteries that incorporated themselves into the art. The tea ceremony especially impressed me. We purified ourselves by washing our hands in a basin of stone. A very low door opened into the tearoom. We entered by putting our fists to the tatami mats and sliding our knees forward. The elegant room had an alcove with a long scroll and the simplest of flower arrangements beside it. Each step required careful preparation, from the cleaning of the utensils to the way the bowl was rotated before the tea was sipped. Then the lip of the cup was wiped with a cloth before being passed to the next guest. Time was taken to admire the cup. Each detail in turn absorbed the attention of the host and the guests. I felt the thinness of my understanding. Even for her, a month was just a beginning."

"You said she was a teacher."

"She was always a student," Andreas replied, "searching and wanting to learn. She didn't set out to teach, but I certainly learned from her. It was just being with her, who she was."

"Why did you trust me with her book?" Thea asked. "I know it's precious to you."

"For the same reason I spoke to you about her. I wanted you to meet her."

He watched Thea intently.

"More than three decades have passed," he went on, "but some memories are so much more immediate and real than others. I needed to speak with someone about her. I shared my experiences, so you would know her in a way. So you might understand what she meant to me. If no one could understand, I wouldn't be able to speak. For me, that silence would have been unbearably painful."

"Silence can be painful," Thea agreed.

"I know she's gone. Yet she remains vivid for me. Living."

He hesitated before adding the last word. Thea struggled to assess his exact meaning.

"Does she . . . come to you?"

The sunlight in its brightness exposed his face, the puffiness, the latticework of lines grooving his forehead and radiating from the corners of his eyes, a heaviness in the flesh of his jaw that gathered to become wattle beneath his chin.

"No."

Thea heard regret in his voice.

"I asked because of what you told me."

"She changed what I believe death to be," Andreas said, "but I don't think she'll return here. If she even could. There was so much she didn't understand. Why she inhabited a body that gloried in sensation. Why she could leave this sensational world and travel to other spheres. Why she could barely describe or recollect those travels. It was her privilege and torment to be born human. I never imagined I could be anything other than human. Through her eyes, I first glimpsed unknowable possibilities of existence. This planet with its billions might be like a campus, a college with a curriculum of physicality, emotion, relationship. If that were true, what kind of worlds did her spirit inhabit? If 'worlds' is even the right word. And her life, the life I'm grieving for because she's gone, was only one of endless lives. Not even that really, because in the realms without death, there's no need to speak of life."

Thea listened for a false note. If she could point to one flaw in what he said, she could deny the entire superstructure of unseen worlds, endless being, and inscrutable purpose. She wanted a lever to lift his universe a few inches in the air, but what could she say with certainty was false?

"Do you think she was right?"

Andreas considered Thea's question. "In some way, she must have been. Those moments with her inside me . . . impossible, yet it happened. As for the rest, learning and so on, I can believe she might be right. Not that learning is easy."

"I never thought of you as a student," Thea said.

"Because I was your teacher."

"But you are a student. I see that now."

"Yes, her student, her lover, the one to share her adventures. For example, this." He lifted the album. "I admired her willingness, her humility, to go to a country and culture she didn't know. To be a novice."

"Do you wish you stayed with her?"

"Looking back," Andreas replied, "maybe she was right. I could have been the one for her. I chose not to stay. I imagined I would find someone younger, be a father, raise a family. It didn't happen.

Would a life with her have been better than the life I did live? I don't know. We stayed connected, even if we didn't visit. I feel her absence. I miss her as a friend. I miss how she was unique, what was vibrant in her. So much of life is practical. She was an antidote to that, an energy rushing among us from somewhere else."

"I enjoyed her poems," Thea offered.

"Yes, I like them too."

"Looking at the pictures, I wished I could go to a school like that."

"It's like coming here, a retreat. I'm sure you'd be welcomed."

After a hesitation, Thea spoke candidly. "I'll never know if what you said is true."

"Never?"

"No, never."

"Nor will anyone else."

There was more to say, but Thea felt comfortable with the quiet.

"Why did you give the bear man into my care?" she finally asked.

"So he would have the best chance to recover. You and he . . . fit together. And I wanted you to belong here."

33

"I read an amazing article."

"About what?" Moritz asked.

"About a bear."

Thea scrutinized the bear man for any sign of interest. His head nodded back and forth, not in response to her words but in the small, quick, repetitive movement that appeared to give him a trancelike pleasure. As far as Thea could tell, he didn't absorb the tree trunks, the leaves, the path, the scatter of stones on the ground, or any of the other details that made the outdoors different from his room. The forest might be a green prison, but his thoughts were inscrutable so she couldn't know.

"About two years ago, a black bear broke into a zoo."

"Into?"

Moritz sounded surprised. The bear man kept on with his self-absorbed rocking.

"He climbed the wall."

"That makes no sense."

"People saw him going up and over the top."

"How did they know it was a male?"

"He was large, at least six hundred pounds."

"Were there bears in the zoo?" Moritz asked.

"Yes, three. A mother and her two daughters."

"It's still hard to believe."

"I have the article right here."

Thea reached toward her pocket, but Moritz waved his hand to stop her.

"What did it do inside the zoo?"

"No one saw the bear inside."

"How can that be? You said it was huge."

"The zoo was closed. It was at night, dark. The people who saw the bear go in called the police. By the time the police alerted the staff and were inside the zoo, thirty or forty minutes might have passed. The keepers counted the bears, thinking there might be four. There were only three."

"Was he somewhere else?"

"The entire zoo was searched. Nothing was found."

They sat silently, the bear man's head tilting forward and back with the perfect rhythm of a metronome.

"Was it mating season?" Moritz finally asked.

"Bears mate in May and June. It was a cool night toward the end of October." Thea paused to wait for Moritz's response. When he didn't speak, she continued. "The zoo isn't that far away. A three-hour drive. You could walk there in less than a week."

"Walk?" His brow crinkled. "Why would anyone want to walk?"

"Two events so improbable," Thea said, resting a hand on the bear man's arm. "A bear who has a man for his companion and a bear who breaks into a zoo. Only a little more than a hundred miles apart. I can't help but make a connection."

Thea watched the bear man, whose expression and rocking remained unchanged.

"It doesn't mean the bear actually walked there," Moritz said, shaking his head.

"It's an intuition."

"You're saying it's the same bear."

"Yes."

"But—" Moritz spoke the single word and stopped.

"It's like knowing something in a dream is true. You simply believe. You can say there's no proof. There'll never be proof. But a bear could easily walk that distance."

Moritz rose, pacing and tossing questions into the air.

"Why would a bear break into the zoo?"

"I don't know."

"But why? What do you think? There must be a reason."

"I believe he went for a visit."

"A visit?"

"One of the bears in the zoo was very ill."

"How could the bear know that? From more than a hundred miles away, how could he possibly . . ."

"I can't explain."

"You believe he went to visit the sick bear?"

"Yes," Thea answered.

"Inside the zoo, did he even go to the bears? You don't know."

"That's right."

"It's just conjecture."

"I don't deny that."

Moritz reversed his pacing just beyond each end of the bench, as if blocked by an invisible wall that made him wheel about and start in the opposite direction.

"Aren't bears solitary?"

"Yes, generally that's true."

"Yet you say he went to visit."

"Yes, I do."

"You don't really know why he went there. Or whether it's the same bear. Or even that he visited the other bears."

"No, I don't know," Thea answered without any effort to resist Moritz.

Moritz stopped. "Then what am I to make of it?"

"Actually," Thea responded, "all the bears were old. The mother was twenty-eight. The daughters had been born in the zoo and were twenty-two. Being safe and receiving good care, they were able to live far longer than would have been likely in the wild. At least, that's what the zoo said."

As she spoke, Thea imagined the safety and good care given the bears was much like the safety and good care the bear man received in his yellow room.

"Did the sick bear survive?" Moritz asked more quietly.

"No." Thea shook her head. "She was euthanized."

"What?"

She heard Moritz but turned her eyes to the bear man. He stiffened beside her. His rocking stopped, his head lifting slightly.

"Yes."

"Was it the mother?"

"No, it was one of the daughters."

"Was that necessary?" Moritz asked.

"I don't know," she replied, still watching the man beside her. "All the bears were old. Their health was failing."

"What happened to the others?"

"They didn't do well. Maybe it was grief. Anyway, in a few months, they were euthanized as well."

The bear man remained in his lifted posture, attentive, ready, but for what? If the bright gleam of his eyes reflected a reverie, it ended abruptly. His eyes became hooded, opaque, and wary. Thea

188

didn't believe he heard as an ordinary person would, the flow of words connecting to make meaning in sentences, the bridges of intention from one sentence to another that amplified ideas, emotions, fantasies. For him, she believed, the words entered beneath conscious understanding and moved not by the logic of speech but by more obscure laws toward destinations inaccessible to everyday thought. Then, like a faint aroma wafting to the nostrils, a thought would enter his awareness. Or it might be entirely different. She couldn't know.

"What nerve! To take life and death into their own hands." Moritz raised his voice. "They're little gods, aren't they?"

"Shall we walk more?" Thea asked Moritz.

"I've had enough."

"Then let's go back."

Rising, she brought the bear man to his feet. Accustomed now to his daily excursions, he walked with a wary stride through the trees to the downward slope of the lawn. Each of the five buildings cast its shadow like the sundial they passed in the center of the walkways. Mounting the steps in Amazon, they found the door to his room ajar. He entered without offering either resistance or a sign of recognizing the yellow room. Resuming his place, he stood staring toward the empty expanse of wall.

Moritz shucked off his sneakers. He sat on the bed and slid back until he supported himself on the wall with his legs crossed in front of him. He didn't look up at Thea, who remained in the doorway. After a few moments, he lifted the open book he had left on the bed and placed it in his lap. Bending his head, he studied the pages.

Suddenly, Thea doubted she should have shared the story of the bear breaking into the zoo. Moritz focused on the killing of the captive bears, not the uncanny connection she sensed between that bear and the bear man. As for the bear man, she was almost certain he had been disturbed. Reading the article, she accepted that the bears were old, ill, and best freed from their suffering. The word "euthanasia" had such a pleasant, lulling sound. It didn't suggest killing, but in the way eugenics might make a better species, so euthanasia might make a better death. Now she wondered if the bears really had to die. Or had it simply been more convenient for the zoo than caring for them?

34

"My mother was sick," Sally said, "before I was born. My father told me it was a miracle she survived my birth."

Thea noted the reverence with which Sally said the words "mother" and "father."

"In all my recollections of my mother," Sally went on, "she is ill. I have very few memories of her walking. Toward the end, she barely moved in her bed. When I went near her, I would hold my breath. I was so afraid of death, of losing her. If I put my fingers on her wrist, her pulse was like a bird beating its wings on the bars of a cage."

"What good did it do to hold your breath?" Thea asked.

"She had trouble breathing," Sally replied. "Each breath marked the passing of time. If I didn't breathe and time didn't pass, she would never die. If I held my breath, I was like her. Even when I breathed, I helped her breathe. But I couldn't really do anything. She died when I was six."

Thea peered at the darkness below her window. The lanterns lit the walkways, but the lawn vanished in the darkness. There was nothing to distract her. Twirling the pen, she watched its motion. If visiting Sally had been useless, why did the details reside so firmly in her memory? Sally's living room was plain. The furniture looked old and worn. They sat on the couch with a space between them. Thea wondered why she'd waited so long to make this visit.

We resist what we can't accept, Andreas had said.

Thea hadn't gone when she found out about Hugh's abuse of Delphina. She hadn't gone when Hugh left her. Only Delphina's breaking off brought her there. Even sitting beside Sally, Thea felt reluctant to speak.

"I don't know how to start, so I'll just start. I'm here to ask for your help." Hearing herself, Thea's eyes filled with tears. "Not to do anything—there's nothing to do now. But I want to understand . . . how it could go so badly."

"You mean with Hugh?"

Thea shook her head. "No, not with Hugh."

"Then what?" Sally looked perplexed, but her eyes glistened in sympathy for Thea's tears.

"You have children."

"Yes."

Sally had two daughters and a son.

"It would be like losing one of your children."

Sally looked alarmed. Thea's tears didn't stop.

"I don't understand."

"Hugh sexually abused my daughter."

Sally's head wagged. Thea couldn't tell if the rapid back-and-forth signaled disbelief, horror, or both. This movement made Thea want to tell her story before Sally could interrupt.

"He touched her, a nine-year-old child. He did it throughout our marriage. He'd enter her bedroom hoping to catch her in bed or dressing. He'd expose himself to her. He was obsessed with her. Why I trusted him, I don't know. I never even thought of such a thing. Yet it went on day after day for years. How could I not know?"

Thea's open hands implored Sally.

"And after I found out, I didn't send him away. I didn't take my daughter's side the way I should have—firmly, completely, raging against what he had done. I couldn't do that. I don't know why. Instead, I made Hugh go to therapy and sent Delphina away to school."

Their teacups rested on the coffee table's marble top, supported by its curving legs.

"Why?" Thea asked. "Why would he do that?"

Tears flowed freely on Sally's cheeks.

"I don't know." Sally looked down as she spoke. "I don't know," she repeated more loudly. "I . . ."

"I haven't spoken about this to anyone," Thea interrupted, "until today. I can't explain why I haven't. I don't feel able. But I had to tell you."

Sally's cheeks had reddened. A silence began that Thea found unbearable and yet wouldn't break.

"There's something I want to tell you," Sally finally said, speaking slowly and quietly while looking down to her teacup with its pattern of blue and yellow hibiscus leaves and rim of gold around the top. "I've only told my husband."

Thea waited without speaking.

"My husband had to know because . . . he just had to. I told him before we married, so he would know everything." Sally kept looking down at the cup. "There are things I can't do. Some are sexual. I just can't. Even if I could, he had to know. He's the only person who does know."

Sally raised her eyes to look directly at Thea.

"After my mother died, I only had my father."

"Yes."

193

"My mother was gone. He was lonely." Sally dropped her eyes again and spoke even more softly. "He wanted to give me pleasure. That's what I think. All the pleasure was for me. He was always dressed. But he touched me. My body was too small to hold that. I couldn't hold it. It was strange, yet he chose me. He could have found a new wife. Eventually, he did. But for that period. . . . He loved dogs—cocker spaniels, beagles, golden retrievers. He treated me like a dog. He petted me to give me pleasure. I know now it was wrong, but I was a child. It was overwhelming, like looking at the bright face of God."

Saying this, Sally kept her eyes averted from Thea, who reached out to take Sally's hands.

"I'm so sorry," Thea said.

"You don't have to be."

Sally took her hands from Thea's to brush away her tears.

"Did Hugh ever touch you?"

"Never in a bad way. Once, I was crying, and he put his arm around me. It frightened me because of my father. I didn't know what he intended. But I think he only wanted to comfort me."

"Did he know what your father was doing?"

"I don't think so."

Sitting with Sally, Thea tried to absorb the meaning of Sally's story. Sally was a victim. Was Hugh in some way a victim as well? Had living in that household harmed him, even if he hadn't been a witness? And if Hugh was a predator and a victim, what of Glenn? If his history were traced back, was he too a victim?

Instead of writing, Thea rose from her desk. The smallness of the room restrained her. She should write, but she lacked the words to move her pen from line to line. The memory of Sally was so rich and immediate. It made writing irrelevant. Thea walked the few steps to the bureau and looked at the photo of the standing bear and the crouching man. That memory of Sally was a puzzle. Something in it resisted understanding.

"It never leaves me," Sally had said. "It has a place inside where it lives. He wounded me more deeply than I can describe or even know." With those words, she raised glittering eyes and bravely, even defiantly, looked right at Thea. "It's embarrassing to feel what I feel. It's embarrassing to tell anyone what I'm going to tell you. I know I shouldn't feel this way. He chose me. He could have found another woman. Later, he did. But at that moment, he chose me. It was wrong but still a choice. I didn't understand as a child. I still don't understand. I'm the special one. He made me the special one."

35

Moving the bear man required only five shopping bags. Two bags held clothing, a third contained art supplies, another contained the stacks of paper on which he had drawn and painted, and the last, and heaviest, was filled with the dozen books Thea had given him. He hadn't yet opened any of them, but Thea hoped this would happen with time.

When Thea finished packing and surveyed the yellow room, it had an emptiness she hadn't expected. Moritz returned to his usual spot on the bed, his back against the wall and his legs crossed, and resumed his reading. Walking the circumference of the small room, Thea made sure nothing had been forgotten. The bear man sat at the foot of the bed and offered neither protest nor acknowledgment as his belongings filled the five bags beside the door. It was ironic to call the contents of the bags his belongings. Naked when captured, he had no possessions. He used what Thea and the institute provided, but he gave no sign of considering himself an owner. Once, Thea plucked a slender paint brush from his hand. Rather than reaching to take it back, he took a different brush so he could

197

continue. In any case, to remove the scattered objects used by the bear man brought a painful vacancy to the space. It alerted her to how his life, his energy and activities, filled this yellow room.

"Shall we go?"

Moritz looked up. "Yes, of course."

He marked his place with an index finger. The book was old, thick, its golden clothbound cover faded. Quickly, he opened the back cover to retrieve a slender bookmark. Rising, he closed the cover and slipped the book into the bag with the art. Then he rose and touched the bear man's elbow to bring him to standing.

Thea picked up the lighter two bags. Moritz lifted the bag with the books in one hand and in the other clasped the handles of the bags with art supplies and the bear man's art. Thea led the way down the hall, followed by Moritz and then the bear man. Only two weeks had passed since his first walk outside, but he had mastered going down and up the stairs and no longer needed their hands to steady him.

The bluestone walk brought them to the sundial. The morning light cast a sharp line of shadow on the Roman numerals of its face. August's oppressive humidity had given way to the crispness of September. Thea moved ahead toward Danube. On the third floor, Andreas had found a small one-bedroom apartment for the bear man. Danube, where Andreas had his office on the first floor and his apartment on the second, was the only building with apartments. Permanent residents, invariably staff, resided in Danube.

Steadily, shopping bags in hand, Thea ascended the flights to the third floor. Glancing back, she saw the bear man climbing the steps with Moritz at his side. She had worried he might be distressed by the change, resist leaving the familiarity of the yellow room, or try to stop her from filling the shopping bags. Instead, he came effortlessly. That was the best word she could find to describe it. He was almost thoughtless, almost trusting. Apparently, nothing attached him to the familiar. Did he expect anything better? She didn't think so. She wasn't sure he knew he was going to new quarters. He simply followed because he followed, because no other thought interceded to prompt him to do otherwise. Or so it seemed to her.

Opening the door, she crossed to the center of the living room and turned to watch the bear man as he entered.

"This is your new home."

She spoke calmly, quietly, knowing he wouldn't respond. Just inside the front door, he stopped and raised his head slightly higher. His nostrils widened. His ears quivered. What he scented or heard, if anything, escaped her. To her, the living room, bigger by half than the entirety of the yellow room he had left, looked bare. There was a couch and an armchair like those in Andreas's apartment. Now the bear man would have a room with the same green walls as Thea and Andreas.

In front of the couch was a square coffee table on which she had placed a vase with wildflowers. Goldenrod, loosestrife, Queen Anne's lace, and other flowers whose names she didn't know grew in profusion in the meadow on the mountain. Later in the morning, the custodial staff would bring the bed, desk, chair, bookcase, drawing board, and fans from the yellow room. Then, for her, the living room and bedroom would feel populated.

"Come," Thea said, slipping her arm across the bear man's lower back, "look at the view."

She brought him to the windows. It was the same view she had seen from Andreas's office and apartment. Danube's walls of stone rose at the very edge of a precipice where the forest declined steeply down to the valley before rising up the flanks of the facing mountain. The bear man stood where Thea positioned him, a few steps from the two large windows. His eyelids fluttered with the brightness of the light. In the sky, mountainous ridges of white clouds floated high above the earthbound mountains, undulating at the horizon. A silver jet gleamed against a patch of blue sky before vanishing into an enormous slope of cloud. Toward the center of the valley, a large bird tilted its wings to turn and skim blackly above the treetops.

She scanned his eyes. Had he seen the bird with outstretched wings moving like a shadow? Did he see the valley, the mountains, the clouds? His gaze seemed fixed neither within nor without. He might be in a trance. Before him were the windows that were meant to free him from the monotony of those yellow walls. Did he take pleasure in this spectacular view of the valley?

"Come with me," Thea said, lightly pushing him forward. "This is the kitchen."

There was a small refrigerator beneath a white countertop, a white sink, a stove with four burners, a microwave mounted above the stove, and white cabinets matching the countertop. As in Andreas's apartment, a pass-through connected the kitchen to the living room.

"Here's the bathroom," she said, moving him down the hall. It had a shower stall instead of a bathtub. At the end of the hallway, she opened the door and moved him forward. Silently, Moritz trailed behind them.

"Your bedroom," she murmured, continuing to play the tour guide.

Instead of pivoting toward the two large windows facing the valley, the bear man focused on the green wall. Its unbroken expanse of color, bright with fresh paint, gleamed in the sunlight. Thea waited to see when he would turn in another direction, but he remained oriented as she originally left him. At last, she gently rotated him toward the windows.

"You can look out."

He squinted in the vivid light. He looked but not out. Had the months without windows made him unable to see beyond where the yellow wall would have been? The bed would come later in the day, but there was an armchair in one corner and a bureau opposite where the bed would be placed. A mirror with a mahogany frame hung above the bureau.

"Stay here."

Thea gestured with her head to make certain Moritz kept a watch over him. Returning to the living room, she picked up the shopping bags with his clothes and carried them back to the bedroom. The bear man stood motionless where she had left him. Moritz had come to his side and rested an arm across his back.

"Look."

Moritz turned the bear man toward Thea.

"This is your bedroom. I'm putting your clothing away."

She opened the top drawer and neatly arranged the underwear on one side and the socks on the other. Bending to open the second drawer, she made one pile of the red, black, and green shirts, setting each back slightly so the colors of all three would be visible. Next to the shirts, she stacked the tan shorts on top of the black trousers. After debating whether to leave the blue sneakers on the floor beside the bureau, she put them in the bottom drawer instead.

It was so little, but if the shirts, shorts, pants, and so on had been multiplied a hundred times, the bear man would be no more interested. He lacked connection to her. Or did she lack connection to him? Certainly, she wanted to heal him. She advocated for him. She paid attention to him, but always in the way she conceptualized him. What did he think of himself?

"That's it." Pushing in the bottom drawer, she rose. "The rest of your furniture will come later. Then we'll put away the art supplies and the books."

Moritz released the bear man, who walked slowly past Thea and out the bedroom door. She and Moritz followed him along the short hallway to the living room where he stopped at the windows. The light cascaded over him. After a few moments, he turned to his left and followed the green walls of the room, past the shut front door, and back along the hallway with his right arm brushing the wall. In the bedroom, he took the same position facing the windows. Another brief interval passed, then he retraced his steps, keeping his right side brushing the walls, until he stood again before the living room windows.

Here he remained as one minute slipped to the next. Thea stood to one side and gazed at his profile. His nose was straight, his lips pressed tight with concentration, his cheeks fuller than when he had been captured. His hair had grown back, dark and trimmed short. Dressed as he was now, he might have been a weekend visitor entranced by his first sight of the spectacular view. It would take so little to make him whole. Words. But if words were so little, how could they be so very much? Without words, without communication, he would never be a man.

The inadequacy of it all! She could move him from yellow room to green, but what would heal him? What infusion of breath would give him the gift of speech? Suddenly, as an inner wind shifted direction, Thea rejoiced to have brought him here. He needed time to accustom himself to the new layout, the large windows, and the absence of a lock on his door, but this was a place of possibility. He belonged here. Certainly not forever, but for as long as he needed.

A rapping sounded on the door. Thea glanced at Moritz, who stood on the far side of the bear man. The rapping sounded again.

"Come in," Thea called.

The door swung open to reveal Andreas filling the doorway. He held a small bag in one hand and raised his other hand to greet them.

"I wanted to see how the move is going," he said, stepping into the living room and closing the door behind him.

"Fine, thanks," Thea replied.

"There's some furniture to come from the old room," Moritz said. "Then he'll be completely moved in."

"It's gone smoothly?"

"Yes," Thea answered.

"Is there anything I can do?" he asked, walking forward to stand by her. His bulk, his weightiness beside her, had a gravitational force.

"Not at the moment."

Andreas moved his eyes from the bear man's head down his torso to his sneakered feet and back up to his face lifted to the light.

"Do let me know if there is."

"Yes, I will."

Andreas's presence surprised her. He had rarely visited the yellow room. She wondered if he would come more frequently to these new quarters. His office was on the ground floor and his apartment on the floor beneath this one, so it would be easy enough to visit. He had spoken of his concern for the bear man, but his solution was to put Thea in charge.

The bear man ignored the newcomer. Andreas, for his part, took the measure of the man standing before him. As still as the bear man, Andreas studied him as he studied the windows, the valley, or perhaps his own inner vistas.

"Don't you think it looks sparse?" Andreas asked at last.

"The other furniture . . ." Moritz started to speak, but Andreas stepped to the center of the room. Smiling, he reached in the bag and with his right hand lifted free a small white Buddha.

"I brought another visitor."

"It's beautiful," Thea said, carefully taking the statue in both hands.

Moritz came to look more closely.

"He makes a good companion," Andreas added. "I promise that."

The statue reminded Thea of the photograph with Andreas standing below the platform supporting the immense Buddha. Seated cross-legged, with pendulous ears, this small Buddha's hands also rested in his lap. A striking artistry had shaped the diminutive figure. Thea could hold it in her palm, but the intensity of its meditation heaped universe upon universe behind its tiny brow. The swirls of its third eye rose in a widening gyre of ever-enlarging consciousness. The Buddha's tranquil expression, the relaxed and youthful roundness of his face, offered a surpassing sweetness. In his lap, the tips of his thumbs and forefingers pressed together to complete circles. For Andreas to bring this when his own apartment lacked decoration of any sort was remarkable.

"Where did you find this?" Thea asked.

"It's marvelous," Moritz said, taking the statue from Thea and holding it aloft. "The perfect companion."

Andreas, smiling at Moritz's response, shook his head at Thea's question.

"It doesn't matter," he replied.

As soon as he spoke, Thea knew the statue had come from one of the drawers of his bureau. It had been hidden there with the small painting, the album of Japan, and the other treasures Andreas kept out of sight. This was precious to him, yet he shared it with the bear man.

Moritz stepped before the bear man and gracefully raised the statue like an offering. The bear man remained motionless except for a small, repetitive up and down movement of his head. After waiting a few moments, Moritz lowered the statue and moved out of the bear man's line of vision.

"We'll return this to you," Thea said.

"When its work is done," Andreas replied genially. "There's no rush."

By the statue's work, Thea knew he meant healing.

"This statue needs a large view," Moritz offered. "He should look over a room. And face the windows."

"You'll find the right place for it." Andreas said, moving toward the door. He paused to look again at the bear man. In this scrutiny was a deep taking in and, as best Thea could imagine, acceptance of the bear man and his mystery. It reminded Thea of long-ago lectures when Andreas spoke of ancient shrines and mystery cults whose initiates descended to the darkness of tunnels and caves and emerged newborn in the fiery light of torches.

"Dr. Henniger."

Moritz's voice interrupted Thea's thoughts. He crossed the room with his hand outstretched.

Andreas gave his hand to Moritz's grip.

"Thank you for being so thoughtful," Moritz said intensely, "and for your kindness."

"I need you to help me," Thea started speaking before she knew what she would say. "Each time we call him the bear man or the wild man, we take away his humanity. Our names are part of who we are. Why should he not have a name when we do? Our names give us a sense of being individuals responsible for living our own lives. His parents gave him a name at birth. If he wanted to change that name, it would be his decision. But we should call him by his birth name. He isn't the wild man or the bear man. We all know his name is Lucas Lamont. His nickname is Luke. If we care for him, if we care what becomes of him, we should call him by his name."

Thea feared Moritz would try to sway Andreas and argue the man no longer was Lucas Lamont, but Moritz kept silent.

Andreas had turned to face Thea.

"Yes," Andreas affirmed, "let's call him by his name."

36

"If my father had never been born, it might have been for the best," Moritz said as he and Thea walked toward the sundial a few days later.

"But you . . ."

"Yes, I wouldn't exist," Moritz finished for her. "I would pay that price."

"You would?" Thea couldn't believe him. "What in your father's life would possibly make you say that?"

"He was a man who never lived."

"But he fathered you. He married. He worked. He—"

"Yes, he did his best. There's no doubt. But life for him was suffocation. Nothing was truly his. He couldn't fill his lungs. This air—free to us all but not to him." Moritz waved his hand through the invisible substance. "He went through the motions, but he was afraid of life. Afraid to breathe deeply."

Thea sat on one of the stone benches facing the sundial while Moritz paced. Gusting breezes played about them. The low lanterns glowed beside the bluestone walkways. Lit windows made irregular patterns on the buildings' facades. And the rising moon waxed brightly, missing only a sliver to be full.

"If you said your grandfather shouldn't have lived, I might understand."

Moritz shook his head and seated himself on the bench again. "The inhumanity, the evil, was so great that one man hardly weighed in the balance."

"And you, if you had never existed?"

"That energy for life would have flowed nonetheless. I wouldn't be, but someone would."

It was too much to answer.

"And your father?" she asked.

"He suffered. It wasn't suffering for any purpose. He didn't sacrifice to make a better future. He suffered for the past, and not even his past. In every way he was diminished, cut short. It was like an illness. The confines in which he lived. His misery, which he did his best not to show. His effort to go through the motions of life. It had no cure. All his life, even as a boy, he was short of breath. There was no reason for it. He never smoked. That shortness of breath became emphysema. He would inhale a steroid from a nebulizer. The mist opened his lungs a little. Much of the time, he was tethered to an oxygen tank. I remember from history class how Caesar ordered a man killed by ritual strangulation. My father's suffocation went on for years, decades really. He died in his late sixties. It was a miracle he held on that long."

"Did you love him?"

Moritz lifted his head to look at the night sky. Following his gaze, Thea saw the lustrous orb of the moon and the twinkling brightness of uncountable stars. In the city, she would have seen much less. The moon, of course, would have been visible as it ripened over the next few nights to be full. But the brightness of streetlamps, the beams of headlights, and the radiance of apartment windows would have obscured the stars. Even here, in the mountains, the truth of the stars wasn't easily perceived. They appeared to cluster and make patterns, but this came from her being fixed to the planet from which she viewed the celestial display. Closeness and smallness meant almost nothing when she considered the burning immensities of suns separated by light-years of space. Who could escape his or her own point of view? So much of what seems to come to us from others depends on the vantage point from which we relate to them. Sky glow or sky dark, something is always lost to sight.

"I loved him, but he never became the man he might have been. I regretted, I regret, what was taken from him. Yet I had to accept that reality. One generation commits crimes and never dares feel the guilt. Or never expresses it. The next generation carries that guilt, but the burden is unbearable. It sucked the very air from my father's lungs. And another generation comes, my generation, determined to heal the generation before."

Thea rested her hand on Moritz's arm. His biceps and triceps clustered thickly beneath her fingers. Here was the strength of a young man, but his form was an illusion. He was a man, yes, but more than a man. He was an impulse, a yearning, a symbol in the inscrutable equation of generations. Where would Moritz be in a thousand years? A crazy thought, which she quickly resized. Where would he be in five years, ten, or thirty? What set him in motion, searching in the world? Would he find, if not an answer, quietude? Whatever force or chance brought them together would soon enough run its course, but she wished she could see the person he would become.

"What was his name?" she finally asked.

"Stefan," he answered. "Stefan Valentin Manz."

"It's a rich name."

"If I ever have a son, I'll name him Stefan."

He spoke the words like a vow.

"Stefan Valentin?"

"Yes. If I have a daughter, her name will be Stefanie Valentine Manz."

"You've thought about it."

"I don't want him to be someone who suffered and simply vanished. At the least, I want to give life to his name."

"And at the most?" Thea asked.

"I want my father's suffering to have a purpose. If I could touch the forgiving spirit of God, I believe my father could be healed. What he went through could help those who come after him. I carry an image of him within me. Healing could certainly happen there."

Thea wanted to speak. Moritz lived with the darkness, the dreadfulness, passed down the generations. To face this with courage, as he did, could lead him to wonder, to the healing he desired, and to awe at the complex magnificence of life. But the words she would speak paled before what he had told her of his life. It was better to be a witness, a simple listener who offered nothing more than to hear.

She waited until she was certain he had finished.

"Stefan or Stefanie will need a mom. Have you thought of that?"

He smiled at her levity, but his reply was grim.

"My having children won't raise up the numberless dead, the innumerable ones killed by men like my grandfather. So many murderers, so many families passing burdens down the generations. If I can play a small role for my own family, cleansing or purging, what little I can do, I want to do, and I will do."

37

"You must have loved him."

Andreas said this to Thea as they strolled on the walk leading from Amazon. When they'd entered for dinner, the golden disk of the sun was balanced on the western mountains. Now a great brush-stroke of lavender tinted the edges of the sky.

"No, it wasn't love," she replied. "Early in the marriage, I tried to convince myself I loved him. But by that day with Delphina in the shower, I had known for years that I wasn't in love. At the beginning, I was sexually attracted to him, but that was long gone too. I thought he was someone he wasn't. A person who could move in the world. A person at ease with himself."

"Yet you stayed."

"I kept thinking it was good enough. It might improve. That Delphina needed a father." She smiled bitterly and shook her head. "After it happened, I told myself he would speak to the therapist. He would admit, confess, and finally understand the despair and rage he made such a part of my life and Delphina's."

"Only he didn't."

"No. Wanting him to speak, I lost my voice. I should have spoken to anyone and everyone, until I couldn't force out another word. But I didn't."

"You wanted to give him a chance. Not a chance to straighten it out, because it couldn't be fixed, but a chance to accept responsibility, become a better person, or at least less blameworthy, less likely to repeat what he had done to your daughter. You believe in therapy. You can't hold that against yourself. You had the best of intentions."

Thea shook her head. "You know I blame myself. Once I knew I had to get him out of my life, out of Delphina's life, sending him to therapy wasn't enough. I was a fool to think he'd tell the truth."

"So you were a fool. You didn't protect your daughter, and this happened. After you knew, you didn't support her by forcing Hugh to leave. You didn't take her side the way you might have. Yet your life has to go on."

The waist-high lanterns flickered. Thea stayed abreast of Andreas, feeling like a smaller celestial body drawn into motion by a larger one. Reaching the sundial, he gestured toward a bench. They sat side by side. Before them, the elegant curve of the gnomon rose in the glow of the lanterns. The upright of polished brass, no longer utilitarian in the absence of the sun, became a sculpture rising from shadows.

"Yes, one way or another," she replied as she settled on the cool stone. "Being by myself, I feel how airless it can be to have only my own thoughts. Repetitive, insubstantial—suffocating really. Then I miss the inner life of another."

"Aren't we all like that? You're talking about sharing."

"Yes, an aspect of sharing."

"It could be sharing with a friend or a therapist."

"Or a child."

"I have no children. But of course, you're right."

212

"Can you see the inscription?" Thea asked, pointing to the edge of the thick stone beneath the rounded dial.

"*A lumine motus*," Andreas answered without bending forward to look.

"Moved by the light," she echoed.

"What moves across the face of the sundial is a shadow," he said, "but you could say the shadow is moved by the light."

"Plato wrote of emerging from darkness into the light of a higher spiritual truth."

"To move into that light," Andreas responded, "is the reason this institute was created. In a profound way, we live in darkness, in shadows, and strive as best we can to be moved by the light. The sundial at the center reminds us. Our passing time isn't mechanical or digital but born of shadow and light."

"The Bible speaks of Christ as the true light."

"*Christos* comes from the Greek and means *anointed one*," Andreas said, sounding as he had when Thea attended his courses. "Images of light bearers survive from the earliest times. We could call it worship of the sun. Pagan perhaps, but ever so sensible in a world overtaken each night by the terrors of darkness."

"The days are growing shorter."

"Yes," he agreed, "we're heading for the solstice."

"It feels like a journey into darkness," Thea went on. "Then, in December, the shortest day finally comes, and we're released. In January, even if the days are short, each day lengthens, and the light grows. We begin again."

They sat in silence. Looking toward the forest, she could see only the silhouette of the treetops in the dwindling light. To be in those woods at night would be terrifying. Even if she had a companion, she couldn't imagine being without light. What had Luke experienced in the wild? Sally came to mind, the memory of Sally that Andreas encouraged her to confront.

"Isn't this sublime?" Andreas gestured toward the last light on the rims of the mountains. "Before people were here to bear witness, the sun set behind mountains like these. The glory of its radiance came before everything, ancient beyond the meaning of the word."

"There are places," Thea said, "where we see darkness and can't bring the light."

"I wonder about the meaning of what is unseen," he said. "Because we are influenced by every part of ourselves. Do the unseen parts have worth and value? Can we be helped by what never becomes visible? The memories we can't bring to mind, the dreams we forget?"

"I told you about Sally, my sister-in-law. She only confided in me about her father's abuse because I told her Hugh abused Delphina. I don't want to think about what happened to her, but I think of it again and again. I can't explain why."

"You engage it," Andreas replied, "or it engages you. That's all any of us can do."

The grayness of twilight faded to the blackness of night. At last, they rose from the stone bench to say good night and separate, Andreas going to Danube and Thea to her room in Nile.

"Will you visit our friend?" Thea asked from the periphery of the circular patio.

"Yes." Andreas turned and raised a hand in farewell. "I'll stop in."

Thea kept to the walk lit by the tawny, diffuse glow of the lanterns. She passed the looming cubes of Mississippi and Amazon, each with a haphazard pattern of bright and dark windows. In the lobby of Nile, she paused before the large, old map of the Nile River. In her coming and going, she had studied the blue stripe portraying the Nile. For its immense length the river was nearly straight except for a back and forth bending in its middle. To the east was the Red Sea and to the north the Mediterranean. Although the map was flat, Thea felt the massive topography of Africa, the heights from which this enormous river sought the level of the sea. That the Nile emptied into the Mediterranean and not the Red Sea struck Thea as a matter of chance, of how the descending flow met obstacles, adjusted its course, found ways to move ahead. All without thought, except for the thoughtless shape of the landscape channeling the river this way and that. Did the inner rivers of her dreams and reflections flow through a similar topography, guiding and yet unseen?

38

What surprised Thea about Luke's new lodgings was how much she enjoyed being there. If she went before hiking, she would find herself reluctant to leave. The yellow room had been a prison and not only for Luke. It imprisoned her and Moritz as well. When all the furniture arrived at the new apartment, Thea decided to position the bookcase just inside the front door. The shelves held art books and piles of papers covered with Luke's creations. Atop the bookcase, Moritz placed the diminutive white Buddha to contemplate the room and the expanse of sky and valley beyond the large windows. Encompassed in the statue's tranquil gaze was Luke, whose drawing board had been set on a table near the windows. Moritz made himself at home in an armchair where he had a view of both the door and the windows. Beside the chair was a side table on which he placed the book currently engrossing him.

"You're still reading that book," Thea said, recognizing the golden cover. "What is it?"

"*Die Stadt hinter dem Strom.* In English, that's *The City Beyond the River.* It was published in 1947."

"I've never heard of it. Who's the author?"

"Hermann Kasack. In Germany, it's considered a classic about the war. There was a translation into English a few years later, but it was never published in the United States. I had to order a copy in German."

"What's it about?"

"After the Second World War ends, a scholar crosses a river to the city on the far side. What he doesn't realize is that all the people in the city are already dead. He meets people he knew, his father who is long dead, an artist who was a close friend, and the married woman he loved. There are so many people in the city, endless multitudes."

"It sounds painful."

"Yes, it is. The quantity of death can't be believed. When the losses are thousands and millions of people, what can the survivors feel? There's a passage that I particularly like. Shall I read it to you?"

"Sure."

"He's given a position as an archivist in the city. Basically, the archive is an attempt to understand and catalogue so many lives and deaths. I want to read a short speech given by the man in charge of the archive to the narrator and the other workers. I'll be translating, so I have to go slowly."

Moritz opened to his bookmark. As he read, he spaced the words he translated. The measured pace of his recital lent certainty to the words.

"Return across the river. Go back, not for yourselves but to help those who still live. Go back as spirits, phantoms, ghosts in their dreams. Capture their sleep, that state so like your own. Warn them, insist, demand, torment them if you must. You possess the key to the Court of Justice. The example of your deaths can save the future of life. Impel them, coerce those who live on earth. Make yourselves known!"

"It's a forceful voice," Thea said.

218

"Yes, but the book was controversial. It was criticized for not being overtly political."

"Do you know how it ends?"

"No," Moritz said, smiling, "I'm reading slowly for some reason."

At first, Luke would restlessly leave his seat every few minutes and follow the perimeter of the apartment. Keeping one shoulder to the wall, he moved slowly but steadily. If he had to digress because of furniture, such as his double bed jutting perpendicularly from the wall, he would keep the side of his calf against the mattress and slow his pace even more. Since he didn't harm himself or bolt from the apartment as he passed the front door, Moritz and Thea quickly lost interest in accompanying him. At last, they hardly noticed as he passed by them on his orbits.

As the days passed, Luke's walking lessened, and he spent more and more time at his drawing board. With the windows open, the strengthening breezes of September brought forest scents from the slopes of the valley. Moritz began using the art books as paperweights to stop the gusts from scattering the heaps of paper beside the drawing board. Occasionally, then more frequently, Luke would stare into the light or focus on the white drift of the clouds. Thea remembered how he had faced the yellow wall, his head rocking front and back, his gaze in some middle space neither within nor really without. He had been guarded, narrowed to what was near him. The openness offered a freedom lacking in the confines of the yellow room. She could see in his eyes how much more he now took in. He could focus on the shape-shifting of the clouds. When it rained, he was drawn to the windows to witness the downpour, the drops splashing on the ledge. But he still didn't engage her. If their eyes met, he continued to turn his head away.

Then, when walking the edges of the apartment, he began to pause in front of the bookcase. He would stand for minutes at a time in front of the Buddha, his head nodding slightly as if with reverence for the holy man. Then he would resume his round only to stop in the same place and continue what Thea imagined to be a silent dialogue. When he began to take the stacks of paper from the bookcase to the table where he worked, Thea realized her mistake. If he had been thinking of the Buddha at all, he had also been thinking of his art. Setting a stack of papers to his left by the drawing board, he would lift one piece at a time. After thoroughly examining the sheet, he would either set it down on his right or begin to tear the page into pieces no bigger than the tip of a finger. Holding the page in front of him, he would grasp the lower left corner and twist off one tiny piece. More pieces followed as he moved up the page and to the right. These pieces he let fall to the floor until his hands were empty, and then he lifted another sheet from the pile on his left. What criteria he used to decide whether to shred or save a sheet, Thea couldn't determine.

The torn bits of colored paper reminded Thea of a patchwork quilt. Luke didn't protest when Moritz cleaned up the fallen paper but continued his sorting and tearing until a new pile covered the floor to the left of his chair. Moritz finally placed a clear plastic wastebasket beneath his left hand. Luke took no notice of it but loosed the tiny scraps in the same place, so most fluttered into the wastebasket.

Watching the bits of paper fill the wastebasket again and again, Thea wanted to understand his inner process. Dressed in tan shorts and a red T-shirt, his short-cropped hair dark except for highlights of gray at his temples, the moist intensity of his eyes revealing what she imagined to be a sensitive nature, he gave no sign of how he made his decisions. Some pages he would hold up for a long view, five seconds or more, before reaching his conclusion.

Gradually, the piles of art in the bookcase diminished, replaced by smaller piles to the right of the drawing board. It was a mystery, both why he created what he did and why he chose to destroy only some of it. Finally, in the bookshelf, the piles of paper had all been removed and only a few art books remained at the bottom. The rest of the books were being used as paperweights to the right of the drawing board.

"Should we put these papers back in the bookcase?" Thea asked, gesturing to the pile on the drawing board.

Luke didn't look up. He had completed his sorting of the papers in the few weeks since his move to the new apartment. Thea didn't expect an answer but sometimes spoke regardless of his silence.

"Let's go for a walk," she said, moving to his side.

After he had sat for a long time at the drawing board, she liked to take him for a walk. A few months earlier, it would have been unthinkable. Now, it had become an easy part of their daily pattern. If she imagined sitting as he did . . . it had to be uncomfortable to maintain the same posture. For him, no second hand swept around the face of a clock. He was lost in his inner world, his images and inscrutable thoughts. Nothing in his body complained that he sat too long. If his lower back was tight, his neck ached, or his hand cramped, these messages didn't rise from his muscles to be shaped into thoughts that might make him shift his posture, rise and stretch, or take one of his walks around the apartment. If she was right, Luke didn't experience time as she did. He didn't count minutes or days but lived in a moment stretching toward eternity.

She placed a hand under his elbow, and he rose with her touch. In a routine that had become familiar, she opened the door, led him along the hallway, pushed through the metal fire door, and started down the stairs. Looking back over her shoulder, she saw him following her, his hand on the railing and his steps an easy flutter of downward movement.

Outside, she started to walk without waiting for him to catch up. She didn't look back but tested him in a way. Would he remain with her today as he had done each day when she took him for a walk? Passing the sundial, she noticed the condensed triangle of shadow cast by the gnomon. Her own shadow pooled at her feet so that, simply by being upright, she was also a marker of time. The stone walls of Amazon and Mississippi passed to her left and right, then she left the bluestone walk to skirt Nile. The lawn sloped upward, but she didn't slow her stride or look back. Entering the forest, she continued another forty or fifty feet to the well-trodden path. Turning left, she walked toward where this path began at the parking lot. Reflecting the brightness of the sun, automobiles gleamed in neat rows demarcated by the white lines of the parking spaces. While the five buildings might appear to rise from the forest, here was their connection to highways, cities, and a world of ingenious artifice far removed from the wild. Hearing nothing behind her, she turned to look back. Luke was no more than five feet from her. Gently, she took his arm and guided him away from the parking lot. Retracing their steps along the path, she stopped at the first bench and made Luke sit with a light downward pressing on his arm.

Joining him, Thea listened to the sound of birds resonating from the green luxuriance of the leaves. She wished she could see the birds and learn the song each throated. The breezes brought a pattering to the leaves like the falling of rain. The clouds gleamed against the clear blue of the sky. Since coming to the institute, she'd found it hard to keep track of dates or even days of the week. Time there couldn't be measured by external markers. The best measurement would be movement within, the time it might take Thea to change from one inner state to another or the time it might take Luke to be healed. Measured by a calendar, those movements might be brief or endlessly long. There was no way to know what would happen, no way to know when Thea would have had enough of the institute, no way to know when, if ever, Luke might change.

She wanted to speak, but speaking to him was beside the point. Just because she spoke didn't mean he understood. It was tempting nonetheless. Couldn't he be like an infant who would learn language by hearing it spoken? But she didn't think him an infant. He was a man and yet something else. That seemed closer to the truth.

Then there was the experience of being with him. Though he didn't speak, he didn't lack intention. She studied him. His head was now still, but his right thigh shook with a constant, nervous movement. If she didn't know him, she would have seen a wiry, handsome man, his face narrow and his eyes bright with the bouncing of his leg. Walking with him was like a ritual by which she helped accustom him to the outdoors. Often, Moritz accompanied them on these excursions, but she didn't need him. She was comfortable alone with Luke. The easy flow of his steps down the stairway and across the lawn showed how the landscape was now familiar and even welcome to him. It made her think of taking him far from the buildings of the institute.

She knew the conscious mind could believe one thing while the unconscious believed the opposite. She had been Luke's advocate from the start. She objected to his treatment. She weaned him from the medications. She purchased the art supplies, the pads of paper, and the books. She asked for the room with windows and an open door. She walked with him on the grounds of the institute. She did whatever she could to help him heal.

Despite all that, she kept thinking of the bear. Was she truly thinking of a wild animal that lived in the forest, the bear that had been the companion of this man? Or was the bear a figure of her imagination? If so, it felt like a gatekeeper and guardian who warned her not to trespass. She couldn't know, yet fear sometimes shocked her spine and radiated to her hands and feet. It could be close to her and remain unseen. It had immense strength and lived from its instincts. Above all, it was free.

She had read that, in Southeast Asia, there were thousands of bears in captivity, their paws and flesh served as dinner delicacies to wealthy Chinese tourists, their bile harvested by tubes, and their bones ground up for use in folk medicines. Some of these bears banged their heads endlessly against the encroaching walls. The commercial farms, disguised as zoos, confined not only bears for slaughter but other species such as deer, porcupines, crocodiles, and endangered tigers. This was the other side of freedom, where everything existed only for its value in serving human appetites.

It would be safer like that. There would be no bears in the forest. It would please at least a small part of her to know that she could be certain of safety. The bear, the bobcat, and the coyote would vanish like the cougar and the gray wolf.

Slipping her hand under Luke's forearm, she felt him rise and stand beside her. Starting along the path, she left him behind in the certainty he would follow. When she turned on the path to look back at him, he was a few paces behind her. Her expectations didn't matter. He mattered. What was healing but to acknowledge the nature of what is? Thinking this, she turned her gaze back to the path.

39

He chose you above everyone. You told me this. You were transformed by his abuse. By the way he brought you to the center of his life. But you were even younger than my daughter. I wish I could have been there to protect you from him, that I could have been the mother you didn't have.

Thea's lips moved as she wrote. She recognized her fantasy. She would protect and save Sally. She would do for Sally the child what she had failed to do for Delphina. Looking at the pages in piles on her desk, she wished she had never written. Nothing, not a single word. It would be easier, then, to forget, to deny, to fabricate what might have been.

She would take the piles of paper on her desk and rip them to confetti. Then she wouldn't have to face Sally the woman and Sally the girl. She wouldn't have to face Delphina, who raged at her and lived with the wounds she and Hugh had inflicted. She wouldn't have to face Hugh and wonder what he had known as a boy of his father and his sister or think of how he lived through his mother's long illness.

She didn't lift a page from the piles. She didn't want to destroy. She wanted to let go. But examining that afternoon with Sally again and again brought her no clarity. Why hadn't she taken Delphina's side as soon as she knew?

Thea rose from the straight-backed desk chair and walked the few steps to sit on her bed. Facing her bureau topped with the photo of the standing bear and the crouching man, she pictured her phone resting in the bottom drawer. She bent to open the drawer and grasp the phone. How easily she could illuminate the dark screen and escape her room, floating on the magic carpet of the internet to countless websites that would pull her away from herself. How easily, if she dared, she could reach out to Delphina.

Thea shook her head to see how eagerly she digressed from her troubling thoughts of Sally.

Anchoring the phone in her left hand, she pressed the button to bring light to the screen, entered her code, and touched the icon for the web browser. With reluctance and foreboding, she used her index finger to tap the letters of her query, "Mauthausen–Gusen."

The search brought a horizontal sequence of photographs to the top of the small screen. She could see a gate open in a stone wall, with a group of men huddled to one side. Another photo showed a long wall of the same stone and behind it a wide yard and dark rows of rectangular barracks. On a sharp incline like the side of a pyramid, winged insects appeared to cover a rising pathway. Flicking the screen made the photographs move to the left. Naked, filthy men, with ribs large beneath sunken flesh, stood in a formation. Another flick of the screen and corpses of starved men were piled high on wagons.

Thea touched the screen to read the Wikipedia entry about the Mauthausen–Gusen concentration camp. Created in 1938 after the annexation of Austria by Germany, by 1940 it had become one of the largest slave-labor camps. Among the prisoners being worked to death were socialists, communists, homosexuals, anarchists, gypsies, Spanish Republicans, Soviet POWs, Jehovah's Witnesses, and, of course, Jews. The camp was "mostly used for the extermination through labor of the intelligentsia—educated people and members of the higher social classes in countries subjugated by the Nazi regime during World War II."

Thea closed her eyes, the bright screen leaving an afterglow on her retinas. This was the camp where Moritz's grandfather worked, the camp that passed its legacy down to Moritz's father and finally Moritz. So many died nameless, their identities concealed, their records lost, or their numbers given to new prisoners. An accurate count of the dead couldn't be compiled. The only question was whether one, two, or three hundred thousand had died. Her pity felt puny on this vast scale.

Reluctantly, she opened her eyes and continued to read of how work in the quarries carried on in unbearable heat or temperatures as low as twenty degrees below freezing. Near the war's end, rations fell to as little as six hundred calories a day; the average inmate weighed eighty-eight pounds. If the inmates didn't die from working in the quarries, factories for munitions and arms, or the mines, senseless and exhausting work would be invented and meted out. One photograph showed guards forcing the prisoners to play leapfrog.

On the Stairs of Death, prisoners were made to carry granite blocks weighing as much as 110 pounds up 186 steps to the top of the quarry walls. If one inmate collapsed and toppled backward, he would fall on others who would tumble in turn under the crushing weight of flesh and granite. Flicking back to the photograph with the figures Thea had seen as winged insects on the side of a pyramid, she realized these were men carrying rectangular blocks of granite up the steep incline of those stairs.

If laboring twelve hours a day on starvation rations made inmates too weak or ill to work, they would be transferred to the "sick barrack" and soon murdered. In 1940, when the number of inmates requiring extermination made transportation to nearby camps with gas chambers too costly, a mobile gas chamber was improvised using a large van with its exhaust pipe connected to the inside. It could kill 120 prisoners at a time. In 1942, a new gas chamber was built, and the Soviet POWs were among the first to be asphyxiated in it. In May 1944, Adolf Eichmann visited the camp. Surrounded by strutting officers in starched uniforms, he surveyed his domains of death and soon after shipped eight thousand Hungarian Jews from Auschwitz to Mauthausen-Gusen.

Thea wanted to look away from the tiny screen. One death would be horror enough, but these multitudes were unimaginable. Moritz had said as much. But she continued to read how the SS guards, having forced the inmates to race up the Stairs of Death carrying blocks of stone, would line the survivors along a cliff at the top of the quarry. This cliff was known as the Parachutists Wall. Here, facing the guns of the SS guards, each prisoner was offered the choice of pushing the inmate ahead into the abyss or being shot. Prisoners were also beaten to death, starved in bunkers, hung, or shot en masse. Other methods of death were to throw prisoners on the electrified barbed wire, drown them in large barrels, or force them to take icy showers and then leave them outside to die of hypothermia.

Enough.

Tapping for her GPS, she entered Mauthausen and then Vienna. The concentration camp was only one hundred miles from the city where Moritz had grown up. The current of the Danube River hurried past both Vienna and Mauthausen. Mauthausen—how could that name exist? Shouldn't the camps have been razed and the name obliterated from every map and record until no lips could ever sound its syllables? But even in her revulsion, Thea understood the thirst to remember. To obliterate the memory, if that were possible, would make the evil more likely to return.

What could one person do in the face of a Mauthausen-Gusen? What could Moritz do? He dreamt of healing the living and the dead. "Dreamt" wasn't even the right word because he lived with this task clearly in his view. But what could he accomplish compared to the hundreds of thousands dead, the millions exterminated during the war? She wanted to imagine him like those prisoners on the Stairs of Death, carrying the granite burden of the past toward a summit where the only completion would be to murder or be murdered. But she saw him in a new way, this young man who took up the burden as a volunteer. Whether his search led to success or failure, might his willingness amplify whatever became of him? And might even failure be other than it appeared? What greater force could there be than an individual determined to heal? Did a logic, a love, link the generations in such a way that a murderer in one gave rise to a healer in a generation to come?

Question upon question. Watching herself think, she recalled how this sequence of thought began with Sally. Was Sally's story so difficult that she preferred the horrors of concentration camps?

Thea wanted another point of view. She wanted to be lovingly challenged, pressed to defend what she believed, contradicted, confronted by the other, as Moritz confronted his father and grand-father. She wanted someone in the room with her. For a moment, she held the image of Moritz's face, but he wasn't the one. Andreas? He trusted her to hear of his long-ago love and his sorrow at that woman's passing. Like Thea, he struggled to understand the nature of the human, but she needed to be understood implicitly, without probing or explanations. Lucas Lamont? Who could say? He lived in a world of his own devising. If he ever spoke, he might say the same of her.

40

Thea returned to her desk. She shuffled through the stack of pages. Innumerable fragments that would never be complete. But she had finished, polished, and come back again and again to the letters. Finding them, she pulled them free. Tomorrow, she would send them on their way.

She glanced to her bureau where the photo of the bear and man leaned against her pile of books. On top of the books, resting against the wall, was her diploma from the Center for Psychotherapeutic Training. There she had sworn "a most solemn oath to seek the wellness and growth of clients" and "to do no harm."

Who could live a life without risking harm to others? She sat and began reading the letters.

Dear Justine,

I am the former wife of Hugh Eustis. I wish that, before I married him, someone had sent me this letter that I'm sending to you. I write you from concern for your well-being and, especially, concern for the well-being of your daughter.

I would prefer not to send this letter, but I have no choice. I can't allow what happened to me and my daughter to happen again. You have a daughter who is nine, the same age as my daughter Delphina when I married Hugh.

If you choose to marry him despite what you read here, you will at least have been warned. Hugh sexually abused my daughter. He spied on her. He would walk into her room without knocking. If he found her in bed, he would touch her where he wanted. Once, he placed a ladder against the outside of our house to look at her through a window while she showered. I don't know all of what took place during the years of my marriage to him. My daughter despises and fears him.

I blame myself. I should have sensed that something was terribly wrong. I never understood why Delphina disliked him. I never thought deeply about it or took it to heart. After he looked in at her while she was naked in the shower, Delphina told me what had been happening in our home for all the years of my marriage.

I failed to protect her before I knew. Even worse, I failed to protect her after I knew. I'm a therapist. I demanded that Hugh go to therapy. I saw him as someone in need of help. But he never admitted to his therapist what he had done. He never worked to gain a deeper under-standing of himself. He never took the hard steps to change whatever compelled him. If you try to speak to him, if you confront him, he will deny everything and blame me for the breakup of our marriage.

My daughter doesn't want me in her life. Maybe that really is best for her. Much as I want her forgiveness, I'm ashamed. I could have been so much better. I could have been on her side.

If I could send this letter back in time to my younger self, I would send it with a prayer for the recipient. What's done is done. I would never marry him knowing what I know, but the choice isn't mine to make.

Sincerely,
Thea Firth

Reading the letter slowly, word by word, Thea found nothing to change. She didn't know Justine or her daughter but had to take what responsibility she could. She folded the thick sheet of stationery, slipped it into the envelope, licked the glue on the flap, and pressed it shut. An email was evanescent, a flash of dots on a screen. She could hold the weight of this letter, wrap her fingers around its rectangular length and height, and touch its smooth texture. Justine would slip a finger beneath the flap to open it, pull out the letter and unfold it, read, and then be left with the sheet of paper to keep or discard.

Placing the envelope for Justine on the side of the desk, she read the next letter she would mail in the morning.

Hugh,

I write you with reluctance. I'm aware of your plan to marry a woman with a daughter the age Delphina was when you married me. I don't know Justine, but I feel compelled to tell her what happened in your marriage to me.

I have sent a letter to Justine about your abuse of Delphina. This is the abuse you denied to me, the abuse you denied to the therapist, the abuse you will undoubtedly deny to Justine.

I've asked myself so many times why I didn't end our marriage the day you looked in on Delphina in the shower. For years, you had been abusing her. I hadn't known that, but I learned about it that day. My daughter, soaking wet and shaking on the toilet seat, accused you. How could I let the marriage continue?

You grew up in a home in which your father abused your sister. In some intuitive way, even before I knew what happened to Sally, I believe I saw you as a victim too. So, when I understood what you had done to Delphina, I chose treatment for you instead of divorce. That was a terrible mistake on my part. No one can choose treatment for someone else. Therapy can only succeed if you choose it. You had to be willing to acknowledge what happened in your childhood and admit what you did to Delphina. You had to be willing to examine the truth of who you are. But you were unwilling.

I wanted you to be healed, but I should have seen that there's a time when healing has no role. I couldn't heal you. The therapist had no way to heal you. Only you had a chance to heal yourself.

I see you differently now. You are a victim. You're also an abuser. Delphina despises you. Do you want another child to feel as she does? I failed her. She refuses to see me or speak to me. I wouldn't wish this on any parent. I don't wish it on Justine.

I make no apologies for contacting Justine. I can't let what happened to Delphina and me happen to another woman and her daughter. I hold you accountable. If she marries you anyway, keep firmly and always in your mind that she knows your secret.

Thea

41

Thea knocked lightly on Lucas Lamont's door. She had instructed Moritz and the other attendants to do this as a sign of respect for the occupant. Opening the door, she was surprised to see Andreas seated on the couch with his back to the door. Neither Moritz nor Luke was in the living room.

Andreas turned with a smile.

"Moritz went out for a few minutes," he said. When Thea looked down the hallway, he added, "Luke's in the bedroom."

"I'm glad you're here," Thea said, settling in the armchair across from Andreas. "I want to thank you again for giving him this apartment. There's so much space. Windows and no lock on the door. What a difference from where he was before."

"It has to be better for him," Andreas agreed. "I'm close by, so I stop in when I can. Moritz reads, and Luke stares at the forest. That is, if he's not at his drawing board."

"He's certainly come back to life," Thea said, remembering the drugged man who had difficulty rising from his bed in the yellow room.

"He's alert, but he still doesn't acknowledge my presence."

"Or mine," Thea said, "or anyone's, for that matter. He's aloof. It's more than that. He's with himself."

Andreas rose slowly, pushing with his hands on the arm of the couch until he stood erect. He walked to the window. Thea turned sideways and watched him raise a forearm to shield his eyes from the bright sun as he surveyed the valley.

"The trees, the pines, the maples, and the oaks . . ." Andreas let his hand glide in an encompassing gesture. "They're aloof. He was close to the wild, it's true, but I feel his presence. How alertly he waits, keeping his vigil at these windows. But what he waits for, I simply don't know."

"When he started choosing what to keep of his art," Thea replied, "I thought he was getting ready to speak, but he hasn't."

Andreas pivoted toward her.

"There's something about the way he looks out," he said. "His intensity. He's like an explorer seeking a new world."

"To me, he's thinking about leaving."

"Why do you say that?"

Thea shrugged. "I just feel it."

"When I sit with him, there's an endlessness to the silence that I find calming. The quiet has its own meaning."

"He can't be cured if he doesn't speak."

Andreas returned to his seat on the couch.

"We're both therapists, worshippers"—Andreas smiled to use the word—"of the talking cure. So you and I naturally think he must speak to be cured. But what if we're wrong? Words aren't the only way to connect. The human endeavor continues with words or without. The spirit that drives us to this or that. Or to the many, I should say. We go in many directions to find our meaning. The ancient Greeks had a word for it, *polytropos*. Homer describes Odysseus as *polytropos*, 'the many-sided one,' the seeker in many directions. We're all *polytropos*, many sided, pulling in many directions. 'Fragmentary' is a good word. The challenge is to achieve the marriage within, an inner harmony of those many sides. Perhaps his silence is a silence of seeking within."

"There's no sign of that."

"Yes, but he isn't fully recovered. Obviously, he isn't . . . normal."

"Speaking would be normal."

Andreas smiled and replied, "If he says normal things."

Normal might be many things, like points falling in a pattern around a line on a graph. She felt her resistance to that. How could he be healed without words to join him in community with others? But couldn't there be a healing that made him whole to himself? A healing that paid no attention to her definitions and hopes but in which she played a role as best she could and surrendered her desire to control the outcome?

"You say he doesn't communicate, but what about his art?" Andreas added. "He doesn't create images like these by accident."

"Can you tell what he's thinking about?"

"I wouldn't try. It speaks for itself."

The art had changed. The hues became more varied and shaded subtly into one another. A harmony entered the abstractions that made Thea feel Luke was returning to an awareness of himself. Also, she realized, many of the pictures he'd saved were recent. Most of the earlier pictures had been torn into fragments and discarded.

"Do you like it?" Thea was surprised.

"You should frame some of his art and hang it on the walls," Andreas said.

"You say that," Thea chided, "yet you have nothing on your own walls."

Andreas shrugged and didn't respond.

"I will have some framed."

"Good."

"What about your drawers?" Thea asked, thinking of the small painting and the album Andreas kept in his bureau. "Have you added anything?"

"It's rare that I find something I care about enough."

"That Buddha came from your drawer, didn't it?"

Thea gestured toward the small white statue staring impassively across the room.

"You're right. It did."

She let her gaze linger for a moment on the white Buddha perched on the bookshelf. If this small figure came alive, nothing it saw or heard would alter the depth of its calm. She needed that larger point of view, the equanimity of a soul that sees the human in a cosmic ebb and flow of being and evolution. It reassured Thea that Andreas brought the statue to Luke's room. It was like a commitment, an intention to do whatever might be best.

"Let me look in on him," Thea said.

Andreas nodded his assent.

Walking along the hallway, Thea imagined how hanging the art would brighten these walls. The door to the bedroom was open, and Thea stopped on the threshold.

Luke stood facing the windows in a waterfall of light. He was at once solitary and transfigured. Thea had an impulse to cross the room and hold him. How she would hold him she wasn't certain, perhaps by pressing to his back and encircling him with her arms. In this way, she would pull him back to earth. Yet she found herself frozen on the threshold, neither inside the bedroom nor outside it. She couldn't bring herself to disturb him, though her fascination made her want to move toward him. Finally, she returned to the living room and sat in the armchair facing Andreas.

"Is he all right?" Andreas asked.

"Yes, yes. He's fine."

What had she seen? Rapture? Profound loneliness? She didn't know. Was he unknowable? It would be easier to offer a name, find a category. Labeling him insane would dispose of every doubt. But that would betray him. She might conceal her expectations from herself, but she couldn't allow that here. If what stirred within him was unknowable, at the very least she needed to let him be what he was and might become. She had taken an oath to do no harm. The cure was his, not hers.

42

"I had a dream." Moritz spoke with animation. "As soon as I woke, I knew I had to tell you—while the experience of it is fresh. I would have knocked on your door, but it was too early."

He had slipped a note under Thea's door. She had come to Luke's apartment in response to this summons. Moritz sat beside her on the couch, and Luke remained in his bedroom.

"Who was in the dream?"

"Oh no." Moritz shook his head. "No one was in the dream. It was strange in that way. I simply heard a voice."

"But you didn't see anything? No people, no place you recognized?"

"It wasn't visual at all."

"The voice," Thea asked, "was it a man's or a woman's?"

"I can't say. Or maybe it wasn't a voice. Maybe the words just sounded in my mind."

"What were the words?"

"Benno *venite*."

Thea didn't understand. "Do you know what that means?" she asked.

"When I heard the words, they meant nothing to me, but I decided to see if they had meaning. I started with the first word, Benno. It sounded like *buono*, so I thought it might mean 'good.' Instead, I found that Benno is a boy's name with German origins. It means 'bear.'"

"Really?"

"I was surprised. I had no idea."

"And the other word?"

"*Venite* is from Latin. It means 'to come.' So the words of my dream, roughly translated, are 'the bear comes.'"

A chill braided Thea's spine. "What could that mean?"

Moritz shook his head.

"I don't know," he answered, "but as soon as I understood I had to tell you."

The bear would return. This thought shocked Thea, but it was followed by another even more preposterous. The bear would call to Luke. This she couldn't explain. How could the bear reach out to the man? These strange thoughts felt true. Thinking of Luke standing like a sentry scrutinizing the wild, she regretted for a moment her decision to move him from the yellow room. The windows tempted him. They freed him to imagine losing himself again in the forest. He would answer the call of the bear. He was ready to go. If these thoughts were absurd, why didn't he speak? He looked like a normal man. What kept him apart?

It was right to move him. In the yellow room, he had been a captive. She had to remember where he started, the progression toward health that had brought him here. Thoughts of the bear were absurd. This was no different from frightening herself with thoughts of the bear while she hiked—the bear nearby, trailing her, coming closer to her. There had been no sightings of a bear. Even

242

if Luke wanted to escape, a word she hesitated to use, winter was coming. She could hardly believe he had survived the last winter, but certainly he knew the cold severity of the months ahead. No rational person would leave the comforts of an apartment and the certainty of three meals a day if the alternative was a life-and-death struggle in the frigid wilderness.

"Are you okay?" Moritz asked, breaking the silence.

"It could have been my dream," she finally managed to say.

"Yes," Moritz agreed, "that's what I felt."

Yet it was a dream. Thea didn't take it lightly, but its meaning might not be obvious. The bear could be lumbering toward them, its hulking darkness hidden in the forest. Or it could be the approach of something else, a new element that Thea couldn't grasp or enflesh with words.

Thea reached out and picked up the book Moritz had placed on the table. It was solid and old, the fabric of its golden cover worn at the edges. To hold the book with its weight, thickness, and texture distanced Thea from the uncanny divination of the dream.

"It looks like you're almost finished," she said, setting the book back on the bedspread.

"Yes. It's a desolate vision. Everyone alive in the city is really dead, except the narrator who is between the living and the dead. It's what war makes, cities of suffering and death. The narrator experiences the pain of returning again and again in memory to encounter those who are gone. I say memory, but in the novel he encounters their phantoms in the city."

"Is it hard for you to read?" Thea asked, thinking of the terrors of Mauthausen-Gusen and how their legacy reverberated from grandfather to father to Moritz.

"In a way, but also fascinating. Death is ubiquitous," Moritz replied. "This city isn't a place where the living can stay. The question is whether the narrator will leave and live or stay and die."

The city was a metaphor of separation from the life before. In Moritz's novel, the separation was of the dead from the living. But the institute was like a small city that also allowed separation from what came before. Thea arrived seeking time away from her daily routine, time for a different way of living. Moritz was drawn by a spiritual magnetism to shrines, ashrams, retreats, and the geography of the sacred. Certainly for Luke as well there had been his separation from the wild, from the bear.

"Don't you wish he would speak?" Thea changed the subject, thinking of her conversation with Andreas about curing the man.

"Do you?"

"Yes," Thea answered. "It's essential."

"If he's going to speak, he'll speak when he's ready."

"But you want him to speak?"

Moritz looked down to where his hand rested on the book.

"You want him to be cured, don't you?" Thea spoke sharply. How could he not give an immediate reply?

"I'll never forget this time," Moritz said, looking at her. "It's very special. To be with him so much. To be entrusted with him. I don't care if he speaks. To be honest, I'm happy he doesn't speak."

"I don't understand," Thea protested. "If he doesn't speak, we'll never know why he went into the wild, how he came to be with the bear, or how he survived the winter. We'll never know if he's sane or simply docile. Don't you want to know?"

"I know what I experience when I sit with him."

"What's that?"

"I feel at peace," Moritz answered, ignoring her challenging tone, "and something more. I feel an energy working in him, moving him in ways I can't know. For me, that energy is divine. It enters him from another dimension. It isn't of this place, this time, this culture. It isn't bound by our limitations. It's unique in a way that defies description. Words would be useless."

"Why useless?"

"What he expresses can't be contained by words."

"Is he a teacher?" Thea asked.

Moritz shook his head. "No, not a teacher. My hope is that he is a living manifestation of God."

"If he spoke," Thea said, "you would know."

"But I wouldn't. I would only know what he said."

"But . . ."

Thea simply wanted Luke to be present in a way she understood. Moritz wanted the presence of God. Surely that had to do with the terrors of the camps, the terror passing down the generations. She didn't know what to say next to him. She saw the irony that their conversation should halt because she lacked the words to continue.

"I want to take some of his art," Thea said, changing the subject again, "to frame and put on the walls."

Quietly, Luke came and took his seat at the drawing board. Thea made her way around the couch and chairs to stand next to him. His head trembled with a rapid but almost imperceptible shaking. Bending her knees to bring her eyes to the level of his, she saw that his gaze was distant. He looked in a reverie, and she doubted he saw anything at all.

She straightened and moved one of the oversized books off a pile of his art. Slowly, head bent over the art, she moved each sheet to a new pile beside the old. She stopped from time to time to linger over one of his creations. When she finished with his first pile, she went on to the others until she had gone though all five, then neatly placed the books back on top of the art. She gathered up the half dozen artworks she'd put aside to be framed. As she did, she feared his hand might suddenly shoot out to grasp her wrist and prevent her from taking his work. That would have been a triumph of sorts, an acknowledgment of her presence. Although he did nothing, Thea sensed a change in him. She could see it in the neat piles of his art. He had taken steps of preparation. But for what?

"I'll have these framed," she said, stopping to show Moritz her choices.

As he looked carefully at each, she couldn't help but think how easily Luke could slip past him while he slept and take flight. The door wasn't locked. Nothing but a desire to stay could prevent him from leaving.

"These are bright," Moritz said.

"Let's think where to hang them."

Outside, Thea followed the walk to the center of the lawn. The morning sun cast a long shadow on the sundial. Sitting on one of the benches, she shivered with the chill of the thick stone slab on the backs of her legs. It was mid-October, not truly cold yet, but she could feel what lay ahead. Between the buildings, she glimpsed the peaking colors of fall—scarlet, yellow, and golden leaves that shook and shifted with the gusting breezes. Despite the brightness of the morning, the days were shortening. She didn't look forward to the darkness of November, the hurtling winds chafing leafless branches.

She liked being at the center of the five buildings. As the line for breakfast spilled out of Amazon, she felt herself the still point around which everyone moved. Some followed the bluestone walks while others strolled on the lawns. They thickened into groups crowding on the steps of Amazon. She nodded occasionally to a staff member or another long-term resident like herself. Many of the people were strangers who had just arrived for a weekend retreat. She knew the hunger for quiet and nature that brought them here. Shifting from one sit bone to the other and lifting through her spine, she scrutinized each passing visitor. From the tightness of a forehead or a brightness in the eyes, she imagined the homing instinct pulling these pilgrims here.

Suddenly, keenly, she missed her daughter. There were cycles and cycles within cycles. The cycle of her love for Delphina would last her lifetime. Within that was the unknown duration of the cycle of their separation and her sorrow. And the cycle of Moritz's efforts to heal his family through the generations. And the cycle of her effort to cure Lucas Lamont. That might end with a cure or with the return of the bear. Did that mean Luke would escape to the wild?

Did it matter if Luke lacked words? She also lacked words. She didn't know what to say to Moritz when he spoke of the divine flowing through their patient. She had lacked the words to tell everyone about Hugh's abuse of Delphina. She sent him to therapy, so he would find the words, but he didn't. She lacked the words to connect to Delphina, who was no farther away than the glowing screen of her iPhone. Much as she might want to, she refrained from reaching out.

That had been the reason for her affair. She couldn't speak, yet she had to act. It wasn't about the particular man or any pleasure she experienced during their few furtive meetings. She barely remembered him or the sex. Any man would have been good enough. It was a protest, a demand that Hugh speak or leave. When she told Hugh, she thought he would finally find the words to discuss their relationship and what had happened. Instead, to her despair and relief, he left.

As for the return of the bear, why not let Luke go? It excited her to think it. Could she protect him from his own desires? Why not take him to the bear?

If only there could be more than one ending. For her, the man would speak and be cured. For Moritz, he would be the glowing embodiment of the divine. For himself . . . what would he do if the choice was his?

43

Thea began to hike with Luke as her regular companion. First, she returned with him to the path looping around the grounds of the institute. From the parking lot to the marble steps rising toward the obelisk to the fence beyond Danube where the land fell away, she walked with him or sat beside him on the benches strategically placed to capture the views. Depending on the weather, Thea chose a light or heavy jacket from Luke's closet, slipped his arms into the sleeves, and zipped up the front. The lighter jacket was bright orange, the heavier a bold red-and-black plaid. Both ensured hunters would never mistake the wearer for prey. She attempted to give him hiking poles, but he simply let them fall from his hands. As she led him away from the familiar paths, she quickly realized he had no need for them.

"Are you ready to hike?" Thea asked one morning when she found Luke at his usual post before the windows. To Thea, the neatly stacked piles of art by his drawing board suggested a bringing into focus, a narrowing and intensifying purpose.

She rested her hand on his shoulder blade. He gave no response, absorbed in the meanings he alone could glean from the landscape. He looked sensitive, his domed forehead promising stores of wisdom and his narrow lips ready to judge the good and the bad. His intensity brought a fiery light to his eyes. Combined with the fineness of his features, it was easy for Thea to imagine him a poet. If she speculated on what he might write, she thought it would be about his inner life, the hidden passions that took him to the wild. That his escape into the vast reaches of the forest happened beneath a sky crisscrossed by satellites in a wilderness protected as a park from the encroachment of subdivisions, supermarkets, schools, and the rest mattered not at all. In a way, this made it more remarkable. When he left that summer house, he crossed more than the boundary of the land. He refused the limitations of the familiar.

He felt her next to him. She was sure he did, although he gave no sign. He might never show delight at her arrival, pleasure in her presence, or even recognition of her. Placing her back against the window frame, she looked into those intelligent eyes fixed so diligently on a distant vision. When she first saw him, he had been in a stupor. Now he was entirely different. Even as he refused to be distracted by her eyes, he showed a tenacity that implied his mind was at work and his will was strong.

She had an impulse to take him in her arms and dance a few steps. It would bring them to a different awareness, the memory in muscles, the shifting of weight, the architecture of torso and limbs in the delight of motion. She almost reached out to place one hand on his waist and the other on his shoulder. Then she would lean away and pull him from his observation post in a flurry of steps. But she couldn't. He wasn't an object to move to her will. She had to be patient. Turning toward the window, she looked at the forest he scrutinized. The trees clung to the mountainside dropping sharply to the valley. The lush curtain of leaves had fallen away to reveal the earth, outcroppings of stone, and the bare trunks and limbs of the trees. She tried to see what he saw. Small birds, probably sparrows, hopped about pecking the ground just before the land fell away. In the forest, she saw nothing alive. Branches trembled with gusts of wind, but there were no deer among the trees. Neither falcons nor vultures floated toward the lofty ridges of cloud.

"Shall we go?"

Placing her hand on his wrist, she gently guided him toward the door. He moved ahead of her like a breeze, her guiding hand barely contacting him. She brought the lighter jacket from the closet by the front door and slipped it over his shoulders. Picking up her hiking poles, she led him into the hallway, down the stairs, and across the lawn to Amazon.

Climbing the three flights of stairs, they stood outside the yellow room he once occupied. Elevating on the balls of her feet, Thea looked through the one-way glass. The room where Luke had spent so many months contained nothing now. Even the mattress and bed frame had been moved to his new apartment. She hoped bringing him here might jar him in some way. He might recognize how far he had come since he first found himself surrounded by these yellow walls.

Opening the door, she entered. The gray floor tiles had been polished to sparkle. The sink and seatless toilet gleamed. A fresh coat of yellow paint smoothed the walls and concealed any blemishes from his occupancy. She couldn't be certain if he recalled his time here. She thought he must, but he didn't hesitate to enter the room and stand beside her.

Thea turned slowly to view the open door and the walls. She faced the wall Luke had so often faced. If the wall had a window, it would reveal the forest. She compared this room to the spaciousness of his new apartment with its windows opening to the valley and the light. Had she been confined in this room, she would have thought endlessly of Delphina. Her sorrow could overtake her without warning. Worse than the sorrow was to be filled with an inescapable love Delphina refused to receive. She could blame herself or Hugh, but blame did no good. It was confining and small like this room. What if the bear was coming? The dreadful thought cheered her. What if the man escaped not just this room but the institute and her agenda to heal him? There had to be another way to exist, a different way to live her life.

Observing Luke, she found him as he always was. He revealed no discomfort at being in the room that once restrained him. Did he see the wall? Was his universe within him, visions and even words he would never share?

"Come." Thea spoke more to hear her own voice than to communicate.

She closed the door behind them. Descending the enclosed staircase, they exited into the daylight. She led the way across the lawn and up the incline. She moved at an angle to the slope to lessen the steepness. Leaves and branches crackled beneath her sneakers. Clambering over the large, lichen-patched boulders, her footfalls became as silent as his. The peak of autumn had passed. The golden leaves and the scarlet had browned and fallen. Only remnants of that display clung to the branches.

They crossed the slender indentation of the stream, its flow reduced to a dark stain on the pebbled bottom. In the shadows, patches of moss with starlike shoots absorbed the impact of their footfalls. Among the tawny leaves were acorns, branches weathered by the wash of the rains, and more of the endless stones. Needling the earth with the sharp points of her hiking poles, Thea used the strength of her arms to help propel her up the final ascent.

On the ridge, sunlight poured over the boulders strewn about the plateau. The windbeaten trees were stunted, the oaks like bushes. Thea moved ahead among the large rocks. At the far side, the level ground sloped down to form a basin from which the mountain rose even more steeply. As they walked, the massive height of the peak beyond was ever present. It towered above them, eclipsing a broad swath of sky. Hiking toward its summit would be far more rigorous than the climb from the institute to the ridge.

Stopping in the boulder-strewn meadow, Thea wondered why the peak challenged her. She had come to the ridge so many times without giving a thought to going farther. The change had to be Luke. He followed her obediently, but in a way he led her. It was his willingness to come at all. He reentered the forest where he had roamed with the bear. It was in this forest that the constables targeted him with their tranquilizer darts. To Thea these hikes were the natural outgrowth of his watching from his window.

Luke joined her in staring at the peak. She had brought him on different paths to the limits of where she usually hiked. She should always bring him back to the spacious apartment in Danube where he would be safe. But what if safety wasn't his goal? What if, what if . . . what if she took him farther than she had gone? If the bear called to him, what if she let him go? What if she went with him? And where would that be?

The blueberries and raspberries were gone. In the thick patches of blueberry bushes, the leaves were mottled green and wine red, and the diminished branches no longer clung to their knees. In the meadow where Thea had feared the bear, the raspberry bushes looked barren, the large thorns only a reminder of the vanished clusters of red berries the thorns had been unable to preserve.

The meadow ended. Moving through the forest, Luke followed close to Thea. She heard nothing but only had to look back to see him just beyond her reach. That he followed her was a connection, but it was more gravitational than personal. He remained unwilling to meet her eyes. He followed but didn't speak. Nonetheless, his staying close made her feel a rapport.

Ahead was the green of the pine grove. The needled branches gave color and shielded the interior of the grove. Thea wanted to speak, to say this was one of her favorite places, but what purpose would that serve? Often when she lost herself in the forest, hiking away from the trails she knew and letting herself be moved by her limbs rather than any plan, her legs brought her here.

She knelt to place her hiking poles on the ground. A breeze found its way through the branches and played lightly over them. Birds called from beyond the pines. Gaps in the trees let columns of light descend, and where there were no gaps there was a more diffuse glow and a deepening of the shadows round the trunks.

Thea wanted to linger in the stillness at the center of the grove. If she had been alone, she would have lowered herself cross-legged to the soft bed of needles. Turning to her companion, she saw that his focus remained on the peak beyond. He looked at the lofty summit in the same way he stared at the yellow wall or out the windows of his apartment. Did he see the peak as a challenge? Or was his intense gaze a reflection of thoughts she would never learn?

Should she take him farther? In a few minutes, they could cross to where the land tilted down before the steep rise to the mountain's peak. It would be terra incognita. At least it would be for her. She couldn't know if he had been there in the company of the bear. Her impulse was to take his arm and lead him toward where he gazed.

But it was too late in the afternoon. Darkness came earlier now. The sun lowered toward the mountains in the west. Picking up her hiking poles, she turned away from the peak and started back to the institute. On the downslopes, the cover of fallen leaves was like ice underfoot. As she had on the walk up, Thea wove back and forth to level the descent. They filed among the tumble of boulders, crossed the indent of the meager stream, and passed the double-trunked tree.

Reaching the polished obelisk at the head of the marble steps, Thea stopped. The institute's buildings rose like massive blocks on

254

the campus below. By the forest's edge, a dogwood had bloomed whitely in the spring. Now, its leaves were mottled ruby and green. Its branches shook beneath a mass of starlings whose beaks tore at the clusters of bright crimson berries. The leaves thrashed, moved by the tornado of the birds' beating wings, until an imperceptible signal made the flock of fifty or more rise as one, wheel through the air, and hurtle into the forest.

44

*T*he bear comes.

Thea sat with her legs crossed beneath her. A candle burning in the blue bowl on the floor cast a faint and flickering light against the mirrored walls of the meditation room. She breathed deeply in, the air opening the depths of her lungs and then seeming to move through her abdomen and settle in the bowl of her pelvis before her slow exhalation emptied her. The flame danced in currents of air too subtle to feel on her skin.

The bear comes.

The words surfaced again and again. Try as she might to be vacant of thought, Moritz's dream remained with her. Closing her eyes and inhaling slowly to fill the spaces within her, she wondered if the blue light playing off the backs of her eyelids came from the translucent glass holding the candle. Would the blue light fill her eyes if the room were in total darkness? Like a swimmer unable to hold her breath, Thea rose to the surface and opened her eyes. The candlelight illumined the reflection of her face. Her body looked rooted in the shadows multiplied by the walls of mirrors.

Closing her eyes again, she breathed deeply. She was with Luke on the mountain. Let the scene go, she told herself. For a moment, exhaling, she freed her mind from images. Inhaling again, she saw him gazing through the pines to the peak. Release the thought. What did Luke search for in that forest? She had to quiet her mind. Her breathing had an even rhythm, slowly in and slowly out. She followed the flow of the air in, the volume and fullness, and out as her chest contracted to vacate the hollows of her lungs.

Did the bear walk in that forest?

She didn't know. She couldn't know.

The bear comes. It had been a dream, a translation of words in a dream. And not even her own dream. But it rang in her. It couldn't be only about flesh and blood, the actual bear walking through the leafless forest. The bear of the dream walked in her imagination. Whether he was close or far depended on her, the meanings she gave to his presence. Did he walk upright or on all fours? Was he majestic? Did he come as a shaman to heal Luke?

Her thoughts rushed one way, then fled another. Her eyelids opened to reveal the flickering of the candle. Searching the shadows in the mirror, she tried to glimpse the largeness of the bear, the darkness of the bear. This was absurd. To see the bear in the mirror, the bear would have to be in the room with her. She was alone, except for the ceaseless multiplication of her thoughts.

Again, she closed her eyes. After only a few cycles of inhaling and exhaling, she saw the intensity of Luke's eyes as he looked at the steep rise of the peak.

She breathed to her depths, letting the air expand her abdomen. Slowly, she released her breath in a steady stream. The relaxation was what she needed. Not going toward, not an intention, but loosening, surrender. Yet every thought pressed her to be active. If she let go, what would become of her? If a force beyond her volition carried her forward, would she be safe? Would she survive?

All nonsense. Safety, survival. She couldn't let go. If she could, she had no idea whether anything would transport her. She knew so little.

The bear comes.

What prompted Moritz to hear those words? Where had those words originated, from what source, from what depths? Why dream? Of course, humans dream. But animals dream too. Why should dreaming be a common thread? Thea could only think reality insufficient. We needed to know our waking lives weren't everything. We needed to be free of daily realities, unbound by familiar truths, larger than the flesh that contained us.

Slowly, she uncrossed her legs, straightening and shaking them to bring back the circulation of blood. Putting her palms on the carpeted floor, she pushed up to her hands and knees, then stood. Towering above the candle, she thought for a moment of never returning. Every effort she made to release her thoughts made her think them more forcefully. It had happened on other days. No doubt it would happen again.

45

Dear Delphina,

I've already apologized, so I write this letter more for me than for you. I've given a lot of thought to what Hugh did.

You always disliked him. That should have warned me. I was responsible to protect you. If I had engaged you with caring and love about your feelings, I might have learned what kind of man I married.

I might have learned the ways in which he abused you. I failed to be intuitive, inquisitive, sensitive to what was taking place in our home.

Once I knew, I made a terrible mistake. I insisted he go to therapy. I should have taken you and gone as far away from him as humanly possible. I should have divorced him.

It's always tempting to offer excuses. I saw him as ill. I believed a sensitive therapist might help him heal. Underneath it all, I experienced him as a victim. But he was also a victimizer, as you know only too well.

A parent's relationship with a child lasts a lifetime. It lasts despite the pain of disappointments, lost opportunities, and even separation.

I've tried to learn, to understand my failings. My love for you and hope for you will always remain. My arms and my heart are always open to you.

Forgive me.
Mom

The letter was finished, but Thea knew she would never put it in an envelope to send. Delphina didn't want to hear from her, but she hoped one day her daughter would begin to heal. Thea couldn't stop her love, but she needed a respite from her endless guilt and sense of failure. She wanted to walk with Luke beyond where they had gone before. If the bear came, she no longer feared.

46

November arrived with a cold front from the north. Leaving Amazon after breakfast, Thea clutched her sweater closed over her chest. It wasn't enough to keep her warm, so she'd have to return to her room for a heavier coat before the day's hike. She hurried up the steps of Danube, relieved to get inside. Barely noticing the map threaded by the blue of the lengthy river, she trotted briskly up the stairs, rapped sharply twice on Luke's door, and entered.

Moritz read in his favorite armchair facing the door. Luke could only be either at his drawing board or his outpost staring through the windows at the forest. This morning he stood at the windows.

Luke gave no sign of hearing the knocks, the closing of the door, or Thea speaking to Moritz.

"A new book?"

"Yes."

"What's it about?"

"A man alone in the wilderness. Later—I haven't gotten that far—he's brought to live in a city."

"Brought?"

"Yes. He's lived with a tribe, but he's the only survivor."

If Luke hadn't been in the room, Thea would have questioned Moritz further.

"You find interesting books," she observed. "Don't let me interrupt."

Moritz bowed his head and returned to his reading. Settling on the couch, Thea stared at the man before the window. Did looking at the valley below make him yearn for the wild where life was stripped of every complexity except survival? He might live in sensation, feeling gravity's press, the upright architecture of bones, the snaking of muscles, and the rivers of rushing blood squeezed with each resonant heartbeat. Or emotion . . . a grief for the time when he moved among men? Or for the time when he kept company with the bear? Did he miss his companion, the beast, the bear?

What would reveal that he had been cured? A meeting of the eyes? Yes, so very little. Yet her caring was a constant. Inevitable caring. It was for him but certainly also for her. She needed to care. She needed the constancy of it, the service to another, the love that it implied. It was the sublime selfishness of altruism. It was about the self, herself made visible through her actions.

Sitting up straight on the couch, her feet planted firmly on the floor, Thea was aware of the Buddha behind her. As the meditation room had mirrors, silence, and the candle with its dim, flickering light, so Luke's living room had the presence of the Buddha, the intensity of both Luke and Moritz, and the rarely broken quiet. This was true of her hikes as well. There would be long periods when she was simply part of the shifting terrain and the lifting trees. Her legs moved her without command. Conscious thought was an unwelcome interruption. If Luke, the bear, or the institute came to mind, she tried to release those mental constructs. She had read of Zen masters who walked for ten hours or more while chanting and reciting sacred texts. If she had the good fortune to forget herself,

264

her hikes in the wild might be like that. In the moments when she forgot her name, her purpose, and her self-reflections, she moved without restraint or any separation from the forest.

Quietly, Luke seated himself at the drawing board. He took one of the piles of paper and looked intently at each sheet. When all the pages had been turned over, he went on to the next pile. When he finished, he left the piles ordered so neatly they appeared untouched. He walked a few steps to stop before the wall to Thea's left. In the center of the wall she had hung one of his framed artworks. He examined this with the same focus he had given to each sheet in the stacks of papers. Thea looked at him looking at the art contained by the black, wooden frame she had chosen. After several minutes, he crossed the room to the opposite wall to study another of his framed works. He lingered for another few minutes, then passed Moritz and Thea to halt at the beginning of the hallway.

Thea rose and joined him in studying the first artwork in the hallway, then moved with him to the second. She accompanied him into the bedroom where two more works hung to the right and left of the door. Moritz said that, since the art went up, Luke made this excursion several times each day. This was the first time Thea had seen him making his survey.

It left her with an elusive feeling of loss. While the art might best be called abstract, she had chosen pieces in which a strong color was dominant. A work made of yellows reminded her of the sun's brightness. She wanted to say how the golden core unleashed its energy into the yellow flares leaping to the boundaries of the pictorial space. She wanted to say she admired the effort he put into his work, that she drew pleasure from what he created. But these ways of sharing with him were foreclosed. To look together but not speak didn't make her feel they shared. She was in his presence but not with him.

He returned to the living room, where he positioned himself in front of the windows and stared out to the forest flowing down into the valley.

Moritz stirred in his chair, stretching and yawning, his arms above his shoulders with the book aloft in a hand. Glancing at the familiar sight of Luke before the windows, he rested back in the armchair and returned to reading his story.

Skirting the couch and armchairs around the coffee table, Thea passed Luke's desk and came to stand beside him at the window. He continued to gaze out, his head rocking ever so slightly. She saw his eyes were alert and intently focused on the forest sloping down into the valley.

He trusted her to be close to him. Each day, he followed her as they hiked the forest.

If he trusted her, she trusted him. Trust was its own substratum, wordless and connecting. Without that trust, why would she feel at ease alone with him, a man brought wild from the forest? She sensed his presence, the intensity with which he inhabited himself. She wanted to anchor him with a hand on his shoulder. To feel his warmth beneath her fingers would be a comfort, but it would hardly solve the puzzle of the man.

47

Thea was used to visiting Luke in the morning, afternoon, and sometimes again in the evenings. It was the afternoon visit that expanded to include their hikes, but as the hikes lengthened, they often returned to the institute in darkness. Thea loved the radiance of the days, the setting forth, the finding of new paths, but the darkness made her hesitate. It agitated her in a way she could barely describe. It was like a sinking, a heaviness. In the quiet she had sought at the institute, there was little to distract her from the stretching fabric of the night. Not only did the blackness lengthen, but each moment within the blackness expanded.

Finally, Thea decided to hike in the mornings. Buoyed by the brightness, she would bring Luke back early in the afternoon. Once this routine of hiking was established, Thea felt his tension when she arrived in his apartment. It was a barely contained energy, an excitement requiring motion.

Invariably, they walked on the ridge beneath the soaring peak of the mountain. Thea had never considered hiking toward the peak until Luke joined her. Now when she paused to gaze upward, he gazed as well. Thea found herself considering how to begin an ascent. Standing atop a boulder in the meadow, she studied the falling off and the peak rising beyond.

Was she taking Luke to the peak or to the bear? If she took him to the bear, then she offered him to the wild. She rebelled against herself, against her belief that he should speak and return to civilization. She wanted to entertain not only her idea of healing but allow whatever his beliefs might be. He might have walked this expanse of forest with the bear. Perhaps he knew where the bear would seek a cave, a crevice, or a leafy nest beneath a fallen tree for the winter hibernation. If he sought the bear, why should she resist him?

These thoughts excited her, and yet she didn't have the certainty, the courage, to lead Luke to this new territory. The land between the ridge and the start of the peak acted like a barrier. She could look for trails, but she had to be rational and take responsibility for what might come from her actions. If he chose to escape, would he survive another winter in the wild? This frustrated her. Without being fully able to explain why, she wanted to go with him to the peak.

On the night when the clocks would be set back, Thea finished her visit with Luke and Moritz, walked down one flight of stairs, and knocked on Andreas's door. In a few moments, Andreas filled the doorway. He wore an elegant silk robe of blue and gold that touched the floor.

"Welcome. What brings you here?" A wide silk sleeve billowed beneath his elbow as he waved to usher her into the living room.

"I said good night upstairs and wanted to stop by."

Thea had visited Andreas on other evenings after leaving Luke's apartment. The bottle of Armagnac and the snifter on the coffee table didn't surprise her.

"May I offer you a brandy?"

"Yes, thanks."

Andreas vanished into the kitchen and returned with another snifter. Setting it on the table, his sleeve draping almost to the floor, he uncorked the Armagnac and filled the bottom of the goblet.

Andreas made small circles with the hand holding his glass before lifting the rim to his lips. Placing the glass on the side table and resting back in his chair, he placed his arms on the armrests. Thea sat on the couch, facing him across the table. She took her first sip of brandy. Piquant on her tongue, its robust aroma rose into her sinuses. It singed her gullet as she swallowed.

"Our friend is well?"

"His art is on the walls now."

"I've seen it."

Thea glanced across the apartment. On each visit, she imagined what would make the place less bare. Ironic that Andreas suggested framing Luke's art and yet preferred no decoration in his own living quarters. An artwork like the one Andreas kept in his drawer or a few tiny Greek statues, an Apollo and a Dionysius, would alleviate the feeling of emptiness.

"The clock goes backward tonight," Thea added. "It's bad enough the days get shorter. Now we lose an hour of sunlight."

"We can't blame the planet for tilting on its axis."

"I just don't like the darkness at this time of year. The light is gone long before the end of the afternoon. We've started hiking in the mornings to make sure it's light when we come back."

"They sound like long hikes. Is he a good companion?"

"In a way, but . . ."

"What?"

"I keep wanting to go farther. It's something about having him with me. I feel he wants to go farther."

"Is that what you want?"

Thea paused before answering.

"Yes, I want to take him farther."

"Then why don't you?"

"I feel like I'm taking him to the bear. Or if not to the bear, to the wild. I'm showing him routes of escape from the institute. But he isn't cured. I'm not sure what's best for his healing."

Andreas looked to be replaying her words in his mind.

"You really aren't in charge of his fate."

"You asked me to care for him."

"In that, he's fortunate. But what becomes of him is uniquely about him. You have a role to play. No more than that."

"I resent him sometimes," Thea admitted. "Not really him so much as the time, the thought, that I give him. I came here for myself. Yet his presence is like a demand for me to take his side and help him. I can't ignore my concern about what will become of him."

"You have to heal him?"

The robe Andreas wore made him look like a celebrant of some ritual. He turned his goblet back and forth on the lathe of his hands. When Thea didn't reply, Andreas continued.

"The world requires nothing from you or anyone. To imagine you're the only one who can do a certain task, save a certain person . . . it's unlikely to be true and too large a burden. If you went home tomorrow, someone else would be given his case."

Thea wanted to protest. After all, she found him incarcerated in the yellow room, drugged, barely able to move. But Andreas offered another view of her situation. Luke was separate from her. He had his own resources, potentials, and failings. She might be helpful. So might others. Whatever help he received, the outcome turned on him, on what he could offer to himself. Andreas's words rankled because she had given every effort to heal him. But there was relief as well. She could only play her role.

"I feel I'm encouraging him to . . ." Thea paused to seek the right word. "Escape. I keep imagining he'll find the bear again. On the ridge above the institute, the mountain peak is visible. I want to take him to the peak. I'm not even sure why."

Andreas inhaled from the snifter and then tipped back the glass. Thea joined him, the brandy burning as she swallowed.

"And you?" he asked. "Do you want to escape?"

She understood what he meant. He didn't refer to the institute or her connection to Luke. It was a larger question.

"I thought I had escaped."

Andreas smiled. "By coming here?"

"No, not really. I knew better."

"Here you confront the demons. It gives you time and a place that's safe."

"I keep trying to remember, but I resist the memories. The feeling returns again and again."

"Which feeling?" Andreas asked.

"That I was wrong, blind." Thea straightened, leaning forward as she spoke. "I hurt my daughter in a way I can never heal. The time came when I had to stand with her. I didn't. I wasn't there for her. Later, when it was too late, I got rid of him."

"The place where you are and the place where you have to go," he replied carefully, "can seem infinitely far apart."

Thea nodded and pressed the rim of the goblet to her lips, letting the brandy roll over her tongue.

"I don't know if she'll ever forgive me."

"It's hard to accept. What we want hasn't happened and may never happen. We can't control or even know the outcome."

Images of Delphina, from little girl to woman, poured over Thea. How many times each day did this happen, this familiar cascade, these snapshots of her daughter's life?

"There's no point in thinking about what I might have done. I didn't do it."

"Keep your imagination open to her return. You don't know the outcome."

Andreas spoke with a kindly tone. It heartened Thea.

"I don't know," she agreed. "You're right."

"Lucas Lamont lived in the forest with a wild animal. If he wants to escape, will it matter whether you're on the ridge or the peak of the mountain? And if he and the bear are going to find each other, won't it happen wherever he is? Whatever blocks you from going farther with Luke, it must be about you. He can escape at any time. The bear can appear at any time. What holds you back?"

Thea pictured the falling away of the forest. It didn't go down steeply. If there were no paths, she could simply walk among the trees. In ten minutes, or twenty at the most, the ascent would begin.

"Is it all right," Thea questioned, not answering Andreas, "that he can escape?"

"It has to be. If that means I've failed, I've failed before. I'm not afraid to fail again." Andreas set his goblet on the table, poured the golden-brown brandy, and continued. "You and I want him to speak. We want to know he's better. In this case, we may never know. We try to understand. What if, after all the understanding, no matter what we know, he remains a mystery? Silent, complete in himself? Can we accept that? Live with that? Even believe in its value? Each generation, each person, carries mysteries into the earth. These mysteries aren't what we consciously hide but what we never bring to the light of awareness. As for our patient, maybe he can't be translated, made acceptable and familiar. Mysteries like his take their own time to resolve. It may not happen during treatment. To expect more diminishes what is. We can only be thankful. Thankful for the mystery that is life. Thankful for this opportunity to be with him, to know him in whatever way is possible."

To be thankful. It answered nothing and everything. The brandy filled her. Her head was light, her stomach afire, her legs weak.

"It's getting late," she said. "I should be going."

Andreas downed the last of his brandy and refilled the snifter. He raised the bottle to Thea, who shook her head.

"That's enough for me," she said, standing to be sure of her legs. "Thanks for the brandy and the talk."

"Yes, of course." Andreas rose in the splendid draping of his robe. "Thank you for the visit. Don't forget to set your clock back an hour."

"I certainly won't forget," Thea said as she stepped into the hallway.

To Thea, the night pressed against the ambience filling the apartment and the hallways. Each day would shorten until the shortest day of the year, the solstice just before Christmas.

"At least you'll get an extra hour's sleep tonight."

"Good night," she called back over her shoulder.

"Sleep well."

48

Thea entered the meadow and stopped to stare toward the peak. Glancing at Luke beside her, she was struck by how normal he appeared. Slender and handsome, he looked rugged in his coat with its red-and-black checks. He gazed intently toward the heights. If she hadn't known his history, his silence, she would have thought him like any other visitor to the institute. Instead, she imagined herself as his accomplice. She brought him to the wild so he could escape. Escape what? The institute, of course, but also her. He would escape her well-meaning attentions, her efforts to make him other than he was.

She walked to the far side of the meadow. The white filigree of Queen Anne's lace was gone. The leaning stalks of yellow goldenrod and purple loosestrife had vanished as well. Except for the stunted evergreens, the meadow had turned to tan and brown broken by jutting gray boulders. Thea stopped where the trees began.

She couldn't detect a path. But unless she imagined the leafless trees as a barrier, nothing prevented her from walking forward. With a feeling of inevitability, she moved ahead with her companion. At first, the land sloped downward but soon began to rise gently and then steepen. The trees were old, their trunks broad and bare until branches began well above a person's reach. Stopping to make sure he followed, she saw the ease of his movement. He looked unhurried, taxed not at all by the pace she set. Straightening to raise his head, his nostrils twitched and his ears perked. Could he really smell or hear better than she could? Intuitively, she wanted him to take the lead. He knew these landscapes. He would be better suited to guide, but he never moved ahead of her. At last, she moved forward, and he followed.

Occasionally, she raised her eyes, seeking the peak of the mountain. That might have been her north star, but she could only see the forested upslope. The larger vision of mountain ranges, valleys, and peaks was lost to her. As they walked farther, she considered the difficulty of finding the way back to the institute. The innumerable trees offered little to distinguish one from another. Ahead, on the rising slope, was simply more forest. She wanted to continue, but she had no idea how long the trek to the peak would take. Nor was she certain of the landmarks that would guide them back to the institute.

Thea halted. The forest ahead looked no different from the forest behind. To be lost on this mountain. . . . She could hardly imagine it. Everything familiar would be gone. There would be no meals in the dining hall, no narrow room to inhabit. The collective endeavor of humanity, the exchange of energies that supported life, would exclude her. Unlike Luke, she would have no bear to guide her. She would have only her silent companion. If that happened, if they wandered off the map of the known, would he protect her? Would he help her survive?

Each day grew shorter. And each day their hikes toward the peak lengthened. Thea memorized landmarks that would make their return to the institute easier on the next day and the day after.

When Thea ended the upward ascent and turned her back to the heights, she would feel regret and the determination to continue. Her companion followed her down with the same easy flow of steps with which he followed her up, until she took his presence as a given, a certainty.

As the middle of November passed and Thanksgiving neared, Thea regretted the moment on each hike when she decided to turn back. She chafed at her own caution. Why not rush to the heights? But she couldn't. If nothing else, she was responsible for Luke.

The shorter days and longer hikes let the deepening shadows of twilight overtake them on their return to the institute. Thea would lead the way to Danube and ascend the steps to Luke's floor. One night, knocking as always to alert Moritz, she entered to find the apartment empty. Luke showed no interest when she slipped off his coat. Hanging it in the closet by the front door, Thea wondered if he even felt its warmth or needed it. Everything in the living room was neatly arranged, from the Buddha on the bookshelf to the piles of paper next to the drawing board. As if they had never walked in the forest, Luke resumed his lookout by the windows and stared into the fading light.

Thea sat on the couch. She was responsible for Luke until Moritz returned, but a wave of fatigue pulled her with its undertow. She had to close her eyes. Luke might keep his vigil until dark and never notice if she slept. If he did notice, would he seize the opportunity to walk out the door and return to the wilderness? As Andreas said, he could depart whenever he chose. What could she really do to prevent him? Not quite convinced by her justification, she rested on her side and put one of the throw pillows under her head. She wanted a brief nap that would refresh her. She pulled her legs up toward her chest and tucked her hands beneath the pillow.

Her sleep was deep. Distantly, she felt hands covering her with a blanket and tucking in its edges. It occurred to her that

Luke had brought the blanket and gently adjusted it around her. That excited her, but she didn't open her eyes and soon slept deeply again.

"Getting hungry?"

The voice came from ever so far away. It was a pleasant voice, a man's voice. She stretched, legs lengthening and arms overhead. The blanket warmed and protected her. Her languor was gone, replaced by an aching in her legs like a memory of the hike and the mountain's steepness. Opening her eyes, she saw the ceiling light was on. Across the coffee table, Moritz sat in one of the armchairs. Behind him, Luke was at his drawing board. And beyond Luke, the windows showed that night had fallen.

"I thought I'd better wake you. They're only serving dinner for a little while longer."

Thea raised herself up on an elbow.

"I didn't mean to sleep so long. It's that late?"

Moritz nodded.

She swung her legs to bring her feet to the floor. Luke could have walked past her and out the front door, but he hadn't. Fear as she might his leaving while she slept, he had stayed.

"We should go eat," Thea agreed, rising to her feet.

Moritz rose too. Going to Luke's side, he touched his arm and brought him to standing. Thea exited the apartment first, followed by Luke and then Moritz.

"Did you cover me with the blanket?" Thea asked as they started down the stairs.

"Yes," Moritz replied, a hand on the banister and his feet taking the steps in flurries. "I thought you might get cold."

"Thanks."

Of course it had been Moritz who covered her. She was disappointed, but Luke had come so far since those first days in the yellow room. She had brought him so far. She could trust him to remain,

278

even while she slept. She expected him to remain. Could the issue no longer be whether he would stay or go? In fact, could the issue no longer be about him but about her, her desire to cure him, her desire to climb to the heights?

49

"I hope I'm not interrupting."

The next evening Thea came late to Luke's apartment. She often escaped the confines of her room and dropped by to be in Luke's presence, chat with Moritz, or visit with Andreas on the floor below. Moritz was making up the couch with sheets, a blanket, and a pillow. He slept in the living room when he was the one assigned to stay overnight.

"You're here late," Moritz said, glancing up from the blanket.

"I wanted to say good night."

"He's gone to sleep."

Moritz plumped the pillow, finished with the bedding, and stood up.

"I needed a walk," Thea said.

Moritz raised his brows, smiled, and sat in one of the armchairs.

"Today's hike wasn't enough walking?"

"Are you enjoying the book?" Thea asked, settling in the other armchair.

The paperback rested on the coffee table. The cover featured an antique black-and-white photograph of a man in profile. Native American, forty-five or fifty, he looked impassively into the distance.

"Yes, I'm engrossed, although the story is harrowing."

"Is it about him?" Thea asked.

"Yes."

"What was his name?"

"He didn't have a name."

"That's strange."

"His story is strange. Maybe I should say he had a name that wasn't his."

"He took someone else's name?"

"No."

"I don't understand."

"He was called Ishi, but that wasn't really a name," Moritz said, gesturing toward the paperback wrapped by the man's portrait. "He belonged to a small tribe in California. Starting in the mid-1800s and continuing into the early years of the next century, Ishi's tribe clashed with white settlers who cut back the forests for their farms. Many Native Americans assimilated with the new settlers, but Ishi's tribe chose to remain in the wild. They hid in the most inaccessible places they could find and tried to continue with their lives. As the settlers controlled more and more of the land, the tribe struggled to survive. On occasion, they stole from the farmers. In turn, the farmers hunted them like animals. Some of the tribe were killed, others died of hunger or illness, some vanished, and finally Ishi was alone. He faced a lifetime by himself in the wild, always hunted, always in hiding. Or he could surrender to the settlers."

"Wouldn't they kill him?"

"He didn't know. They might kill him. To surrender would certainly be risking his life. More than that, it would be giving up his culture. He would surrender the life that he and his tribe had lived for generations. He would be cut off from his own past."

"But he was cut off from that anyway," Thea said.

"Yes, that's true. He couldn't return to what had been. His choices looked unbearable. He could be alone until life's end or surrender to those who destroyed his way of life and killed his loved ones. Can loneliness, and despair, be so great that the risk of death or imprisonment is better than continuing alone?"

"What do you think?" Thea asked.

"That it's a forbidden topic. You and I have never experienced such losses. It isn't our reality. To speculate about what we might do is just a pretense."

"What did he do?"

"He came in from the wild," Moritz replied. "He gave himself up."

"Was he killed?"

"No. Anthropologists had become interested in his . . . case." Moritz spoke the last word with disdain. "He was turned over to them. Through their connections, he was hired to work in a museum."

"What work?"

"He became an exhibit."

"What?" Thea was stunned. "That sounds awful."

"He would demonstrate the crafts his tribe had practiced. He could fashion clothing, make bows and arrows, weave baskets. Crowds would gather to watch him. He was free to come and go. And he was paid for his work. He had friends on the staff . . ."

"But his world was gone," Thea protested.

"Yes, it was gone. He was utterly singular. There were no others like him."

She couldn't help but compare Ishi to Luke. Each defied the dominant culture, the highway of ideas that brought into being the highways woven through the land. Over those highways came endless goods for consumption in the cities. But Ishi and Luke refused this urban magnetism. Ishi had been raised in a different culture; Luke for his secret reasons sought the company of a wild animal. If possible, both would have remained outliers, signs of the different ways life can be lived.

"Did he live happily ever after?" Thea asked, surprised by her bitter tone.

"He made the best of it."

What more could have been done? The museum employed Ishi to demonstrate a way of life that had once been his. It contained him. Wasn't Luke contained by the institute in much the same way?

"What became of him?"

"Ishi spent five years working at the museum."

"Happily?"

"Who can say? It was a risk for him to work there. Really, it was a risk for him to live in our society. He had no immunity to our diseases. After five years, he died of tuberculosis."

"You really do find unusual books to read," Thea said.

"The books are endless. There's so much to learn, so many people whose lives are different from mine."

"But the book about the man who crosses the river to the land of the dead . . ."

"*The City Beyond the River*," Moritz said.

"That man and Ishi are both alone."

"I see it differently. Ishi comes to the people who destroyed everything he loved. But he lives among them. Whatever you think of his work at the museum, he took pride in it. The man in the city of the dead moves in the opposite direction. He's swept away in an undertow of memories. Much of his remembering is of the dead and relationships that found no realization. He leaves the living behind."

"I still don't understand . . ."

"Yes?"

"You said Ishi had a name that wasn't his."

"That's right."

"Then why was he called Ishi?"

"By tribal custom, he could only reveal his name if he was introduced to someone by a friend. But when he came out of the wild, he had no friends. Ishi, in the language of the Yahi people, meant 'man.' He was the last of his people and took a collective name as his own. If names have magical power, the concealment was to protect him."

To have no friends . . . to live among enemies . . . to take "man" as a name. It was, as Moritz had said, a life barely understood by those more fortunate.

50

The day before Thanksgiving was warm for November. Thea selected the lighter jacket for Luke. Slipping it over his shoulders, she imagined a pilot high above seeing the bright orange jacket like a beacon set on the summit. After she filled her backpack with sandwiches she'd made in his kitchen and a bottle of water apiece, she led him out of Danube and started toward the ridge at a rapid pace. Her urgency was irrational, but by moving quickly, she felt she would have more time to climb to the peak. She panted on the steep slope, the backs of her legs burning as she reached the ridge and started across the meadow. Faithful as a shadow, Luke followed a few steps behind.

The far side of the meadow had grown familiar. Entering the encompassment of the forest, she felt the leafy floor slope gently down until it lifted and led to the sharp rise of the mountainside. Their past hikes had taken them through the woods for three hours and more. Now she knew a sequence of landmarks to bring them safely up and back down. She hoped going a little farther through the forest would bring them close to the summit. There, on the highest promontory, she could look in any direction and see as far as the eye is capable of seeing.

They walked steadily, yet the forest continued. Thea had returned to the institute at twilight often enough not to want to do it again. Even with their early start, another hour of pressing ahead might bring them back in darkness. She could imagine a darkness different and new in which her eyes would adjust and become acute in discovering the slightest hint of light, one whose intimate wrap would encourage her to ask questions that in daylight went unspoken. But she didn't want the actual darkness of the forest, the terror of not knowing which way to go or where to find safety. Recognizing how her thoughts rushed away from her, Thea struggled to identify what, beyond the boundary of her awareness, spurred their flight.

At last, the landscape transformed. A maze of boulders and soaring cliffs opened before them. Trees, sporadic and stunted, clung to the shallow soil in crevices and indentations in the faces of stones. Thea wove one way and then another through the outcroppings. Blocked by a sheer drop to the forest far below, she retreated to the safety of the heaped boulders. Fearless of the heights, Luke followed her.

Thea stopped in a small clearing bounded on its far side by ridges that gave no hint of what might be concealed above. It was difficult to measure how far they had come or how much longer they would have to walk to reach the summit. She had no certainty they could go higher.

Gently, she pressed on Luke's shoulders to seat him on a flat rock. The moment she sat beside him, she felt her own fatigue. Simply to cease moving gave her pleasure. Slipping off her backpack, she brought out the sandwiches wrapped in tinfoil and the water. His pantry hadn't been well stocked, so the sandwiches were peanut butter and jelly. Opening the silver wrapping, she placed the sandwich on his lap. She uncapped a bottle of water and set it beside him.

Taking a bite of her own sandwich, she chewed slowly. In a landscape like this, piled with boulders, bounded by cliffs, presumably filled with crannies, the bear might now be searching for his winter abode. Like a great clock, the lessening of the light shifted an inner balance and moved him toward hibernation. Did he dream in those slumbering depths? Thea imagined he must. If he dreamt, did he dream of the world he had departed, of this world where she sat with Luke, or of a destination beyond her imagining?

Looking at Luke, she felt, despite his silence, such a sense of his presence. Was he with her, she wondered, or only with himself?

Tired as she was, Thea had a longing. Not for what had been but for a new and undeniable life. What did she mean? Strangely, she felt her past belonged less and less to her. Hugh. Her first husband. With age, even her earliest memories had come to feel like they might just as well belong to someone else. How present could the past truly be? She had always wanted to connect with another person at a depth that brought wordless understanding, a touching of the deepest of roots, natural and accepting. She longed for the living presence, the companionship, the undeniable other who could inhabit their own private depths and yet be with her.

She finished eating before Luke. Crumpling the tinfoil in a ball, she capped her bottle after a long swallow of the water. Then she returned the tinfoil and the nearly empty bottle to her backpack. When Luke finished with his sandwich, he tossed back his head to drink until he emptied his bottle. Thea took the bottle and the tinfoil from his lap and put both in her backpack. Rising, she slipped the pack's padded straps over her shoulders.

She turned to retrace the path to the institute. After a dozen steps, she looked back to Luke. She had taken for granted he would follow. He faced toward the heights with his back to her. Suddenly, she wasn't sure he would come. His following had been so automatic. She waited, but he didn't pivot toward her. Walking to his side, she saw how intently he looked at the ridges blocking their way forward. He had that same look when staring out the windows in his apartment. It could be rapture, hunger, or searching. His intensity made her doubt she could move him. She wanted to speak, but he didn't respond to words.

Gently, she reached out and placed her hand on his biceps. His muscle was taut. His whole body was tense, ready to move. She didn't like to think of him as an animal, but he strained like a hound on a leash. Only there was no leash, so what prevented him from rushing ahead and vanishing among the boulders? It could be the light restraint of her hand, the comfort of his apartment, or the neat piles of paper by his drawing board. Might he feel a closeness to her, Moritz, and the others at the institute?

He was lean, but she couldn't encircle his biceps. Gripping his arm, she gradually brought pressure to move him in her direction. She wanted her holding to be experienced as a reminder and not a demand. Although he didn't look at her, he softened beneath her touch and at last turned toward her. She started downhill again, looking back frequently to make sure he followed. Andreas had lectured on the dangers of looking back. Orpheus was warned by Hades but looked back at Eurydice and lost her to death. Lot's wife was warned by angels but lingered to see the destruction of Sodom and lost her life. The warning in these stories, Andreas concluded, was against nostalgia. Yearning for what was loses what is, the present.

When she had looked back enough to trust that Luke walked behind her, she turned her attention to finding her waymarks through the forest. Slowing her pace or pausing, she located a cliff, a grove of white birches, a toppled tree with its roots aloft like hands thrown up in terror.

By the time Thea and Luke emerged in the meadow, the sky had faded from lavender to purple. To Thea, darkness rose from

290

the twilight with the intensity of a sunrise. Crossing to the pine grove where she had often sat to meditate, she raised her eyes to the black limbs of the pines. The darkness, like a narrowing passage, obscured their surroundings. She picked her way carefully among the rocks and trees on the downslope. It was a relief to see the scatter of lit windows when the buildings at last came into sight. The low lanterns illuminated the walks.

Her legs ached. She didn't know how close to the summit they'd come, but they had gone above the trees. Her exhaustion didn't matter. The one certainty was that she would return. The return was always easier. If they started early enough, they would find a way.

51

On Thanksgiving, early in the afternoon, the community convened in the institute's dining hall. With few weekend visitors, the gathering was small. Thea counted a dozen tables draped with white tablecloths. Each had ten chairs, but not every chair was occupied, so at most one hundred staff, residents, and guests were gathered in the hall. Standing with Moritz and Luke, Thea noticed how people greeting her or Moritz would rest their hand for a moment on Luke's arm or shoulder. This had begun during their walks when others encountered him. He didn't respond, but a quality in his presence let people reach out to him.

The tables were laden with covered dishes. Because of the festive occasion, white wine filled the glasses beside each place setting. The buzz of conversation rose everywhere until Andreas stood and tapped his spoon against his wineglass. The chiming gradually reached to the corners of the hall. There was a pulling out of chairs and a final burst of conversation. Thea sat on one side of Luke and Moritz on the other. When the room was silent, Andreas began to speak.

"On behalf of the institute and myself, I welcome you all today. Thanksgiving is, as the name so clearly shows, a special day, a day for giving thanks. It's an opportunity to feel gratitude for what we appreciate in our lives. It's an opportunity to contemplate the gifts given to us, including the gift of life itself."

Andreas's voice was deep and resonant, easily carrying to the four corners of the hall. Portly and imposing, he played his role as the institute's director. Thea looked sideways at Luke, who sat with downturned eyes and a slight rocking of his head.

"We are told the Pilgrims celebrated the first Thanksgiving. Certainly they gave thanks for having survived in a world that was new to them. One hundred Pilgrims had come in 1620, but the two-month voyage on the Atlantic weakened them, and fifty died during the winter. In 1621, using seeds given them by the Wampanoag tribe, with whom they had made a treaty, their harvest was successful. Shooting rifles and cannons to celebrate, they alarmed the Wampanoag who sent ninety warriors to investigate. The warriors remained for three days, hunting and feasting with the Pilgrims."

Andreas paused and scrutinized his audience. This technique, which Thea recalled from his lectures, gave gravitas to the words to follow.

"To imagine this was the first Thanksgiving would be short-sighted. The Wampanoag, for example, gave thanks many times during the year. This thankfulness for the arrival of migrating fish such as the shad, the striped bass, and the sturgeon, for the whales, for the green corn, for the first snow, for a new year in May, and so much more, connected them to the larger spirit of creation. In this, the Wampanoag shared with peoples across the world the desire to give thanks. These festivals of thanks acknowledge the larger fount from which the blessing of life flows.

"Close to the Pilgrims' roots are the harvest festivals in the England from which they fled. The word 'harvest' came from 'hoerfest,' which meant 'autumn' in Old English. It referred to the season for bringing in the grain and other crops that had ripened."

Andreas moved easily from the harvest in England to the Moon Festival celebrated by the Chinese and the Vietnamese. As in England, the Moon Festival was held on the full moon, the harvest moon, in thanksgiving for the crop. Celebrants feasted on bean-filled mooncakes, and lanterns of marvelous shapes would be lofted above them to show their desire for the return of the warmth and light of the sun after the cold night of winter. Even as Andreas delved further, his command of the subject matter appeared effortless. His lectures had always been lively.

"The Incas," he continued, "gave thanks for the harvest in May with the celebration of Aymoray. For the Inca, maize was a living entity. Harvest dances offered thanks to the land and the maize. Carrying maize to their homes, the people sang songs begging it to last a long time and not leave before the next harvest. Then the maize would be put in a special bin and covered with the finest cloth. Called the 'mother of the maize,' for three nights the bin would be watched over and worshipped. By the virtue of the bin, it was said, the maize was given life. Sacrifices of alcohol and cocoa leaves would be offered in return for the gift of the harvest.

"This giving of thanks was universal. We can look to almost any culture at any time in history and find profound thankfulness. To take a last example, in India, the feast of Makar Sankranti falls in January. It celebrates the growth of the light after the winter solstice. In most of India, the spring crops have been sown, and there is a respite from the hard labor in the fields. There are colorful decorations, kite flying, dances, bonfires, and feasts. Children go from house to house asking for candies. Many people visit sacred rivers or lakes to immerse themselves and give thanks to the sun for its return."

From the corner of her eye, Thea watched Luke. Andreas went on speaking. Every twelfth year as many as 100 million people celebrated Makar Sankranti by making a pilgrimage to bathe at the confluence of the Ganges and Yamuna Rivers. Luke continued the minute front-and-back rocking of his head. His eyes rose and fell. His look was of absorption. She couldn't know whether he heard Andreas speaking of the pilgrims offering prayers to the sun. He might be deep in thought, be deaf to Andreas's voice, or hear the words but find no meaning in them.

"Makar Sankranti is mentioned in the great Hindu epic the *Mahabharata*, which means the festival is at least five thousand years old. Sweets are given to all the celebrants. It's a time to speak sweetly, forgive, and release any grudges.

"All these festivals"—Andreas opened his arms in a gesture of inclusion—"come from our human condition, our yearning to connect to the source that gives us life. Because of this, I doubt any culture has ever existed without the profound need and desire to give thanks. Societies whose names we will never know, societies existing at the dawn of humankind and for millennia thereafter, people utterly lost to history—all gave thanks.

"We are gathered together today in a holy union. To give thanks is holy. To feast together is holy. But it is not so easy to give thanks today. We no longer view ourselves as beneficiaries of the harvest. The enormous farms cultivated by large agricultural companies have little to do with people whose hands once brought crops from field to home. With the slaughterhouses out of our sight, why should we sacrifice a llama, a goat, or a chicken to an unseen divinity? What was ever so tangible—the sheaved ear of corn attached to its stalk, the feast animal with its warm blood and heart that beat like our own—these are gone from our experience. The labor of the

Incas forged their relationship with the livingness of the land and the maize. They fostered this relationship with their respect, prayers, and sacrifices.

"But the reward for our work is money. With the computer and internet, all of us have become city dwellers. Even if we live among the natural beauty of the mountains, we labor over abstractions. For these abstract labors, we are rewarded by the abstraction of money. Its value comes only from our belief that it has value. Perhaps this is too familiar, and I linger here too long, but in our society of plenty, we suffer from a scarcity of thankfulness. To give thanks today, we must make an extra effort."

Andreas paused, frowning over some calculation. Finishing his train of thought, he looked slowly across the faces before him. His eyes held Thea's for a moment.

"Life isn't a certainty. It's a remarkable gift. It's a feast of which this shared meal is a reminder. Never forget the miracle of being here, alive with energies, thoughts, and memories that might never have been.

"I could say more, but I've spoken long enough. Some might say too long," he added, smiling and bowing his head. "Let us give thanks."

His listeners lowered their heads.

"Bless this food before us and the source from which it comes," Andreas intoned. "Bless life itself. Now let's eat."

Andreas's one voice gave way to many voices. A rising cacophony quickly filled the hall. Around the table, busy hands offered platters and bowls of squash, creamed onions, string beans, sweet potatoes, stuffing, cranberry relish, and gravy. The turkey came in mounds of neatly sliced white meat with enormous drumsticks acting as bookends. From this cornucopia, Thea parsed out small portions for herself and Luke.

Knife in her right hand and fork in her left, Thea carefully cut Luke's meat into bite-size pieces. He picked up his fork with his left hand, switched it to his right hand, and began to eat with careful precision. It was a social grace to move the fork from left hand to right, but where in his awareness did graces like this survive?

She looked across to where Andreas spoke to his neighbors while holding his wineglass aloft. It was so like him to draw together celebrations of prayer and thanks from around the world. She was thankful to be alive. Thankful for this time at the institute. Thankful for Andreas and Moritz. Thankful to have a career. She was thankful for Luke, for his strangeness, his mystery, and that he had been given to her care. Above all, whatever her sorrow, she was thankful for Delphina.

As Andreas said, in giving thanks, she joined with people from all places and times, people long dead and very much living, speakers of innumerable tongues, inhabitants of far-flung lands with cultures alien to her own.

I could say more.

She kept returning to those words near the end of his talk. If he had more to say, what had been left unspoken?

52

Thea paced in her room. Five steps brought her from door to window. Five steps took her back from window to door. Five steps weren't nearly enough to release what was pent up in her. A cold, rainy spell after Thanksgiving had kept her from hiking on most days. When she did hike, she took Luke with her but made no attempt to climb toward the summit of the mountain.

Stopping at the window, she glanced at her desktop. The piles of paper remained, but she had no desire to write. More than that, she desired not to write. She desired a vigorous walk, but she couldn't quench that thirst in her small room.

She passed her narrow bed to one side and the bureau to the other. Slowing in midstride, she scrutinized the pile of books, her diploma from the Center for Psychotherapeutic Training, and the photograph of the man beside the bear. She saw nothing new in this small shrine. The books she had read long ago when she attended classes at the center. The photograph kept its fundamental mystery. Walking from the door to the window, she stopped again by her desk. She should write. She believed writing concentrated thoughts and opened pathways.

But she could only think again that she had no desire to write. She didn't want to sit in the straight-backed chair and hold her hand above the pad of paper. It was like an imprisonment, this feeling she ought to return to memories of Delphina, Hugh, Sally, and the rest. To hike on the mountain was to escape, to be in her body, focused on where to step, on the stones and the leaves underfoot, and on the silent presence of the trees surrounding her.

As much as she wanted to avoid her memories, she couldn't escape a part of herself that wanted to plumb the past. She recalled a photograph. Her legs tensed, and she began to walk more vigorously, but the length of the room didn't allow it. The photograph was in the bottom drawer with the other photographs she had brought with her. She easily recalled the image another part of her had pushed away. Four couples, dressed for an evening out, sitting at a round table. To get everyone in the picture, the couples had shifted to be closer together and left the part of the table closest to the photographer vacant. Thea remembered how they had shuffled the chairs. She and Hugh had separated, leaving the empty table, its white tablecloth falling to the floor, between them.

Interrupting her pacing, Thea squatted before the bureau and pulled out the bottom drawer. Taking out a small pile of photographs, she sat on the bed and dealt the pictures in a stack until she came to the photograph. Six people, three men and three women, smiled for the camera. Hugh appeared to have forgotten everything—the group he had come with, the nightclub, Thea. He gazed at nothing. He might not have been part of the group at all. He wasn't her date, her husband. He wasn't even in the room. Or in his body. He had been carried away, but why and to where? She studied her own expression. She didn't remember her thoughts in that moment when the flash of light preserved this record. It showed her looking across the emptied section of table at Hugh. There was a gleam in her eye and a smile on her lips. But the gleam now struck her as predatory, merciless, and the smile about realization rather than connection. He stood on the edge of an abyss. He might stand there forever, but she couldn't stand with him. She smiled because her illusions had vanished. She knew this man was not a companion for her.

His eyes found nothing on which to rest. They divorced him from her and from all the others with them. He forgot to shape an expression for his face to accompany those eyes. It would have been useless in any case. An incongruous smile, an inadequate frown. The eyes burned. The man seeing through those eyes was utterly alone.

She shook her head and spread the other photographs on the brown blanket stretched tight on her bed. Why did she want to cure when she could accept what was? The images of her daughter looked out from the rectangles of the photographs. Thea felt joy, but she felt painful regret as well. Memory was weightless, unlike flesh and muscle, unlike a father's hands touching a daughter's skin. Sally was so sweet, so devoted. But the memory of her father would always be part of Sally's being. Always a part of Delphina's being.

Thea swept up the photographs and returned them to the half-open drawer. Rising to stand, she considered whether to walk to the window or the door. To go in either direction admitted her confinement. She could walk out the door, but would she be free? Yes, to visit Moritz and Luke, Andreas, or all of them, but not truly free. Her room seemed as much a container as the yellow room had been for Luke. But the container wasn't that room, the meditation hall, or the institute. She was the container, the creator of her own limitations. She didn't have to stay at the institute. Yet she remained.

Thea walked to the window and put her face on the cold glass. Peering into the darkness, she saw the lanterns next to the walks and the lights in the windows of the other buildings. Strings of white Christmas lights outlined the doorways and railings of each entrance.

Lights strung on the benches and around the sundial floated in the night. Thea felt the darkness enlarge as the days shortened. These Christmas lights affirmed that the growing darkness would reach its limits and retreat. The shortest day, the winter solstice, would come. Then Christmas would bring the new birth of the sun and the light of lengthening days.

She thought of the rituals that were once at the heart of everything. Rituals responding to inevitable change, rituals facilitating change. "A sacred child is born!" the worshippers cried in the torchlight, emerging from the underground passages of Eleusis. Andreas had lectured about the ancient sites, now reduced to ruins but still living in the need to rise above the profane and quotidian, in the craving to worship, in the notion of the human as more than merely human. It was the reservoir of spirit brimming in the baptismal font, the solemn sprinkling of sacred water or the immersion beneath it that raises the human toward the sacred.

Abruptly, Thea pictured Luke with such clarity that he might have been standing before her. His eyes held hers. Not pleading but self-contained, self-assured. Could she offer healing that takes the healer beyond the safety of the familiar? Could she offer healing that accepts the other?

53

"Why didn't you say more?" Thea asked. "I mean on Thanksgiving. If you had more to say, I certainly wanted to hear it."

The dining hall had emptied except for Thea and Andreas sitting at one end of a long table and a few stragglers scattered among the other tables.

"I'd spoken enough. It was my way of saying grace. I wanted to be celebratory."

"What could be more important than giving thanks? To live with a sense of gratitude. It was wonderful, truly."

Andreas smiled at her words. "I didn't want it to be even longer," he said. "It was already a bit of a lecture."

"Giving thanks was the reason for the celebration," Thea pressed. "That was why we gathered for the meal. It was a ritual. You said it yourself. What didn't you say? I'd like to know."

Andreas hesitated.

"No one can fault thanksgiving . . ."

"You do believe in it?" Thea asked, ferreting beneath his words.

"Yes, I do, but each meal we devour requires death. Death of the animals whose flesh we eat. Death of the plants. And those deaths, in a sense, require our deaths. Death is the rule governing all that lives."

Every life ended in death. That was obvious. But the intensity with which Andreas spoke showed this familiar truth afflicted him with power and immediacy.

"All those who love will lose their beloved," he continued. "Even if the beloved is healing itself. This is a fact, a certainty of human experience. In youth, it's a truth easy to ignore, but at my age it's no longer so easy. If we live and love long enough, we will lose what we love."

Thea thought of the woman with whom he'd traveled in Japan, the older woman who loved him. He chose not to live his life with her, and now she was gone.

"But you praised thanksgiving," she said. "If we lose what we love, why should we be thankful?"

"I meant what I said," Andreas replied, raising his coffee cup and taking a sip before replacing it on the saucer. "The shadow of life, of course, is death. Sacrifice of a chicken, a goat, or a child isn't only a gift of thanks. It offers a life in substitution for our own lives. It buys us some time, but certainly not forever. It also admits the ubiquity of death. This gift of life is limited in duration. Even Lazarus, whom Jesus raised from the dead, didn't live forever. He was given a second chance and lived to old age, but then he died like everyone else."

"That isn't in the Bible, is it?"

"It's in the traditions of the church," Andreas answered. "Nor was Jesus the first healer to find his work undone by death. Asklepios, a gifted healer in ancient Greece, not only raised the dead but gave them immortality. At last, the god of death complained the underworld was empty. Zeus, the highest of the gods, sided with death and struck Asklepios down with a thunderbolt. In death, Asklepios became the god of healing."

Andreas spoke too much of death for Thea's liking, but he continued with barely a pause.

"Healing reflects our longing to live without the boundary of death. It has a special meaning for you and me."

"Why do you say that?"

"Because we imagine ourselves to be healers. This is what I wanted to say but didn't. So many of the people in the dining hall were healers of one sort or another. But to be a healer is to try to be larger than death. The inevitable outcome of healing is failure."

"I can't agree," Thea said firmly. "Think about relationships. Just because a relationship ends doesn't mean the entire relationship was a failure. It's about the process, the passing moments. Was there joy, understanding, love, and more? If a doctor operates and saves a life, that must be good. The patient will still die at the end of his or her life, but would it have been better to suffer from ill health or die sooner? Or a therapist who talks patients through difficult times? Life can be made more meaningful. It can be lived with greater depth."

Andreas smiled to hear Thea disagree with him. "What you say is true," he agreed, "yet what I say is also true. The healer's task is an impossible one. Utterly necessary, utterly human, well intended, but the healer must always remember the limits of the powers we command. There are injunctions for those who heal. The first is do no harm. For that, we must accept that we are imperfect. If we exaggerate our power to heal, we may injure those we seek to help. Another injunction is to heal ourselves. For that, we must accept that we will fail. Failure is the certainty we bear as best we can. Because no matter what tools we possess, there will always be what cannot be healed. To practice healing is to accept these boundaries."

"You're speaking of humility."

"Yes, certainly, and self-awareness."

"To raise someone from the dead is also about development. At times we feel dead within. Then we're raised up again to life."

Andreas nodded. "I've certainly felt despair so dark it can only be compared to death," he said. "Somehow the human spirit overcomes this."

Was he referring to his role as a therapist and healer? It might be that, but he didn't limit his experience of despair to one episode or another.

"When we emerge to life again," he continued, "we're filled with awe for our finitude in the vastness surrounding us."

"Yes," Thea agreed, "I know that feeling."

"These patterns come from what we are as humans. Even the institute is an example of the forces shaping us. In trying to cure physical and mental ills, we are healers. That role is larger than any individual. To a greater or lesser degree, the desire to heal is in each of us. For those drawn to healing, the institute has a magnetism. We seek to change the natural outcome of disease, the perpetual motion of life toward deterioration and death. If we're fortunate, we gain wisdom before the inevitable decline."

"You could have said all that," Thea replied. "It's a challenge to look more closely at the lives we choose to lead."

"Often we have good reasons for what we hide from ourselves. Nonetheless, it's important to look directly at what's hidden."

"Can you give an example?"

"Take your relationship to Delphina."

Thea's body tightened when he said her daughter's name.

"What about it?"

"You only speak of love for her."

"Yes."

"Isn't there more?"

Thea didn't want to continue the conversation, but she trusted in Andreas's caring. If he spoke of what he knew she didn't want to hear, he had good reason.

"Does there have to be more?" she finally replied.

"You told me how you slapped her. It was brave of you to be so honest. But what made you do that?"

"Rage. Suddenly it would take me over."

"Why?"

"To me, at those moments, she made everything I wanted impossible."

"How could a child do that?"

"I wanted a happy family, a good husband, a loving daughter. She refused to love. She refused to approve. She was obstinate, so stubborn. That's what I experienced. Now I know better. She was abused. She was in pain. I'm humiliated to speak of how I felt and acted."

"Why? I'm not blaming you, just trying to understand."

"What I did was wrong, totally wrong."

"But you had reasons, feelings. We aren't gods or angels. No matter how much we love, we never love perfectly. I don't minimize the pain you caused Delphina or the pain you suffered, but your life continues."

He spoke with kindness. As much as Thea hadn't wanted to speak, she felt relief to confide in him.

"That's why I came here. To find a way forward."

Andreas lifted his cup and sipped his coffee. Setting the cup and saucer back on the table, he perched on the front edge of his seat.

"In my Thanksgiving talk," he said, "I spoke of harvest festivals. The harvest brings together the death of what is consumed and the lives of those who consume. Of course, we're thankful to live, but why not rage against the certainty that we too will one day be the harvest? If we could feel that rage, that fear, would we still give thanks?"

Thea parted her lips to say she would, but Andreas continued before she could speak.

"I believe we would," he affirmed. "If we can cease to exist, if we aren't immortal, then we can understand that we might never have been. That, to me, is far more terrifying than a life certain to end in death."

54

"We're going to hike," Thea announced.

"You're early," Moritz replied.

"It's a long hike."

"Where are you headed?"

"To the top."

Luke leaned over the drawing board with intensity, his hand moving like a conductor's in service to a brain seized by a swelling music yet unshared. He gave no reaction to what she said.

"We've eaten breakfast, so he's ready."

The heat from the parka made her shrug it off. Her legs were warm in the ski pants, but she left them on.

"I'm going to make some sandwiches."

Swiftly, she made the usual peanut butter and jelly sandwiches, added bottles of water, and filled her backpack. In the living room, she slipped into her coat, then pulled the straps of the backpack over her shoulders. Moritz rose, but Luke appeared oblivious to her preparations. She went beside him and gently slipped a hand under his elbow. He rose easily and followed her to the door. Dressing him in his red-and-black plaid coat, she crossed a scarf around his neck.

Having hiked so often on the slopes above the institute, Thea didn't seek the same route to start but inevitably encountered familiar landmarks and trails. Luke, as always, refused to lead. The only sounds were the leaves crackling underfoot. She glanced back from time to time to reassure herself that he faithfully followed her. Her lungs filled with chill air. Steadying herself with her hiking poles, she was surprised by the intensity and speed with which they moved. On the ridge, she tilted back her head to take in the imposing height of the mountain.

The streams of vapor from their breathing made Thea think of the large nostrils of horses, the pull of freezing air into mammoth lungs and the gray exhalations pouring warmly out, the shifting of weight from hoof to hoof in a muscular tension relieved only by movement. Quickly, they crossed the boulder-strewn meadow sloping downward from the ridge. They moved among the leafless trees. The ground began its steep rise, but Thea continued her brisk pace. The winds racing about the circumference of the mountain grew in force, and she pulled her hood over her head.

Silent as her companion, Thea no longer thought his quiet a deficiency. His presence told of his desire to go with her to the heights. This walking was like a meditation to a mantra of footfalls. The trees thinned and shortened. A few trees clung to the rock walls rising before them. They moved among boulders piled high at the foot of the cliffs.

At last, Thea sought shelter where the cliff face and a boulder formed a niche that diminished the cutting winds. She shrugged off her backpack and offered a sandwich to Luke. She sat on a rock to eat, and Luke did the same. Pushing off her hood, Thea realized she shouldn't sit for long. Once she stopped moving, the cold penetrated her. Luke's cheeks were flushed. At least the scarf remained around his neck. He refused to wear both hat and gloves. He chewed slowly, looking unmoved by the cold.

When Thea rose and pulled the hood over her head again, she waited for Luke to finish. She gave a sidelong glance to see his expression when he realized they would go higher. He didn't meet her eyes or smile, but the quickness with which he followed her suggested he was eager. He hiked behind her, but his energy urged her forward. In a way she didn't understand, it was easier to hike together.

They entered the maze of stone. Passages dwindled. Spaces between boulders opened only to end in impassable rock. As Thea tried to lead one way and then another, the ground narrowed between the rise of cliffs to the left and a precipitous falling away to the right. Picking her way among the boulders, Thea doubted they would ever find a way through. She didn't want to skirt the boulders by risking the precipice, but on the other side the cliffs looked massive. That left only the boulders bunched in the narrowing space between. An ancient flood of unimaginable force had tossed these giant stones like pebbles. She climbed up to the top of a boulder. Ahead, the piled stones rose nearly to the top of the cliff, but the climb looked hazardous.

Thea could evaluate the danger, the smooth surfaces hard to grasp, the heights, the strength required to climb. She didn't know if she could reach the top and if that, indeed, would be the summit.

She wavered. She couldn't see a way to the top. It was impassable. As much as she wanted to go higher, she couldn't. Even if the rocks didn't block her path, it would take hours to descend to the institute. If she was sensible, she would stop for the day and turn back. If she turned back, there would be no returning. No other day would be better. It was a loss. Perhaps it was her fatigue, but her eyes slicked with tears. She should turn, take Luke's elbow, and start down the mountain. It was unbearable to submit. She remained frozen, unwilling to surrender and unable to go forward.

Luke came beside her. Looking alert and single-minded, he stared intently toward the stone architecture rising above. The mountain was unfamiliar to Thea, but he had roamed this forest and might well have trekked here with the bear as his companion.

She reached out to him. She might have wanted to take his elbow to start back toward the institute. Or perhaps she wanted to hold him, to comfort him for a moment or be comforted by him.

Suddenly, he rushed past her. She parted her lips to call out, but the cry caught in her throat. Leaping agilely from boulder to boulder, he climbed until she couldn't see him. Her poles were of no use on the stone. She dropped them to scramble after him. Her gloves slipped on the faces of stone. She feared the heights and feared he was gone. With each grip of a hand and placement of a foot, she risked a fall. If she reached the promontory where he vanished, and he wasn't there, she didn't know what she would do.

Her fingers burned from gripping small ledges of stone. He appeared to have moved effortlessly, but she needed all her strength to climb after him. He had scampered up, but she didn't think she could. For a few moments, she was immobilized, her gloved hands resting on the stone of the boulder. Then she simply went on. She found handholds and footholds to lift and push herself upward. At last, shaking and breathing violently, she reached a plateau.

Ridges of stone like steps for giants rose to where Luke stood facing away from her, his arms outstretched, his spine arched, his head tilted downward. To her, he looked like a man crucified. Slowly, she climbed higher, traversing a wide circle around him. For the first time, she saw the far side of the mountain. It was this falling away that his gaze encompassed. As she came to face him, she realized that his arms were open to embrace these plunging slopes and, beyond, mountain after mountain flowing to the horizon. His outstretched arms drew energy from the wilderness. He reminded her of a sail puffed full by a forceful breeze.

She was uncertain how to approach him, then wondered why she had to approach him at all. To bring him back to the institute? Why couldn't they remain here until he was ready to leave? If they had to walk in darkness, they would walk in darkness. Slowly, she lowered herself to sit on a shelf of rock.

The joy in him was visible. Whatever he took in through his outstretched arms, he returned in the sparkling outflow of his eyes. They hadn't reached the summit, but this view had been what he sought.

To see him here made his stay in the yellow room all the crueler. To her, he was a circuit drawing and releasing energy. There was a dialogue between Luke and the far side of the mountain. She didn't count the minutes stretching away but drifted from Luke to the mountainside to elusive thoughts more like fragments of dreams. What now was definite, known, and mapped would one day be uncertain and unknown. By a reciprocal process, what was unknown, the maze of boulders through which they had come or the paths on the mountain's far side, became more certain. This great flux of knowing and unknowing was at the heart of meaning. Memories flowed in fragments. The child didn't know the adult. The adult forgot so much of what was the child.

These thoughts welled up and slipped away. She looked at the furrowed ridges of clouds. A pale light penetrated the gray firmament with long pennants of silver. She felt impervious to the biting surges of the winds. She could see a woman and a girl of nine or ten. Not Thea and Delphina, but Hugh's future wife, Justine, and her daughter. In sending the letter to Justine, Thea had done what she could.

At last, Luke straightened, lowered his arms, and leveled his head. Without thinking, Thea stood and walked to him. His eyes were liquid, bright, but as always without connection to her. She pressed his arm to bring him after her. Crossing the peak of stone, she counted the hours to hike back to the institute. If night did fall, only Luke would be with her. Thinking this, she turned to look back. An arm's reach away, like her shadow, he followed.

55

Thea experienced the journey to the solstice as a descent into darkness. If she could walk beneath the ocean waves, ten thousand steps down a circular staircase to a soft, absolute black, that was how these nights enclosed her. The light in the ceiling of her room, the lamp on top of the desk she sat facing: how could they resist the gathering of the dark?

One idea returned again and again. After this darkest of nights, the light would grow. Ever so slightly, each day would be longer than the last. The strings of tiny Christmas lights outlining the buildings' entrances, wound about the wrought-iron banisters, and highlighting the shapes of the table and benches by the sundial promised this brightening of the light. She would walk up the spiral staircase until the black depths were a memory.

Rising from her desk, she went to her closet. She pushed the light-blue parka aside, wrapped a lavender scarf around her neck, and slipped into a knee-length brown topcoat. Outside, she cut across the lawn toward the dining hall in Amazon. Her hunger wasn't for food but for light. The dining hall stopped serving dinner earlier in the evening, but a ten-foot Christmas tree set in the center of the tables glowed with yellow, blue, and red bulbs reflecting on the densely hung ornaments. An angel topped the tree, her flowing gown elongating her body.

To Thea, the angel looked ready to rise heavenward. The fragrance of the fir tree drew her closer to the needled branches. It was evergreen, symbolic of the eternal life of the spirit. This large room was usually devoted to what was daily and unremarkable. People came with their hunger, filled their trays, talked with those who sat near them at the many tables. Tonight, in the absence of those crowds, the large room was dimly lit. There was an emptiness, a silence, that Thea welcomed. Stepping closer to look at the lifted face of the angel, she felt carried away from the appetites of daily life. A stillness emanated from the angel. Breathing in the fragrant balm of the evergreen, Thea sensed eternity coiling about her as the moments slowed and ceased their endless progression.

She passed beyond careful measurements. Atomic time, digital time, mechanical time—none of these could measure the physics of the human spirit. A vastness surrounded her. It expanded within her. In the vastness was a completion, but of what? Could it be this longest night ending the cycle of darkness? For that completion, the enormous mass of the planet spun through the heavens. Populated by billions. Infinitesimal amid countless planets, countless suns, countless galaxies.

Tomorrow, the light would grow. In a few more days and nights, Christmas would celebrate the birth of this physical light, the birth of the divine light that could shine through all of humanity. It had only to be allowed.

She wanted to linger, but a gravitational force pulled her toward Danube. Leaving, Thea took the bluestone walk past the sundial. Despite the darkness, she could see the golden upright rising from the flatness of its platform.

She knocked on the door of Luke's apartment, then entered. Moritz looked up from the book in his lap. The chair was empty at the drawing board.

She took off her coat and scarf and sat on the couch across from Moritz.

"Where is he?" she asked.

"In the bedroom," he replied, placing his open book on the coffee table.

"I wanted to see him."

"He'll come out soon enough. He always does."

"And you," Thea added. "I wanted to see you too."

Moritz smiled at her words and replied with a question.

"What happened on the mountain? He's been different since that hike. He had torn up so many pages, I thought he was finished with that. Now he's focused on them again. He's always at his drawing board. If he goes to the windows, it's only for a few minutes."

"Near the top, he got away from me," Thea admitted. "I couldn't see where he went. I wasn't sure I could even climb after him. When I found him, he was looking at the far side of the mountain."

"Just looking?"

"Maybe he was having a vision. I can't say what he saw. I knew I should bring him back, but part of me resisted. I didn't want to rush him. I was afraid it would get dark, but I wanted to trust that we would be all right. Even if I didn't understand him, I wanted to let him be as he was. I sat down and waited for him."

"What did you see?"

"Energy flowed into him. From the mountain. That's the best I can describe it."

"Energy?"

"I'm not sure I'm even right," she said, shrugging and not trying to explain further. "It doesn't make sense, but I felt a completion for him."

"Of what?"

"He wanted to reach that place. He had to go there."

"Then what happened?"

"We came back."

"In the dark."

"Yes." Thea smiled at having taken the risk.

Moritz rose, placed his palms on his lower back, and leaned back first to one side and then the other.

"Too much reading," he said of his stiffness.

"You can't mean that."

He bent forward from the waist and swayed side to side with his hands brushing the floor.

"You're right," he agreed, his head by his knees. "I don't really mean it."

Straightening, he shrugged his shoulders four or five times toward his ears and then circled his head in a luxurious rolling. When he finished, he remained standing with his spine straight and his head lifted.

"Do you think he's intoxicated with God?"

His earnest question revealed his desire for that intoxication.

"You know better than I."

She wished she could have said more, assured him Luke was flooded by the divine. That Moritz asked at all made her think this longest night oppressed him. On an impulse, she rose, stepped close to him, and encircled him with her arms. At her touch, his body softened, but he didn't bring his arms around her, and after a moment, she stepped back.

"It's such a dark night," she said, adding with a bob of her head in the direction of the bedroom. "If only we could ask our friend."

"Yes." Moritz nodded. "If only."

"I'm going to say good night to Andreas. Then I'll come back."

"I'm sure," Moritz replied, "Luke will join us then."

56

The flames burned steadily above two tapered white candles set on the table by Andreas's windows. The lamps and ceiling light were off, so Thea could barely see the empty bookshelves and the undecorated walls. Between the candles, a frame held a picture, but from across the room she couldn't make out the image. Otherwise, the apartment was in darkness.

"Am I interrupting?" Thea asked.

"It's a welcome interruption," Andreas replied. "Come. Watch your step."

He wore a formal black Japanese dinner jacket. Its sleeves billowed at the elbows. He led her toward the table and gestured to have her sit in one of the dining chairs.

"That's the woman you traveled with in Japan," Thea said, recognizing her from the book of poems and photos she had made for Andreas.

"Tonight," he said, looking at the picture as he sat beside Thea, "I wanted to be with her."

Their movements as they sat made the flames undulate. Then, in the stillness of the shadowed room, the flames resumed their upright postures. Andreas didn't speak. No doubt the photograph had come from the small cache of treasures he kept in his bureau. She wanted to question him, but a single question, however innocuous, would amplify in the silence and feel like a cross-examination.

She could only wait. As she waited, she brought Moritz side by side with Andreas. This was not to choose who was better or whom she liked more. On this long night, Andreas prayed—what else could she consider his communing with the dead? Moritz also prayed, but in an utterly different way. His time with Luke was a prayer. Even his reading was a prayer.

"I wonder at the meaning of it."

With those words Andreas broke the silence. Thea wanted to speak, but he continued before she could shape her questions.

"There are so many ways the dead live."

"Live?" Thea echoed.

"Yes."

Andreas gazed at the photo, his face lit by the warm light of the candles.

"How earthbound I feel much of the time," he finally said, turning to look at Thea. "I went to a monastery once. Only for a week, just a taste of what a monk would experience. I had to take a vow of silence. And we weren't allowed to look at anyone. I kept my eyes on the floor. I recognized others by their shoes, sandals, and sneakers. Sounds ridiculous, doesn't it?"

Thea didn't respond.

"When I left after the week, I missed the silence. I didn't want to look at people's faces. I wanted the freedom of my isolation. It must have been another week before I began to enjoy faces again and welcome the sound of voices."

"Why do you say 'earthbound'?"

320

"She"—he looked to the face in the frame and back to Thea—"lived here and beyond here. She wanted me for her lover, but she wanted much more than that. She wanted a companion to go with her where she traveled. When she moved in and out of her body, I felt the stirring of her leaving and her return. She had a higher soul. Not perfected but in touch with an ecstasy I believe waits for all of us."

Thea frowned and opened a palm toward him. This might have meant he should stop, but he continued.

"She jolted me out of my safe life."

"You said there are so many ways the dead live."

"They live in our memories. But I'm sure they also live in another form, in a life after this life. It's a common enough belief, but I experienced it. Because of how she entered my body that first night. We can leave the body and travel to other destinations. Night after night, I could feel the vibrations of her leaving and returning to her body. So much more is possible than we imagine. Viewed from that perspective, 'dead' is a curious word. What could it possibly mean?"

"You can say that," she answered, recalling their conversation the night she stayed with him. "I never had that experience."

"I understand so little. Even she could scarcely recall where she traveled. Strange how I can believe when I know almost nothing."

"What do you believe?"

"I believe," he began carefully, "that after our lives end here, everything is explained to us. This world is so wonderfully physical, but it's a place for learning. Where we're going, energy rules. Freed from all these stimulations, we can understand why we lived at a certain time, why we knew these other spirits encased in flesh, and the purpose of this journey of spirit through flesh. Effortlessly, our spirits advance in a natural evolution. It isn't the movement of individual souls but a much larger merging. To say the movement is toward a goal would be meaningless. Words no longer suffice. Every soul is merged in an ineffable brightness like that at the moment of creation."

Thea liked that he trusted her to be his confidant. She couldn't know the truth of what he said, but his words created a vision for her. He returned his gaze to the photo. She hadn't known the woman, but she felt her absence. She pictured the woman in that album of photos and poems. To be in Japan, in a school for the sacred arts. The hours spent arranging flowers, the tea ceremony, and making the bold black strokes of her calligraphy. One of the short poems came to Thea:

He does not see with eyes,
seeker of the boundless Love
within.

She had been a seeker. Andreas had spoken of the keyhole in her right eye. How she looked over the left shoulder of a person to see his or her soul. Now, gazing from the photo, she looked over the left shoulder of the person viewing her image. She looked over Thea's left shoulder. The photographic print was a thin piece of chemically treated paper. It was too dark for Thea to see the tiny keyhole in the woman's eye. Yet Thea considered what was above her own left shoulder, what the woman would have seen if she gazed at Thea.

Andreas's head was bowed in meditation. He spent this darkest night in communion with his memories. Thea realized the woman offered a mirror to him, a vision of his own soul. In being her companion, in following her to Japan, he had shown that he too was a seeker. It made Thea wonder about her devotion to Luke. In her desire to heal him, she could feel her own need to be healed. Forgiveness had its own immutable rules. It was beyond her power to forgive herself for failing Delphina. Only Delphina could forgive.

The thought of Luke made her rise to her feet. She stood for a few moments before Andreas took his eyes away from the woman's face and rose to stand beside her.

"Thanks for inviting me in," Thea said.

She stepped forward and stretched her arms around his middle. Pressing herself to the smooth silk of his jacket and the cushion of his girth, she rose on the balls of her feet and lifted her lips to kiss one plump cheek and then the other before releasing him. She crossed the living room and turned in the open doorway to say good night. No doubt he would resume his meditation once she had gone.

"This night feels it will never end," he said, his resonant voice carrying across the room. "I'm so thankful to have known her, to have experienced her caring and had a glimpse of what might be. I'm old enough that I might as easily have died as lived. Then I would know if the mysteries are as I imagine. Yet I'm alive, conscious, in need of a purpose. My early passions no longer have the same appeal. I'm finished with sex, but companionship? Love? Who can say?"

57

Thea walked up the flight of stairs and rapped sharply on Luke's door. Entering, she stopped by the bookcase where the watchful Buddha surveyed the room and its occupants. Moritz glanced up, nodded and smiled to greet her, and bent his head to continue his reading. Luke had returned and sat at his drawing board with his back to Thea. He didn't turn to see her enter and settle herself on the couch.

She hadn't noticed before her visit to Andreas, but light flooded the room. The ceiling globe, the lamps on the end tables of the couch, and the floor lamps on either wall to the sides of the drawing board poured forth their illumination.

To sit silently while Moritz read and Luke sifted through his art was peaceful. Nothing was required of her. She had a sense of belonging. When Luke finished with an old page, he would either use his thumbs and forefingers to tear it into tiny pieces or place it on a growing pile to his right.

Sitting so near Luke, Thea questioned whether her vision was adequate. It was easy to feel she and Moritz shared the room with him, but his closeness might be an illusion. Her thoughts returned to that moment when he rushed ahead of her to scale the massive boulders. If he had vanished, returned to the bear, to the wild, it would have been his choice. She didn't want him back for the institute, for the constables, or because no civilized man should find companionship with an animal in the wild. It was for herself. She wanted him to return because of her connection to him, her friendship for him. Her love for him. He might never speak. Certainly, her life would flow forward and eventually she would leave the institute. Others would care for him, give their own meanings to his silence and his presence. She hoped they would feel friendship as she did. If one day he walked away, disappeared into the wilderness, it would be his decision to abandon the human.

What kind of god would bring a man to such profound silence? For Thea, there was a way his not speaking made him like every unknown other, every stranger who should be welcomed at the door. So much was left unexpressed. Even Andreas and Moritz possessed unseen depths like silences. Only faith allowed the facing of those silences, of the divine.

What was Luke? What would he become? Why didn't she admit to the immensities she couldn't know? She was overcome by a sudden sense of smallness. She felt herself a mote, a scintilla in the infinitude of the cosmos. So much was beyond her power to control, change, or heal.

Lowering the lids of her eyes until Luke and Moritz vanished, Thea brought together the tips of her index finger and thumb and rested her hands on her thighs. She breathed in and out, again and again, deeply, her focus on the air entering and departing. The room enlarged, the ceiling gaining height and the walls bending away. She waited for a vibration like the movement of angels from world to world, a stirring that would make her tremble within. Or Luke's god-intoxicated spirit might be rising, the walls immaterial

326

and passed through as easily as a breeze slips through the forest. She wanted the quiet to be boundless, a sense of presence everywhere about her in the air.

She didn't make prayers of words. She didn't entreat a higher power. She didn't ask for relief from this or help with that. She wanted to be the sacrifice, to give herself over, to be merged in a god who made "I" an irrelevancy, to vanish and yet remain. She couldn't fully express this, but she experienced her incapacity to be as she wished. She was like a rock, not a dove, not an energy in flight toward a boundary beyond which the very idea of flesh would be a forgotten oddity. She didn't feel the vibration that would transport her. She didn't feel the energy of Luke or even Moritz, whatever might lift them free of their flesh to meet in an unimaginable realm.

It was hard to tell how much time passed. When she opened her eyes, little had changed. Luke let his hands rest on the paper and, as he often did, rocked his head slightly back and forth. Moritz still read with concentration. It was like stepping outside time.

Rising, she skirted the coffee table and walked to stand behind Luke. Gently she rested her hands on his shoulders. His back felt warm. He breathed in and out with an even rhythm. Thea shifted her palms, placing the right between his shoulder blades and the left on his upper arm. The bony knots of his spine moved with his rocking.

"Do you miss the bear?" She asked this question in her mind but didn't say the words aloud. "Do you think of loved ones far away?" She wanted to give and receive words like gifts in an easy back-and-forth with him, but she also wanted to give up what she wanted. Slowly, she increased the pressure of her hands.

He lifted his head to gaze at the dark windows before him. The muscles of his upper back thickened. When he had gazed for thirty seconds or a little more, he lowered his eyes until he hunched forward over his desk and again stared at the whiteness of the page beneath his hand. His rocking resumed.

For what purpose had she lavished so much thought and care on him? To be allowed to love. To be allowed to heal. To be given the humility and thankfulness of offering what the other might never acknowledge. Pleasure filled her like a breath drawn not only into her lungs but into the farthest reaches of her body. It poured down her trunk, branched into her arms and legs, flowed to her toes and the tips of her fingers. It released itself back to the air, too much to hold within her, an exquisite wind that rushed against the boundary of her flesh and swept onward into the world. If she no longer had control of what might happen, would she be safe? Could she trust, not in the power of love, but in its mercy?

About the Author

TAD CRAWFORD is the author of the novels *A Floating Life* and *On Wine-Dark Seas* as well as *The Secret Life of Money* and a dozen other nonfiction books. His stories and articles have appeared in *American Artist*, *Art in America*, *The Café Irreal*, *Confrontation*, *Communication Arts*, *Family Circle*, *Glamour*, *Guernica*, *The Nation*, and *Writer's Digest*. Crawford is the founder and publisher of Allworth Press. The recipient of a National Endowment for the Arts award, he grew up in the artists' colony of Woodstock, New York. He now lives in New York City and the Hudson Highlands.